BOUND OVER

by

DEREK SHANNON

Published by **CHIMERA**
ISBN 9781780807317

CHAPTER ONE

The van hit yet another pothole in the road. Tiffany Welborne was counting them - eighty-three so far - as she had precious little else to occupy her mind. She was going mad, actually. Two hours cooped up in a windowless van with a feckless idiot for company was threatening to fray the shred of sanity she had managed to hold on to over the past hellish month. Another bump... eighty-four...

A meek nudge to her side interrupted her thoughts like water dripping from the ceiling. 'Yes, Jude?' she sighed.

Jude Forrester was a ginger-haired, dark-eyed, pouty-mouthed girl around Tiffany's age, with a tall and ample frame squeezed into a multi-coloured T-shirt and cheap counterfeit versions of expensive jeans and trainers. She was a typical working-class native destined to become fast-food counter fodder. Tiffany had to admit, however, that there was an unconventional prettiness about the girl's long face and full lips, individual detriments that together seemed to work for her. If only she was not so annoyingly effusive.

'Isn't this great?' Jude beamed.

Tiffany groaned inwardly and wished they had not made her pack her cigarettes along with the rest of her belongings in her luggage, which was now in the van's storage compartment... eighty-five...

'I couldn't believe I managed to get a place in a correction house,' Jude continued, relentless in her enthusiasm. 'They don't take just anybody, you know. It's supposed to be brilliant, like holiday camp, we—'

'Yes, yes.' The solicitors advised Tiffany to keep a low profile, and gave her some bullshit story about not wanting her to be exploited because of her connections, but she suspected daddy was simply ashamed of having a jailbird daughter. It was all academic, anyway; the time she had spent in various police stations, courts and holding facilities over the last four weeks under the media's spotlight had proved she was now famous, or infamous, in her own right... eighty-six...

'I suppose I was lucky,' Jude mused, 'being charged with car theft instead of something serious like armed robbery, or they wouldn't have accepted me.'

'You'd have been luckier not to get charged at all,' Tiffany pointed out. Another bump. Was that eighty-six or eighty-seven? Damn! She wished an end to Jude's chatter, wished an end to the journey, wished the past thirty days had just been some terrible nightmare.

'Can you get me your dad's autograph?'

Tiffany grimaced. How the mighty have fallen...

Not long ago, the greatest problem for Tiffany Welborne, Baroness of Wrightwood, had been ensuring her make-up was still perfect. A quick check in the rear-view mirror reassured her it was. She left the mirror as it was - she was not using it for anything else anyway - and checked her nails, which were also perfect. Adding to her impeccable look was her wardrobe. Tonight's adventure had called for her finest black leather *Rifat Ozbek* strapless mini-dress and matching knee-high boots from *Manolo Blahnik*. She thought she looked hot, and she wanted to celebrate. She was back from England and the academy and still on a high both from her eighteenth birthday party and her academy football team's victory in the British Regional Championship's, a victory that would not have been possible were it not for Tiffany's impressive on-the-pitch skills. If a tree fell in the forest and no one heard it, as far as Tiffany was concerned it made no noise, and likewise, superiority was pointless if no one was around to covet it.

Above and around her the lights of Cascara City dazzled, as they did every time she cruised its streets. She was British born and would always think of herself as such, but she could not wait to settle down here permanently. The city had everything; the golden, beckoning sparkle of Vegas, the skyscrapers and bustling kinetic energy of Manhattan - over ninety percent of the island's million-plus population lived here - the chic of Paris and the exotic spice of Hong Kong.

The metropolis rose like cathedral spires from between the crescent arms of Cascara's Hammer Bay, just as the island itself, a lush green plateau, rose from the waters east of Africa and north of the Seychelles. It had a colourful history as a one-time haven to corsairs who prowled the Indian Ocean to the east, and it had subsequently been colonised by the French before being usurped by the British. It achieved independence following the Second World War, and then left the Commonwealth a decade later to become a Republic. Its economic and strategic status made it a key player in the area, and its status as the world's best tax haven drew rich and powerful emigrants in the form of both corporations and individuals.

Individuals like Tiffany's daddy, Zak Welborne, lead singer of the *Armageddon Choir* and one of the top twenty richest musicians in the world. He divided his time between touring with his band of fellow shaggy-haired pensioner rockers, and living here, particularly when Tiffany was on holiday from the academy. Tiffany loved it in Cascara and she held dual citizenship as part of one of daddy's tax evasion schemes, even while retaining her baronial title.

Her window was rolled down, and despite the air-conditioner operating at full blast the sultry evening air outside was like a warm flannel embrace, but she ignored the discomfort in order to enjoy the admiring catcalls from pedestrians and fellow drivers. It was not just her considerable beauty people noticed, but also the first edition Lamborghini Diablo it was framed by. She loved the hunger in their eyes as they spotted the Diablo's immaculate cherry-red finish and long, low body as wide as a manta ray, and would gun the engine as if to confirm that, yes, both the driver and the car were real.

Daddy had presented her with the keys to a black Porsche 911, his present for her. A Porsche. How dare he present her with a mere Porsche? Other girls at the academy had received a Porsche just for getting good grades. It had been her eighteenth birthday, for Christ's sake! It was meant to be *special*. So she had cursed, thrown the cakes and buffet trays at the walls and at the servants, ordered the guests away, and demanded daddy give her the Diablo as well as the Porsche. He could afford it, he never drove it, and he knew she wanted it. She was the Baroness of Wrightwood. She deserved the best.

But daddy did not see it that way. The uncaring, unfeeling bastard tried to fob her off with every explanation under the sun, reminding her of the sky-high insurance following her last few accidents with the BMW, his favourite car. But she did not give a damn how much he had to pay for insurance; that was his problem. She tried all her tricks - crying, begging, stamping her foot, threatening to get pregnant, threatening to go find mummy, now living in California - but he remained resolute. So she stole it, and her victory tasted sweet. She drove to the French quarter of the city, which boasted all night jazz clubs, pubs, cinemas, shops, and the *Enclave*. That night, the former French embassy was illuminated by spotlights of lime green and shocking pink, giving the illusion of an inner glow that made her think of some exotic bioluminescent deep sea creature. If you watched long enough, you could see the colours melt and slide over one another like a massive lava lamp.

One valet, and a fistful of hundred rupee notes to the doormen, and she was past the queue and in the rear courtyard, where the action took place. A hot clutch of humanity swirled like seaweed to the sonic currents of the live band, some popular locals performing their own interpretation of the latest European top-twenty hits. She orbited the dance floor on her way to the bar surrounding the courtyard, where drinkers collected like barnacles.

Tiffany resisted the siren spell of the music, resisted diving onto the crowded dance floor to find a guy for the night. She had other things on her mind, other reasons for being there. Her boot heels clicked against the immaculate white steps leading up to the building's side door.

One of the two doormen, tall, tanned, granite-jawed bouncers in smart fake Armani suits, immediately and effectively blocked her way. 'May I help you, miss?'

'I've been invited to visit the catacombs,' she announced, hoping she was not the victim of an elaborate joke.

'Looks like a nice ride,' remarked his companion.

'Maybe we could take care of her ourselves,' his friend suggested. They spoke in full Creole, in a *patois* from the days of French occupation and African slavery which had survived, despite the fact that English was Cascara's official language. They obviously thought she was a tourist with her academy-honed accent and that she would not understand them.

She held her tongue and produced the bold red plastic card with gold lettering she had received in the post soon after her arrival in Cascara at the beginning of the week. The card invited her to visit *The Catacombs* on her eighteenth birthday, an inner circle based within the *Enclave*. The elite association was so exclusive it was not even listed in the directory.

The bouncer stole a quick glance at the card. 'If you'll follow me, miss,' he said respectfully.

The blessedly air-conditioned interior made her think of an Edwardian gentleman's club. The furniture was polished mahogany high-backed chairs upholstered in walnut-coloured leather, and decorative bookshelves rose from the patterned burgundy carpets framed by brocade drapes hung over darkened windows. Hardly any of the music blasting out in the courtyard filtered into this cultured interior; obviously a fortune had been spent soundproofing and treble glazing. Most unnervingly of all, the room was empty except for a man standing behind the bar.

'Where the hell is everybody?' Tiffany wondered out loud.

'Downstairs,' the doorman replied. 'In the catacombs.'

'They're for real?' She had thought the name was merely poetic, designed to conjure up images of ancient secret societies.

'They were part of an attempt by an ambassador in the late nineteenth century to break into the neighbouring embassies. When that failed, they expanded them into storage cellars. And now...' He stopped by the bar and indicated a dark-red door ahead of them. 'You must proceed alone. Have a drink or two beforehand, if you wish. As a member, it's all on the house.'

A member? 'Wait, can't you tell me anything more about—?' She stopped in mid-sentence when she realised he was gone. She glanced at the bar, tempted to just sit there for the rest of the night. She felt a frisson of excitement, the gut feeling she always experienced before a match, or before she spent more of daddy's money. Something special awaited her...

The door led to a darkly panelled hall and a set of stairs. As she descended, electric lights gave way to oil lamps and shadows flickering on the blackened stone walls. The smell of oil hung in the air even though she felt a current of ventilation coming from somewhere.

She found herself in a wide tunnel, a black, gaping hole in the earth lit from the sides by open doorways cut into the rock. From these doors poured golden lamplight and the muted sound of voices and laughter.

A wave of claustrophobia washed over her. She was afraid, even though she had no reason to be. With its draconian attitudes towards crime, Cascara was one of the safest industrialised nations on earth; the rich paid well for their security. She peered through the first doorway, and her breath caught in her throat. She was looking into a stark cell like one found in a prison or a monastery. More oil lamps flickered on the bare walls, and clothing lay crumpled in one corner. The owners of the clothing stood in the centre of the room, a man and woman. The man was naked, his arms bound over his head to iron manacles hanging from the ceiling. He was young and tall, lean and fit. His skin shone with perspiration and tawny curls clustered in a diamond on his chest. His penis was soft, curled forward over his balls, its foreskin partially retracted to reveal a lilac head, the tip glistening in the soft light.

The woman, a curvaceous, raven-haired beauty, was nearly naked, clad only in a glistening black leather basque elaborately tied down the front which scarcely confined her breasts and left her long legs, and the dark patch of her pubic hair, bare. Her stiletto heels clicked against the stone floor as she circled the man, the tip of a riding crop gently slapping into her open palm before suddenly striking his firm bottom cheeks.

Tiffany was struck by the rawness of the scene, and the colour rushed to her lovely face, surrounded by strawberry-blonde curls. Though she had always sported a licentious attitude amongst her contemporaries, in truth she was a sexual neophyte. She had only had three lovers since she turned sixteen, none of the encounters lasted more than one night, and they all failed to arouse and satisfy her in the way she hoped they would. Now here were people putting into practice what she had only read about, and she mumbled an awkward apology as they both turned their heads to look at her.

The man whispered something in what sounded like German, his tone heavy with nervous expectancy.

'Um, sorry,' she said, 'I don't understand.'

The woman pointed at her with the crop, then at the man's cock, which was stirring to life.

Tiffany's mouth went dry, and she was suddenly aware of her nipples stiffening against her dress. She had never seen a beautiful young man bound and eager to serve, and the sight was intriguing. Still, she disregarded the woman's apparent invitation to join them and remained rooted to the spot, watching as the dominatrix reached down and took the man's penis in her hand, squeezing and rolling until it hardened. The woman purred some incomprehensible words like a cat toying with her prey, and Tiffany shuddered. Her strokes grew quicker, more wanton, as the foreskin glided over the young man's glans. Tiffany watched intently, imagining she was the one nursing his erection and controlling him. She scarcely realised her hand had drifted between her thighs and beneath her dress. She had never experienced such an immediate physical response to anything in her life.

The man arched his back, cursing. He was ready to come as Tiffany silently urged him onward. But the woman released her hold on him at the crucial moment. He jerked and moaned, his frustration coming across quite clearly despite the language barrier, but his beautiful tormentor only laughed and tapped his throbbing erection with the riding crop.

Overwhelmed, Tiffany backed away. They appeared to have forgotten her, and curiosity and desire drew her onwards down the corridor.

In another chamber along the dark tunnel, a second naked couple lay on a white fur. The man was a lithe, dark-skinned Adonis with a shaved head, and he was spreading the legs of a plump brunette woman murmuring something in Creole. His cock bobbed long and thick between his legs as his partner drew her knees up eagerly. He positioned himself at her entrance, and gently slid into her pussy as she sighed and accommodated him, taking him in to the hilt.

Tiffany fought to ignore the growing warmth in her panties, utterly absorbed by the sight of the powerful man thrusting into the moaning woman - two handsome rutting beasts oblivious of her presence.

She moved breathlessly on to another chamber, and discovered a man dressed in leather from head to toe, held together with zippers and belts and buckles. He looked like a mummy, only his sapphire eyes showing and blazing with an intensity of purpose. He rose from his armless wooden chair and pointed to her, speaking in a language she did not recognise. But the tone was familiar enough, the tone of someone accustomed to getting his way, just like her.

She stepped back. 'I shouldn't be here...'

More quickly than she would have believed possible he was on her, grasping her wrist and pulling her into the cell, gently but insistently. She should have screamed and fought him, but piggybacked onto her fear was an equally potent measure of curiosity and excitement, which made it impossible for her to resist as he pulled her facedown across his lap. He settled her neatly across his knees even as he drew the hem of her dress up to her waist, exposing her tight black satin panties to his gloved touch and naked gaze. He roughly squeezed her right bottom cheek, and she moaned, overcome with an acute sensation of pleasure mixed with discomfort.

He pulled down her panties, fully exposing her plump cheeks, and Tiffany blushed to her roots as she felt his eyes feasting on her. This was not right. She was Tiffany Welborne, Baroness of Wrightwood, daughter of Zak Welborne, for God's sake. No one, but no one, was supposed to treat her like this... and she certainly was not supposed to enjoy it...

His hand moved lightly across her bottom as his other steadied her by pressing into the small of her back. He continued to speak, his tone patronising, and she flinched as one of his thumbs dug into the soft downy skin between her buttocks, finding her dampness and the perimeter of her pussy. She became intensely aware of how her sex opened to him, and she could actually smell her own arousal. Then, suddenly, he spanked her. She cried out but promptly bit her lip, unwilling to concede that much to this man, a total stranger who had the audacity to continue spanking her while she felt his erection growing beneath her. And as the blows kept coming, the pain was overwhelmed by a warm, almost comforting glow spreading outwards from her bottom, bridging and reinforcing perverse points of arousal in the rest of her body. And her reluctant yelps after each strike melted into a long, low moan rising from the very core of her being...

Finally he stopped punishing her and caressed her burning cheeks, making her wriggle and groan. Dizzy and distracted by the smouldering ache in her buttocks, she could barely keep herself steady on her feet as he released her and let her struggle up off his lap. Her face felt flushed, and she wished she could curl up on herself she was so ashamed. Her hair felt mussed up, and her make-up was probably smeared panda-like under her eyes by now. She bent over to retrieve her panties unable to believe she had just allowed a complete stranger to spank her.

Without glancing back at her tormentor, Tiffany fled the room, the swift clicking of her heels matching the pounding of her heart.

She returned to the above ground club, had the valet fetch her Diablo, and sped out of the car park. She got about ten metres before being halted by members of Cascara's security police, doing another random check. Flustered and angry, she did not have the patience to answer questions from some uniformed subordinate with an attitude about why she had no ownership papers for the car. Therefore, ignoring urgent cries for her to halt, she pulled out of the queue and took off towards daddy's estate in the foothills. She had to get home to daddy.

She blew all four tyres on the nail strips the police set out on the road. It was an abrupt end to a bizarre night. Then she heard the troopers approaching and realised the night had only just begun.

The night lasted an entire month. Drugs were found in the car, and she found herself facing multiple convictions. Now she was on her way to prison. She would be spending the next three years - she could get out sooner, daddy's solicitor's insisted, with good behaviour - in one of Cascara's many correction houses, private franchises licensed to help reduce the high prisonpopulation that results from a zero tolerance towards crime. Many foreigners bought their way into these facilities rather than serve in the far harsher state prisons. It would not be like a holiday camp, however, whatever Jude might hope. They could not leave the premises, and communication with the outside world would be limited to letters. Otherwise, daddy's solicitors assured her, it would be like being back at the academy.

Well, at least she would be away from daddy, who had spent every waking moment lecturing her on the potential loss of life that could have occurred as a result of her actions, and on the millions he would be spending on damages and compensation, blah, blah, blah, blah. All that mattered to her was that he had not been able to get her off with just a fine and a caution, which showed just how much he really loved her - not!

The van lurched to a halt, and after a few moments voices could be heard outside. Then the doors opened onto bright sunlight.

Chapter Two

Tiffany blinked against the brightness of the outside world even as she relished the fresh air caressing her face.

The driver and his escort stood in their traditional blue uniforms beside a third man, clad in a short-sleeved black shirt, black trousers and shiny black leather boots. He was a tall, physically imposing Asian with skin the colour of polished walnut. A goatee heightened his strong jaw, his hair was cut short, and he wore a thick black equipment belt around his waist. 'Come along, girls,' he said with a scowl. 'You're home.'

Tiffany rose as best she could. The van's height, or lack thereof, meant she could not stand up straight. She was wearing a new aquamarine *Ralph Lauren* suit she had bought for the occasion. She knew enough about Cascara to guess they were in the verdant interior of the island. The large white two-story building before her was a restored version of one of the many plantation houses built in the last century, complete with front and side porches on both levels, marble steps, and plants hanging from the central arches. It sat before a well-kept garden with intricate and vibrant flower displays, and all around it huge dark trees stood like sentries. Such trees once covered all of Cascara, but centuries of deforestation for agriculture and shipbuilding meant they had only survived in remote places like this. With cicada chirping loudly in the background, the location was much more serene and civilised than she had expected. Maybe it was going to be like the academy, after all.

The Asian man clamped a hand on her shoulder. 'This way,' he ordered.

She made a show of wriggling out of his grasp. 'Do you mind?' she said indignantly. 'This suit's worth more than you make in a month.'

He smiled. 'You must be Tiffany Welborne.' His voice was suddenly silky. 'I am Armin Singh, head of security at *Rache Correction House*. Shall we get your luggage?'

She watched them pull the prisoners' suitcases out of the van compartment and drop them carelessly on the ground, including her best *Gucci* bag. Then, after a moment of waiting for someone to actually take her luggage inside, she realised they were going to make her do it herself. Jude had only brought a simple duffel bag.

The foyer was dominated by a broad and elegant wooden stairway leading up to an interior balcony on the second floor. A short but shapely dark-skinned young woman with burgundy hair wearing an ash-grey military-like outfit sat behind what resembled a hotel's reception desk. She rose when she saw Singh, who ignored her.

'Are you taking us to our rooms now?' Tiffany asked him. 'Because I'm famished and I'd like to have dinner before I take a bath.'

Singh paused, and seemed to mentally count to ten before replying, 'I'm taking you to meet the house director, *Miss* Welborne. Dinner will wait.' He strode away, fully expecting his charges to follow, which they did.

They traversed a wide corridor running the length of the building, and glancing through open doorways, Tiffany saw other young women like herself all dressed in old-fashioned uniforms and performing a variety of chores.

The director's office was at the very end of the building's west wing, and Singh led them directly inside. The room was spacious, air-conditioned and well decorated, reminding Tiffany of the academy headmistress's office. There was a large mahogany desk, leather-backed chairs, glass-fronted bookcases, a drink's cabinet, a tall grandfather clock and burgundy drapes. There was also the lingering scent of brandy in the air. The man behind the desk appeared to be in his mid-fifties, but he was still attractive and debonair. He wore a uniform much like Singh's, but with long sleeves and a tie. A large snow-white cat with almond-shaped eyes and wearing a diamond-studded collar sat in his lap purring as he stroked it. There was something magnetic about the man's aura, which made the white hairs in his neatly trimmed beard look distinguished rather than out of place.

He smiled. '*Bonapremidi, Manmzels* Forrester, Welborne. Have a seat.' He rested his attention on Tiffany, staring at her intently. His greeting had been in

Creole, yet his accent was more French than Cascaran, perhaps the result of an overseas education. 'I am Doctor Cyrus Rache, owner and operator of this establishment. Please sit down.' He let the cat jump off his lap. 'You still have to be officially processed, so we'll keep this as brief as possible and be done in time for dinner.' He folded his hands together on the desk, and looked at each girl in turn as he spoke. 'I'm certain you've heard many rumours about correction houses. Well, I think you'll find that life here will be either far easier than you expected, or far worse than you imagined.' He paused to offer them a brilliant smile. 'Perhaps even a little of both.'

'Facilities like ours are small scale,' he went on, 'almost family run operations when compared with the state prisons, and we never usually keep more than thirty-two subjects here at any one time. That way, we are able to devote a significant and appropriate amount of time to your reformation. We do not refer to you as prisoners here, by the way, or as inmates, but rather as *subjects*. Our purpose is twofold. Firstly, you are here to be punished for the crimes you committed.' His expression changed from cordial to cold with such ease that it sent a chill down Tiffany's spine, despite the affection she was receiving from his cat, which was rubbing its body around her shins. 'Don't bore the staff or myself with protests of your innocence,' he warned. 'Even if we believed you, we could not, and would not, treat you any differently. And have no illusions, there may not be any cells here like the kind you find in a prison, but you are still confined to these grounds for the duration of your sentence. In fact, in some ways you will have even less rights here than you would have in more traditional institutions. As will already have been explained to you, all correspondence in and out is vetted, and there will be no visitors or telephone calls—'

'About *that*,' Tiffany interrupted him. 'I'll absolutely *need* a phone.'

'No, Miss Welborne,' Rache replied simply, 'you won't. Weren't the restrictions explained to you beforehand?'

'Yes, but I didn't think they'd be applied to me.' She leaned towards him in confidence, separating herself from Jude. 'You know who I am, after all...'

'Yes, Miss Welborne, I know who you are, and the answer remains *no phone*.'

Tiffany surged to her feet. 'When the British Consulate finds out about this—'

'They'll do nothing. You're listed as having Cascaran citizenship. Besides, you weren't exactly dragged here kicking and screaming. Now sit down.'

She did so at once without even realising it.

'Forget what you had before today.' Now he looked at Jude as he spoke. 'Forget all your assumptions and preconceptions about what you think you should expect or deserve. All that matters is what we expect and deserve from you. And what we expect and deserve is obedience, full, unhesitating, unadulterated obedience. Which brings me to the second reason for your being here, *reformation*. The word *reformation* means more than just making you into law-abiding citizens. We intend to reform your very way of thinking. And we have numerous facilities here to do just that. There are sports activities, landscaping projects, garage and workshop areas, and accredited computer based academic courses available. I hope you will both avail yourselves of these during your stay. We even have the facility to place you in new, appropriate positions following the fulfilment of your sentence. Your personal, psychiatric and criminal records were thoroughly examined to determine the efficacy of our methods on you. In other words, you would not be here today if we did not believe we could help you. The daily schedule here is basic and unchanging, except on special occasions. You awake at six o'clock for assembly—'

'Excuse me?' Tiffany half raised her hand, not quite certain she had heard him correctly. 'You expect me to get up at six o'clock in the morning?'

'Don't interrupt me again, Welborne.' Rache no longer displayed even a hint of geniality; his voice was as hard as concrete. 'Following assembly there will be exercise, and then breakfast at seven-thirty. The rest of the morning will be spent working on one of the labour crews, either inside or outside. You must work in some capacity if you wish to earn credits for luxuries such as sweets, toiletries and make-up.'

'You call those luxuries?' Tiffany muttered to herself. 'Talk about hell on earth.'

Rache did not respond to her this time, merely looked at Singh and said, 'Thirty by hand later.'

'Yes, doctor.'

'Following lunch at noon,' Rache continued as if there had been no check in his speech, 'depending upon your schedule you might either return to your work crew, or you may engage in some of the aforementioned activities, classes, sports, etcetera. Dinner is at eight o'clock, and from eight-thirty to lights out at eleven o'clock your time will be yours, although you will not be permitted to leave the immediate area of the main house except on official business. Your dormitory is on the second floor alongside the classrooms in the east wing. Following processing, you will meet the housekeeper, Anne-Marie Colbert, who will instruct you in the finer details of life here.' He paused a moment for his words to sink in, and then asked, 'Are there any questions?'

Tiffany took the initiative, ignoring her curiosity over Rache's earlier remark about 'thirty by hand' to enquire as politely as she could manage, 'May I make a final phone call, please?'

'And whom would you phone?'

'My daddy.'

'You're eighteen, Miss Welborne, a little too old to be phoning daddy. And neither he nor his solicitors could get you out of here now. In fact, they already moved legal mountains to get you sent here for three years instead of to a state prison for six years. Of course, if you wish, we can have you transferred to a more conventional facility right away. They wouldn't offer the activities available to you here, but perhaps you find the concept of spending twenty-three out of every twenty-four hours locked up in a crowded, windowless cell with rats and roaches for company appealing?'

Tiffany did not respond.

'I thought so. Remember, you're here of your own free will.' He rose abruptly. 'Now we will take you to be processed. And remember what I said, obey the regime, obey us, and I promise you will attain fulfilment such as you have never known before.' He fixed a withering gaze on Tiffany. 'Disobey, and you'll soon learn the true meaning of the phrase *hell on earth*, young lady.'

They were led back down the hall again towards the foyer. Jude, walking beside Tiffany, whispered, 'Are you okay? You look pale.'

'Me? You were the one who looked like she was going to wet herself in there.' Then she relented slightly, thinking she might need an ally, no matter how dull-witted. 'I'm just angry. This isn't turning out like it was described.'

'Maybe he just does that speech to put the wind up us? It might not actually be so bad once we're into it.'

Tiffany grunted cynically, but inwardly she grasped at this crumb of hope. Jude might be stupid, but she also might be right.

The two new arrivals were ushered into a large, stark room in which even the frosted windows were painted white. The only colours on the floor were three crimson squares. A table covered with cardboard boxes and envelopes sat near an open door, and an expectant-looking young woman in a grey suit stood behind it. Fluorescent tubes lined the ceiling alongside a slow moving ceiling fan, and some flickered occasionally. The smell of cleaning fluids hung heavily in the air.

Rache slipped into the white medical smock lying on the table, his manner businesslike. 'We will be conducting your processing here,' he said. 'This will involve the confiscation of all contraband items, an examination, disinfecting and the allotment of uniforms and possessions. Understood?'

Singh took over without waiting for a response. 'Right, each of you stand in front of a box. Move it!'

Tiffany and Jude obeyed. The girl behind the table was a fresh-faced redhead, and her eyes were glowing strangely with anticipation.

'You will set your luggage on the tables to be searched before storage,' Singh went on. 'You will then empty your pockets of all items and remove your watches and all jewellery. You will witness them being listed and sealed in the envelopes, and you will sign the appropriate form declaring your witness.'

Tiffany's disbelief afforded her momentary courage. 'Our luggage? Do you mean we won't see any of our possessions until—'

'Until you leave here.' Singh smiled coldly.

She looked to Rache for confirmation. 'But you said you were only taking contraband items.'

'Everything not supplied by us is contraband,' he explained with infuriating simplicity.

Once the girls' bags were searched and security-tagged, and the envelopes were sealed and placed in the boxes, Singh pointed to them and said, 'Lift those and carry them with you to the red squares on the floor behind you.' He moved to stand beside the doctor as they obeyed him. 'Now, remove your clothing and place it in your box.'

There was a pregnant silence, and then Tiffany cried, 'You're not serious?'

'I'm dead serious, Welborne.'

'Take my clothes off in front of you? You're a *man*.'

'Thank you for reminding me.'

'It's a violation of my civil rights,' she protested desperately.

'Rights you happily signed away to come here,' Rache pointed out patiently.

Panic welled up inside her unchecked. Even after she was arrested all they did was empty her pockets; nothing before or since had prepared her for this. She started towards the door. 'That's it, I'm going!'

Singh was on her in a flash, clutching her wrist and pulling her back. With an easy twist of her arm he had her bent over until she could nearly touch her toes, and with his free hand he smacked her across the bottom, the force of the blow easily penetrating her slacks and panties. Tiffany squealed and struggled as he spanked her again, and again, but to no avail. His punishing hand was hard, steady and swift in its power and rhythm. She felt the shock and pain coursing through her body, suffused with a curious warmth spreading up from her buttocks. It was like the incident in the catacombs weeks before, which she had managed to forget until now.

At last Singh stopped spanking her and let her straighten up. He turned her to face him, and his eyes burned into hers. She could not look away as he said quietly, 'It hasn't quite sunk in yet, has it, Welborne? If you don't obey us, you don't go home to daddy in three years, you go to a real jail. Understood?'

Tiffany felt numb, but she had heard every word, and understood. Unable to sort out the miasma of feelings raging inside her, she nodded mutely.

Singh released her. 'Now return to your square and strip,' he commanded.

She returned to the box, and saw that Jude had already removed her T-shirt, revealing full breasts snugly encased in a white bra.

There was an acutely uncomfortable silence for about a minute, alleviated only by the rustle of clothing being removed. Tiffany was not crying yet, but her eyes felt hot as she carefully deposited her four hundred pound *Manolo Blahnik* shoes and her eight hundred pound *Ralph Lauren* suit in the box as if they were charity donations. Yet at the same time a primal sexual thrill rushed through her like an electric charge. Stripping before strangers had always been restricted to the sort of teenage magazine fantasy you laughed at with your mates over a few drinks, now she was actually being forced to do it...

'Stop dawdling, Welborne!' Singh barked.

Tiffany unbuttoned her one hundred pound blue silk blouse, looking over at Jude as she did so. The girl was a pale-skinned, broad-framed Amazon who should have looked imposing, but without the benefit of clothing she seemed smaller. She had one arm draped across her breasts, and her other hand was shielding the copper-haired delta of her pussy.

'Welborne!' Singh barked again, and took a warning step forward.

Tiffany took the less than subtle hint, quickly removing her blouse, which was followed into the box by her blue lace brassiere and matching panties. Then, naked at last, she adopted a pose very similar to Jude's in a vain effort to conceal herself.

Singh made a show of running his eyes up and down her, exacerbating her embarrassment, before looking to Rache. 'Hardly worth the wait, was she?' Then he was all business again. 'Okay, Forrester, you're first. Pick up your box, place it on the table, witness my sealing it, sign the appropriate form, and then stand before the doctor.'

Jude did not hesitate to obey. She stepped forward, revealing a fleshy bottom crowned by two deep dimples. Singh sealed the box and she signed the form, still making an effort to cover herself with her hands.

'Stand with your legs apart, eyes forward, arms over your head,' Rache instructed, slipping on a pair of thin rubber surgical gloves.

Jude hesitated, but a look from Singh spurred her into complying.

Rache circled her slowly, running his hands over every part of her body from her head to her toes, inspecting the soles of her feet and even the skin beneath her pubic curls. And as he did so he made comments about birthmarks, and other distinguishing features of her body, while the girl behind the table took notes on a clipboard. Then he reached out and lifted first one breast and then the other, looking underneath each as Jude gasped but said and did nothing. And as the doctor let her breasts go her nipples began puckering and hardening.

Watching the procedure, a mixture of dread and fascination twisted Tiffany's insides.

Jude continued to blush furiously as Rache checked inside her ears, under her arms, and opened her mouth to run a forefinger around her teeth and gums. Then he ran his gloved fingers through her hair, feeling her scalp. After that there was only one area left to inspect. 'Turn around and touch your toes,' he said.

Weeping silently to herself, Jude obeyed as best she could, crushing her full breasts against her thighs. Tiffany could not actually see Rache's hand penetrating the other girl, but the mere thought excited her. Her pussy was unfathomably warm and moist, and she found herself rubbing her thighs together like greedy hands preparing to count her fortune. Yet she should not feel this way, she should be horribly upset...

'Straighten up, Forrester,' Rache commanded, apparently finished with the examination.

Singh pointed to the open doorway. 'In there you'll be disinfected. If you try to struggle or run off, you will be bound and scrubbed. Once you've showered and dried off, remain where you are.'

Rache waited until Jude had left the room before addressing Tiffany. 'Your turn, Welborne.'

She took her cue, turning several shades of red as she raised her arms over her head, fully revealing herself to the doctor's gaze and touch. He focused intently on her bosom, or rather on the star-shaped birthmark decorating the inner curve of her right breast, a birthmark identical to her mother's. She looked to the girl behind the table for some sympathy, but whatever the other young woman was feeling, it certainly was not sympathy.

Encased in rubber gloves, Rache's hands felt coldly inhuman and sent shivers down her spine, yet all the while the moist heat of her sex was a sweet distraction that made her want to touch herself. Then came the dreaded command to assume the position.

She complied, and felt the doctor lay one hand on her buttocks, and firmly part them while reaching under with his other hand to cup her pubic mound. He squeezed it almost gently, and then his forefinger pierced the aroused lips of her sex, parting them in search of her swollen clitoris.

Tiffany shuddered and nearly toppled over, her blood hopelessly confused about which part of her body to rush to, her head or her vulva. Rache could not fail to notice how aroused she was, how lost she was to his domination, and she desperately quelled the climax building inside her as he probed. Finally, he withdrew his finger and moved up to her bottom's little puckered opening. She caught her breath in disbelief when he penetrated it, thrusting his digit inside her with far more ease and far less discomfort than she would have believed possible, using her own shameful juices as a lubricant.

Then, suddenly, it was all over. 'Straighten up, Miss Welborne.' He broke contact, leaving her feeling strangely empty and unsatisfied. 'Follow Miss Forrester to the next room.' His voice was impersonal as he removed the tight gloves.

Shame added to her frustration, and she covered herself with her hands again as best she could as she left the processing chamber.

The adjacent room was smaller. That was all she had time to notice before two women appeared holding sponges and buckets of a foul-smelling, bubbly pink liquid, and one of them was the ugliest, most menacing woman Tiffany had ever seen in her life. She took Tiffany by the arm and immediately began scrubbing and lathering every inch of her, stopping only to re-soak her sponge. Then she wiped the suds off her face and pushed her away. 'Get going,' she snapped.

There was a running showerhead. The water was ice-cold, and struck Tiffany like a thousand tiny spears. Yet she endured it in order to wash the disinfectant off her skin as quickly as possible. Her body shook with cold and outrage, and her tears were lost in the chilly downpour.

Afterwards she padded over to the other side of the room to a table set before a wall of shelves filled to capacity with cardboard boxes of all sizes. Another young woman stood behind the table. Jude was there, still naked and drying herself off with a thin, barely adequate towel. She looked subdued and defeated yet also oddly invigorated, which was just how Tiffany felt. Jude finished drying herself, and tried to cover as much of her body as possible with the towel, an impossible task given their respective sizes. She did not meet Tiffany's enquiring gaze.

Singh appeared in another doorway, roughly took the wet towels from them and threw them under the table. He then looked Jude over carefully. 'Olivia, size twenty-two, size ten and size forty-B.'

The girl behind the table responded to his words by removing several boxes of varying sizes from the shelves behind her, and placing them in front of Jude. Tiffany understood what was happening, and knowing her own measurements, she was impressed by Singh's accuracy when it was her turn.

'These contain all the clothes you will be wearing during your time here,'

Olivia explained, opening the top of one of the boxes and removing some of the items. 'They include sunhats for outdoor work, exercise clothes, boots and trainers, a towel, and one basic toilet kit. You will now be shown how to identity mark your new possessions using the numbers Mr Singh will assign to each of you, and you will be responsible for their security and care. You're advised to put aside as many of the work credits you earn as possible, as you will be paying for any replacements you might need later on, and won't be allowed to borrow off each other.'

'And don't ask for credit,' Singh added.

Tiffany opened one of the boxes and stared down in dismay at the ash-grey garments.

Singh saw the look in her eyes, and grinned. 'It's what everyone's wearing this year, and guaranteed not to go out of fashion for the duration of your sentence. But chin up, how long will that be for you? Three years? A thousand days? Twenty-six thousand hours?'

He was right. How bizarre, she thought, that it had only begun to sink in.

CHAPTER THREE

Tiffany and Jude were silent as they carried their new belongings up to the second floor. One of the house guards, a tall, broad-shouldered, brown-skinned young man named Stuart Knowles clad in the staff's black outfits, was speaking. 'The west wing is the staff and guards' quarters and is off-limits unless you're authorised or summoned there.'

Tiffany was only half-listening; she was still too distracted by the experiences of the last half-hour to concentrate. Her outfit - a collarless, lightweight uniform with reinforced patches on the knees and elbows and buttons extending down to the navel - was absolutely hideous.

The corridor led directly into the dormitory, an open area where three of the four were walls lined with high, narrow windows fitted with insect screens and overlooking the woods. Sixteen sets of bunk beds with olive coloured metal frames were lined up in two rows. Metal lockers, painted a dull olive colour and numbered in white, served as a headboard for each bed. What captured Tiffany's attention, however, was how spotlessly clean the room was. The white sheets on the cots were perfectly taut, the beds were precisely aligned, and the polished floor shone almost blindingly.

Stuart knocked on a door just outside the dorm entrance. 'Miss Colbert, it's the new arrivals.'

From within the office came a muffled voice, 'Thank you, Stuart, send them in.'

He smiled as he opened the door slightly, and waived them in. 'See ya, girls.'

Tiffany huffed, setting her boxes down on the nearest bed and pushing past Jude to be the first one inside.

The housekeeper's office was starkly furnished with a desk and chair and a large magnetic wall chart with movable names, times and locations. A window looked out into the dorm. There was a leather couch, a small refrigerator and a portable air-conditioner unit upon which sat a television and video player. A black-clad woman, somewhere in her thirties, stood by the desk stubbing out the remains of a cigarette in a metal ashtray. She was tall and her skin was the colour of coffee-and-cream. A mass of curly mahogany hair was tied back in a neat bun that set off her full, rosy lips, turned-up nose, and large, challenging eyes. 'You're letting the heat in,' she said.

Tiffany quickly closed the door, and then held out her hand in greeting, desperately feeling the need to take command of the situation. 'This is Jude Forrester,' she announced, 'and I'm—'

'Welborne.' The housekeeper ignored the proffered hand, and moved behind her desk for a clipboard.

Tiffany let her hand fall and put aside her indignation at the woman's lack of manners in order to make a good impression on her.

'My name is Anne-Marie Colbert, and my friends call me Anne-Marie,' the housekeeper announced. 'But you will address me as "madam".'

A door at the back of the office opened suddenly and a young woman stepped into the room. She was a timid looking creature with frizzy blonde hair and apple-red cheeks. Casting a furtive glance at the newcomers, she moved by them towards the door leading into the dorm.

Ann-Marie Colbert waited until the girl's hand was on the doorknob before asking cryptically, 'Well, Bonnie?'

The girl froze, and then turned to face the housekeeper without actually meeting her eyes. 'Thank you, madam.' Her voice was as soft as tissue.

Colbert treated herself to a slight, enigmatic smile. 'You may leave now,' she said.

Bonnie obeyed with alacrity.

'Now, as my job title might lead you to expect,' the housekeeper went on pleasantly, 'I keep the house running to Dr Rache's high standards. Apart from the staff and the guards, there are no maids or cooks or cleaners. We're responsible for all that, and though you may be assigned to other work crews or have academic or athletic requirements, all of you will at some stage be helping me out. I also act as intermediary. If you have a problem with someone here, staff, guards or fellow inmates, then you take it up with me first, or with my subordinate, Bonnie, whom you've just met. Understood?'

Tiffany and Jude nodded.

'Good. Time for your first lesson. From now on when I ask a question, I expect to hear "yes, madam", "no, madam", or whatever is appropriate. Do we have a problem with that?'

'No, madam,' Tiffany found herself saying in unison with Jude. This woman was arrogance itself; she acted as though she owned the place. Tiffany had known a hundred women like her, and few were worth a second glance, let alone any measure of respect.

'Of course, we may already have a problem,' Colbert informed them, looking directly at Tiffany. 'One thing you'll notice in places like this is that everyone here drives a luxury car on the outside and everyone has celebrities for lovers, family members, and so on. Yet they all become obedient girls, more or less, who have learned their place, and they don't need a duchess trying to throw her weight around.'

Tiffany straightened her back and squared her shoulders. 'I'm a baroness, actually.'

'You *were* a baroness, now you're nothing more than a subject of *Rache House* and subject to its authority here. Understand?'

The statement rankled Tiffany, but she nodded. 'Yes, madam,' she said through gritted teeth.

'Good.' Suddenly, the housekeeper's expression and voice softened somewhat. 'Look, Welborne, just behave, okay. You do that, and I won't treat you any differently than I do the other girls.' She walked around to the front of the desk. 'Now let's get your bed assignments. You can leave your things in my office here. Dinner's over at half-six, but wait for me in the TV room afterwards. We'll teach you how to properly store everything in your lockers.' She frowned abruptly. 'Where's your gear, Welborne?'

Tiffany indicated the door. 'On a bed outside.'

'What?' Colbert reached out, grabbed her wrist, and pulled her out into the dorm. When she saw the boxes piled on the bed she released her, stormed over to them, and began flinging them off the bed in Tiffany's direction. 'Stupid bitch! You'll ruin the covers!'

Tiffany let the boxes slide along the floor on either side of her like curling stones, making no attempt to stop or catch them.

Colbert's fingers played on the corners of the bed, drawing taut the sheets as she shot a venomous glance back at Tiffany. 'The doctor likes to make surprise inspections in the afternoon! If he saw this he could mark the whole dorm for twenty by switch. Do you know what that means?'

Swallowing as she recalled the thirty by hand she had just received from Singh, Tiffany nodded reluctantly. 'It was a mistake,' she admitted. 'Sorry.'

'A mistake that could cost you beatings from the doctor and from me. Understood?'

Anger and dread fought for dominance inside the young baroness. How could she possibly tolerate all this authority, all these petty, meaningless rules, and the constant threat of punishment - *corporal* punishment - for three years? Did they truly expect her to surrender her individuality and her willpower? This was a nightmare that just kept getting worse. Yet all she said was, 'Yes, madam.'

'Then collect your belongings. And try not to make a habit of this, Welborne.'

Two long tables, one large for the subjects and one smaller for the staff, dominated the dining room. Plates of food were distributed from an opening in the wall leading into the kitchen. Subjects brought the staff their food first and then queued up for their own. Each subject carried her plate and cutlery to a seat at the table, then stood and waited. Tiffany, separated from Jude, was not quite sure what everyone was waiting for, and no one bothered to tell her. Then she saw an almost imperceptible nod from Rache relayed to Colbert. The nod was passed on, and only then did everyone sit and begin eating. The subjects talked freely amongst themselves, albeit in relatively hushed tones. Tiffany's appetite had awoken with a vengeance when she first smelled the food cooking in the kitchen. Dinner was curried fish with rice and vegetables, typical Creole cuisine and substandard fare compared with daddy's chef's creations, but she was hungry enough that it tasted delicious to her.

Afterwards the subjects gathered in the TV room, and lounged in the several couches and armchairs strewn around the small screen. Sitting alone, Tiffany became aware of a group of girls in a corner staring at her. The apparent leader of the clique was the ugly, menacing woman who had scrubbed her down during processing, and the look of bold appraisal she was giving Tiffany was unnerving.

'That's Shazza.'

Tiffany looked up to enquire further, and then forgot her question. The young man who had spoken was a guard, a wild-haired creature with thick lips and sleepy eyes who somehow managed to be good-looking despite his fierce aura. 'She's king girl in the dorm,' he added in a sexy Creole drawl.

'King girl?'

'Queen Bee, if you like. The pecking order extends throughout the house.' He smiled again at her expression. 'Don't worry, it gets better.'

She grunted. 'It can't get much worse.'

'My name's Rembrandt Baptiste, but everyone calls me Remy.'

'I'm Tiffany.'

'I know.' He leaned against the wall, partly facing the TV as if he was not supposed to be talking to her. 'I've heard you've had a hard time so far. If there's anything I can do for you, just let me know.'

'I don't suppose you have the keys to the front gate?'

He made a show of patting his pockets. 'Sorry, the senior staff have all the important keys. You'll understand, if you get assigned to Singh's work crew.'

'Assigned? You mean I might get to work with you?'

'On a limited basis,' he clarified, sounding almost apologetic, 'if Singh wants you. You've probably already met some of his crew in processing.'

She felt herself blush. 'They're sadists, all of them.'

'Yes,' he agreed simply. 'But if you trust them, you can't imagine what...' He stopped himself as if he had almost divulged a forbidden secret.

His attitude piqued Tiffany's interest. 'What do they do to us here, Remy?'

He frowned, and then looking around furtively he asked, 'Fancy a chocolate?'

It astonished her to realise how quickly the simplest pleasures became valuable. 'You have some?' she whispered eagerly, momentarily forgetting her more important question.

'Uh-huh.' He reached into a pocket and produced something that remained hidden in his hand but which made slight crackling sounds. 'Don't let anyone see you eat it,' he warned.

Tiffany was not listening. She snatched the treat from his hand and tore open the foil wrapper. She did not see Remy stiffen, but she did heard him mutter, 'No!'

A hand reached out from her other side and grabbed what remained of the chocolate.

'Where'd you get that?' Colbert demanded.

Tiffany did not answer; the melting remains of the chocolate were coating the inside of her mouth and making speech difficult.

Remy straightened up. 'I gave it to her, Miss Colbert.'

The housekeeper nodded, and pocketed the remains of the chocolate. 'You know better, Remy. Let's go, Welborne. You too, Forrester.'

Tiffany, confused by the exchange, nevertheless obeyed.

The following hour was interminable. Tiffany and Jude were instructed by Colbert and Bonnie on how to properly store their clothes and toilet kits in their lockers, and were taught how to make their beds and tighten the sheets into crisp hospital corners. There was even a proper way of aligning shoes and boots beneath the head of the bed, and the boots had to be polished until they possessed a mirror finish. It was a humiliating experience for Tiffany, who fumed silently as Colbert insulted her efforts.

'There, now you can't claim ignorance if you screw up,' the housekeeper taunted. 'Not that it would help, since Dr Rache doesn't suffer ignorance gladly. And speaking of him...' She glanced at the wall clock. 'It's nearly eight. Go downstairs and wait outside his office, Welborne.'

Tiffany started to ask why she should do that, but then thought better of it.

Downstairs there were other subjects standing or sitting in the gloomy corridor outside Rache's office, and Remy was there, too.

'Hi,' she said, and started as Rache's door opened abruptly and a subject emerged looking exhausted.

From within the room came the doctor's impatient voice. 'French!'

One of the girls waiting in the corridor rose from her seat and entered the office without delay, taking care to close the door quietly behind her.

'He sounds worse than usual because he has to rush things tonight,' Remy informed Tiffany. 'There's a staff meeting scheduled. How'd your training go?'

She shrugged. 'Why am I here?'

'By giving you some of my chocolate, I broke the rule against trafficking.'

'Trafficking? It was hardly drugs we exchanged.'

'Same principle, though. No giving or lending of clothes, goods, *anything*. Keeps people from exercising undue power over others.' He smiled as if at a private joke, and then looked contrite. 'Sorry.'

'What's going to happen?' She tried not to sound anxious.

He leaned back against the wall and folded his arms over his chest. 'He'll call you in, like you just saw. He may ask about the offence, even ask for your side of the story, but that's unlikely. Then comes the punishment.'

The door opened again, the girl emerged teary-eyed, and beat a hasty retreat down the corridor.

Rache summoned the next victim, and once the door closed on her, Remy went on. 'Since he's rushing it, he's probably using the switch.'

'The switch?' It took a moment for Tiffany to comprehend what he meant. 'He expects me to just walk in there and let him beat me? And you're here to witness it?'

He frowned. 'No, more'n likely I'll get switched as well.'

'What? But you're a guard. He can't do that to you. You can quit anytime.'

Remy opened his mouth to reply, and then seemed to think better of it. 'You'll understand soon enough,' he said instead.

The office door opened again, the latest victim walked out sniffling, and Rache called out, 'Baptiste! You and Welborne!'

Remy nodded to Tiffany and she followed him into the room, prepared to give the doctor a piece of her mind while she had the chance.

Rache was not behind his desk; he was pacing the floor before it like a man waiting for an overdue taxi, while his cat regally occupied his leather chair. He was holding a long thin wooden switch he occasionally snapped through the air. He waited until the door closed before saying, 'I don't have time to go over the stupidity of your actions, Baptiste. Nor should there be a need to, either. You've done well enough up until now. And as for you, young lady, I knew this was inevitable, albeit not so quickly. I did so want to savour your first time before me at punishment.'

Tiffany's anger chilled into apprehension.

'Doctor, I must take full responsibility,' Remy said quietly. 'Miss Welborne didn't know—'

'You know what I say about ignorance, don't you, Baptiste?' He did not wait for an answer. 'You're very gallant, Remy, but your gallantry is misplaced. Now both of you kiss the desk. Baptiste, show her how it's done.'

Tiffany started when Remy touched her arm and guided her to a sinisterly well-worn spot in the burgundy carpet. Then, standing beside her, he unbuckled and unzipped his trousers and let them drop to his ankles. A moment later his briefs followed. The lower half of his body was matted with dark hair running up from his shins to collect and thrive like wild flora around his groin. And as if to mirror this display of vitality, his penis, long and thick even at rest, was pulsing gently to life, the shaft hardening and pointing towards the desk as the head emerged glistening from its hood. His balls hung beneath his pubic hair, their sac pink, wrinkled and heavy looking. He bent forward, gripped the edge of the desk, and stared straight down at the carpet, presenting his buttocks for punishment, for only the tops of his bottom cheeks were covered by the tail of his shirt.

'Follow his lead, Welborne,' Rache commanded.

Slowly, Tiffany opened her uniform and let it fall around her boots, exposing her plain white cotton panties. Then she froze.

'You're still not ready, Welborne.'

Fighting back tears of outrage, she slid her thumbs beneath the elastic of her panties, and pushed them down to her knees, quickly bending over and gripping the edge of the desk before either man could see her dusting of pubic hair.

Rache alternated between Tiffany and Remy, striking each one with the switch in turn. Tiffany bit her lip as the evil stick bit into her tender flesh and sent flashes of pain up her spine, followed by waves of heat. In the corner of her eye she could see Remy's penis swiftly rising into full attentiveness. She had never expected to see a man in this humiliating position, much less expected to see him react in such a way, and then she realised her pussy was growing sympathetically hot and wet...

Rache stopped beating them and moved away as if the incident had been supremely distasteful to him. 'You may dress again now,' he said.

'Thank you, doctor.' Remy reached down and drew up his briefs and trousers, burying his erection, as Tiffany silently covered herself again and turned towards the door, eager to escape.

Rache moved quickly and grabbed her chin in his hand. 'Your pupils are dilated,' he said, studying her lovely face intently. 'Your cheeks are flushed, your breathing is rapid... you enjoyed that. Is your pussy wet?'

Tiffany defiantly pulled her chin free of his possessive hold. 'You sick bastard,' she said quietly, and he slapped her cheek; a light blow born more out of contempt than anger.

'Return Welborne to the dorm, Baptiste, then get back to work,' he said flatly. 'And watch yourself. This hellion could ruin you without batting an eyelash.'

'Yes, doctor.' Remy motioned with his head for her to follow him out of the office, and before they parted on the second floor landing, he asked her, 'Did you enjoy that?'

'My feelings are my own business,' she muttered, unable to meet his eyes.

'Not here,' he corrected her. His tone was unnerving precisely because there was no malice in it, just what sounded like the simple truth. 'Here there are no secrets, no privacy, Tiffany. Sooner or later everyone will know you inside and out, literally and otherwise. You thought your clothes and possessions were the most they could strip from you, but they're nothing. You'd better be prepared. It's the price you pay to be here and not in a state prison.' And with this warning he left her alone with her mounting confusion and anxiety.

CHAPTER FOUR

The dorm was abuzz with activity, and although Tiffany had seen most of them before in the dining room, now was the first time the other girls really began noticing her. They whispered furtively to each other as they glanced her way, and there was the occasional childish giggle. Most of the subjects appeared ready for bed dressed in T-shirts and panties, and Tiffany was surprised by the open displays of affection amongst some of them. She also tried not to notice the marks on many of their backs and buttocks.

The lavatory was filled with the collective scents of soap, shampoo, and femininity. She considered showering, particularly to rid herself of any lingering traces of that awful disinfectant used on her during processing, but she decided to wait until morning. She was washing her hands at one of the basins when she saw Jude in the mirror standing behind her.

'They sent me in,' Jude said, as if apologising for daring to infringe upon Tiffany's personal space. 'They want us,' she added, looking nervous.

'What's wrong with you, Jude?'

'I was in borstal once, and I remember the welcome the girls gave me there. I'd still love to escape from here.'

Tiffany's gaze met hers in the mirror. 'Me, too,' she agreed sullenly.

'Forrester! Welborne!' A mocking voice echoed hollowly into the lavatory from the open doorway. 'Don't keep us waiting!'

Jude smiled anxiously, and gently squeezed Tiffany's shoulder. 'Well, here goes,' she said ominously.

Tiffany shrugged angrily. 'Stop being so dramatic,' she said, trying to sound braver than she actually felt.

They stepped out into the open area at one end of the dorm. Tiffany and the head girl appeared to be the only ones still in uniform as the two new arrivals floated into the centre of the semicircle of women.

Shazza approached them, her eyes bright. 'Girls, we're here to welcome you to our little family, and to make sure you know your place.' She nodded towards Tiffany. 'You're a princess, aren't you?'

'A baroness.'

Shazza feigned an apology. 'Oh, please forgive me. Being king girl around here, I should have recognised you even without your crown. They say real nobility shines through no matter what you wear, or don't wear. So let's test the theory. Strip, both of you.'

Wordlessly and immediately Jude began to comply with the order while the girls around them jeered and cheered.

Tiffany remained coolly defiant. 'Is that how you get your kicks around here?' she asked scornfully.

Shazza smiled venomously. 'For a start, yes,' she said threateningly.

'Filthy dykes,' Tiffany sneered.

Shazza raised a hand, and the girls around her swarmed towards Tiffany. Some grabbed her by the hair. Others held her firmly by her limbs and supported her back as they lifted her up off the floor while the rest tugged at her uniform. She cursed and swore, and someone stuffed something - panties, she found out later - into her mouth. The cheers of the girls pounded her eardrums as they removed her uniform, her boots and socks, and finally her panties. Only when she was completely naked did the frenzied mob set her down beside Jude and retreat slightly, jubilantly congratulating each other on their good work.

Tiffany stood with her arms crossed over her breasts, scowling, and when the girls' raucous laughter and catcalls finally subsided, Shazza stepped forward again and looked the new arrivals over with the critical eye of a woman considering purchasing two new knickknacks for her collection. Then she stepped behind Tiffany and brushed a palm over her bottom. 'Yes, princess,' she whispered, 'some of us are dykes, while some aren't and yet indulge anyway. But our masters and mistresses will not let us be restricted to those pigeonholes. We've learned to serve both sexes equally here just as you'll learn to.'

'Fuck you!' Tiffany snapped, bristling with defiance.

'You'd do well to copy her, Welborne,' Shazza said calmly, indicating Jude. 'She'll get by with a minimum of bother here and a maximum of pleasure. But maybe you think you're different, special somehow, superior perhaps?' She chuckled, slowly prowling around Tiffany as she addressed her subsequent words to the crowd. 'We forgot about her nobility, didn't we, girls? But what Welborne hasn't bothered to mention, and which Dr Rache told me tonight, is that the baronial title she likes to flaunt wasn't inherited, it was bought. It was a present from her daddy for her twelfth birthday.'

There was more raucous laughter, and Tiffany was ready to burst into tears at the revelation. It was true; the title had come with the estate at Wrightwood daddy purchased before emigrating to Cascara. Yet even now she stubbornly refused to accept the true origins of her title, and it was this passionate refusal that enabled her to retain her dignity.

Shazza turned to the other girls. 'Get in position,' she commanded, and Tiffany watched them scattering to stand beside their beds facing the path running between the twin rows of bunks, and suddenly she noticed the wet towels and T-shirts lying everywhere.

'We've welcomed you,' Shazza said with a formal note in her voice. 'Now we have to make sure you know your place.' She pointed to the opposite end of the runway. 'I'll be standing down there. Crawl to me on all fours, and when you arrive,' she pointed at her feet, 'lick my boots. Got it?'

Again Jude nodded, but Tiffany, although less arrogant than before, asked stubbornly, 'And if I refuse?'

'Then I'll make you lick me somewhere else.' The bully strode down the runway, her voice carrying over the clack of her boot heels on the polished floor. 'I expect you both on all fours before I turn around.'

Jude, as usual, obeyed at once. Tiffany was slower to do so, but she yielded just in time as the other girls lifted their wet towels and shirts in preparation. Then suddenly the dorm fell silent, and all that could be heard was a faint, steady, slow dripping of water from the shower room.

Shazza was some ten metres away, but her triumphant leer burned bright as ever. 'Now start crawling, bitches.'

The polished floor hard against their hands and knees, Tiffany and Jude began crawling down the runway between the beds. The first of the wet towels striking their backs added to their discomfort, and soon their buttocks and thighs were burning from the sting of soaking wet cotton. Jude pressed doggedly onward, her head bowed, but Tiffany faltered and paused. A torrent of blows rained down on her then like sharks attacking one of their own in a feeding frenzy, and encouraged her to keep moving.

The two initiates crawled through the gauntlet of pain and humiliation as their new dorm-mates transformed into fervent savages, then after what felt like an eternity, Tiffany found her progress impeded by one of Shazza's boots. The beating stopped, and her senses focused on the strong smell of leather and polish. She looked to her right. Jude was crouched before the other boot, running her tongue along the polished sides from toe to heel, and back again, as devotedly as a lover, only stopping to remoisten her tongue. The sight should have triggered the expected reaction of disgust and humiliation, but when she searched for those feelings, Tiffany found instead an acute hunger she could not define.

Shazza's foot began to tap the floor, keeping pace with Tiffany's racing heart as with an ease that would continue to surprise her for days to come she bent forward and began licking the boot before her, ignoring the unpleasant taste. And as she licked, her laps became longer, more drawn out, until she was lovingly covering the entire boot with her tongue as if possessed by a demon she could not even name.

The morning bell cut through Tiffany's befuddled brain like a knife, and she cringed beneath her sheet while all around her she could hear the unbelievable fact that many of the other girls were already up and about. After last night's humiliation, she could not bear to face anyone.

Then the sheet was rudely pulled off her and Colbert's voice pierced her eardrums almost as sharply as the bell. 'Welborne! Get up and get dressed! Assembly and exercise in five minutes!'

Assembly was in the living room on the first floor, with the subjects all wearing T-shirts, shorts and trainers and lined up in quasi-military fashion. Tiffany was in the back row, which made it easier for her to slip away and tiptoe down the corridor towards the offices, her heart pounding, her hands shaking as she tried each doorknob until she finally found one that opened and let her inside.

She found herself in a nondescript office, but she did not have the time or the patience to notice anything more than the telephone on the desk. She rushed towards it, her mind recalling one of the numbers to daddy's estate. She had to speak to him. She had to convince him to get her out of this lunatic asylum. Lifting the receiver, she began hitting the buttons, and received nothing but a strange set of beeps. Was the phone broken? She tried again, cursing more loudly with each successive failure.

The door opened behind her, and she turned to see Remy standing on the threshold, his expression neutral. 'Security access numbers are required for outside lines,' he informed her.

Her face glum with defeat, she set the receiver back down and followed him out of the office.

Back in the living room she took her place in the assembly formation again while Remy had a quick word with Rache, who nodded and looked to Quinn, the house's official trainer. 'They're yours now,' he said.

Outside, behind the house, stretched a large clearing sectioned off for various sporting activities with white lines and markers set in the well-manicured pitch. There was even a three metre wide oval running track encircling the clearing lined with maroon gravel. A morning mist hung in the air, settling amidst the surrounding trees and floodlight poles so they looked as though they were submerged in snow, and the air was electric with the sound of busy insects and birds.

The subjects lined up in the clearing as they had inside the house. Quinn appeared before them, and the exercises began. Stretches, jumping jacks, deep-knee bends and half a dozen other tortures. Too late, Tiffany realised she was not wearing her allotted sports bra, and cursed herself for the oversight. She was very glad when the ordeal finally ended, but then she found out those were only the warm-ups.

There were push-ups and sit-ups made even more difficult by the tropical humidity. She tried to cheat, and was rewarded by Quinn's immediate presence beside her. The exercise mistress blew her whistle and prodded her on verbally as well as physically with her boot. She would not let her stop, so Tiffany called upon her remaining reserves of energy to carry on and bring the ordeal to an end. And just when she thought it was at an end, there was the track run.

By the end of her jog she was sore everywhere, and yet she surprised herself by completing the required laps without collapsing. Only when the whistle blew, a million miles away, and she knew for certain it was all over, did fatigue finally come crashing over her like the rear cars of a train colliding into the engine after a sudden halt. She sank to her knees, and then onto all fours on the adjacent dew covered pitch as her lungs desperately fought for air.

After a moment she became aware of someone crouching beside her, and then helping her into a sitting position with her head between her knees, keeping her centred. It was Quinn supporting her, and she was saying something Tiffany had to concentrate on very hard to understand. 'You've done well for a first-timer. I've seen your athletic record, and I'd like you on my football team. Maybe we can get together sometime this week and talk about it. Okay?'

She nodded in acknowledgement, and let the older woman help her back up to her feet, her touch strong and comforting.

She was preparing to enter the showers when she was called into Colbert's office. The woman was sitting behind her desk, and she did not look up from her computer as she said, 'Close the door behind you, Tiffany.'

'Yes, madam.' She was too exhausted to notice right away that the imperious housekeeper had addressed her by her first name. 'Is there a problem, madam?'

Colbert looked up. 'I'll not keep you long. Did you attempt to use one of the downstairs phones before assembly?'

Tiffany breathed in deeply, and sighed resignedly. 'Yes, madam,' she admitted.

'The doctor will want to see you tonight at eight o'clock about it. As I may have explained to you last night, it is my policy to inflict additional punishment for infractions within the house, but not in this case.'

Tiffany frowned, confused. 'Madam?' she queried.

Colbert's face softened almost sympathetically, and rising, she stepped around her desk to stand before Tiffany.

'I was unduly harsh with you yesterday,' she said. 'Please accept my apologies.

I also believe Shazza was unnecessarily cruel to you during your initiation last night, and I hope you weren't too distressed by it. I will reprimand her for you.'

'I...' Tiffany felt her face colouring at the memories, which coupled with the abrupt change in the housekeeper's attitude, left her at a loss for words.

'I want you to know that you are not without allies here, Tiffany,' the woman went on. 'Should you have any problems or any questions whatsoever, please do not hesitate to approach me.'

'I... um, thank you, madam,' she stammered.

Colbert smiled affably. 'Now run along. We don't have an infinite amount of hot water for the showers.'

'Yes, madam.' More confused than ever Tiffany left the office, quietly closing the door behind her.

After showering, changing and having breakfast, Tiffany was informed that she and Jude were on Eric Kemp's ground-keeping crew. They met the man and the rest of the assigned crew outside, and he led them away from the house along a well-worn path between the sand dragon trees, their high wigs of generous green fronds providing temporary shelter from the sun and heat.

They emerged into a large rectangular clearing bordered on two sides by a high granite wall, and by trees on the other two sides. As befitting the estate's agricultural origins, this area had probably been used for cultivation, most likely of spices, but had since been allowed to become overgrown and weed-ridden.

Kemp then led them to a small building sitting at the edge of the field, with a corrugated steel roof and shutters on the windows. The size of the locked and bolted door indicated it had once been a stable, even though its size suggested an old groundskeeper's cottage.

Kemp opened the door and ordered his subjects to begin bringing out shovels, hoes and other gardening implements, including primitive ploughs complete with harnesses for a horse, though Tiffany had yet to see any around.

Kemp, handsome and frightening all in black, wearing a large-brimmed hat and wielding an ominous riding crop in one of his gloved hands, motioned to Tiffany and Jude, who had remained detached from the others, unsure of what was expected of them. 'Forrester, Welborne, get over here and pick up that plough.'

'Yes, Mr Kemp,' Jude said, quickly moving to obey his order. Tiffany watched her in disgust. She had recovered from the morning's arduous callisthenics, and the idea of behaving as subserviently as that stupid cow turned her stomach.

The plough, a simple but sturdy tool consisting of the arrowhead-shaped share blade, a few supports and a harness, was heavier than it looked, but Tiffany let Jude do the lion's share of the carting.

Kemp looked the field over before he began speaking, while pointing at girls and places with his crop. 'You workers with the tools, start digging up all the rushes, weeds and rocks you find, then carry them over to that wall for disposal. And watch out for snakes and ants. Holbert, Morrow, Forrester and Welborne, you'll be manning the ploughs.'

'Where are the horses?' Tiffany blurted without thinking. No one answered her, for there was no need as she watched Georgette Holbert and Monica Morrow - respectively a tall, gaunt girl with doe eyes and buttery-blonde hair, and a shorter, chunkier young woman with bobbed raven hair - nod to each other with a professional air and begin helping each other into the harnesses.

'That's barbaric,' said Tiffany, and then added to Jude, 'Well, we know which end you'll be taking.'

Jude nodded dumbly, and even moved towards the harness, but Kemp addressed Tiffany. 'What was that, Welborne?'

She suddenly felt like a child caught with her hand in the biscuit barrel. 'Um, nothing, Mr Kemp...'

He approached her, smacking the crop absently against his strong thigh. 'You said you knew which end your partner would be taking on the plough. Would you care to enlighten me, seeing as how I'm just your humble supervisor?'

The sarcasm was biting, and Tiffany found herself squirming beneath his, and everyone else's, regard. 'I - I only thought, seeing as how Jude is such a big girl—'

'Then she'd be ideal for directing the plough, wouldn't she?' He smiled. 'And you pull, right?'

Tiffany raised her chin sulkily. 'No,' she said.

'And you pull, right?' Kemp repeated, and smacked her right thigh with the crop.

She yelped and quickly nodded reluctantly, and Kemp signalled to Holbert. 'Show them both how to attach the harness,' he ordered, and then turned his attention back to Jude and Tiffany, who was pouting and ruefully rubbing her sore thigh. 'Watch and learn; you'll be expected to do this yourselves from now on, and if you get it wrong you'll dislocate something. Or worse, you'll annoy me.'

Tiffany, her stomach churning, watched intently as Holbert laconically fitted the thickly-padded leather bridle - obviously too small even for a pony, Tiffany now realised - over her head until it rested heavily on her shoulders. Leather cords reached under her arms, and down between her legs.

'Lean forward when you pull,' Holbert instructed Tiffany, taking her hands and binding them by the wrist on the front portion of the bridle. 'Pull with your upper body, keeping as steady a motion as you can.' She lifted something shiny and long from the front of the bridle. 'Open your mouth.' It was a bit; she wanted to put a horse's bit in her mouth.

Tiffany backed away. 'Fuck off!' she challenged.

'You have to wear it, it's part of the outfit,' Holbert insisted, glancing nervously in Kemp's direction as if she might be blamed for Tiffany's rebelliousness. 'Try it,' she urged, lowering her voice. 'Believe me, you'll like it.'

There was conviction in her eyes, an arresting conviction that somehow made Tiffany open her mouth like a child finally accepting her medicine while the other girl placed the cold bit on her tongue, and then fit the rest of the straps around and over her head.

Her mouth clamped down on the metal bar as best it could, and moving her head around told her it did not seem to be connected to anything controllable by the person behind the plough. It was a prop to acerbate the humiliated status of the one in the harness. With her hands bound at the level of her breasts, she had to fight the distraction to claw at her restraints, and she had even less success ignoring the sweet warmth in her sex, a pulsing moist heat as much out of her control as the degrading object in her mouth.

Kemp returned and inspected Tiffany, occasionally tapping her with the tip of his crop while he looked her up and down. 'Good work, Holbert. I hope the new mare wasn't too difficult.' He rapped Tiffany playfully on her bottom, and then he was all business again, pointing to one end of the field. 'I want both teams working side by side. Forrester, watch and listen to Holbert as she guides Morrow along. And don't let your mare off lightly. She's supposed to be doing most of the work.'

'Yes, Mr Kemp,' Jude agreed sycophantically.

Tiffany swore through the bit more than once during the hours that followed, which proved a body and mind-numbing experience. It was backbreaking work even though the earth beneath her boots was soft from recent rains and easily furrowed. The smell of cleaved soil filled her nostrils, but did not do much to refresh her straining and overheated senses. Perspiration soaked every fibre of her uniform, and the merciless sun above seemed to burn into her skull. The only positive notes in this symphony of misery were the facts that it was too hot for the insects, and she managed to keep up with her fellow plough-horse, Morrow, who set an exhausting pace. But then Holbert was not out to berate and chastise her partner as Jude seemed to be intent on doing to Tiffany whenever she faltered. Jude had taken on the role of plough-girl with obvious relish.

At last it was noon and lunchtime, and Tiffany was freed from her bonds. Her right calf felt as if she had pulled a muscle there, and her shoulders and chest felt peculiarly light without the restraints. She straightened her back and stretched, moaning with relief.

'Tiffany?'

She glanced derisively at Jude, who looked contrite now that she was no longer behind the plough.

Jude averted her eyes, looking ashamed of herself. 'Tiffany, I... I don't—'

'Piss off, bitch,' Tiffany hissed.

While Kemp employed the inside of the cottage for his meal, enjoying the shade, most of the crew took shelter behind it to eat, drink and rest. Nearby stood the rusted skeletal frame of a shower, and Tiffany watched as some of the girls took turns working the hand pump to draw water up into the pipes from an adjacent drum, while other girls, Jude included, casually stripped off their uniforms and cooled themselves down, squealing and giggling like children. It looked delightful, and Tiffany was tempted to join them, but she refrained from doing so because she did not want to appear to be settling into the oppressive regime.

Holbert sat down beside her. 'We weren't properly introduced before,' she said.

'Everyone calls me Georgie.'

Tiffany finished off her water. 'I thought everyone got a good introduction to me last night,' she said belligerently.

'Oh, you're not still sore about that, are you?' Georgie said breezily. 'Everybody goes through it with Shazza. And once everyone understands their place, things run smoothly around here.'

'It's awful!' Tiffany insisted, unwilling to accept what had happened that easily.

But Georgie just smiled. 'Hey, Tiff, you stick with me and I'll teach you everything you need to know. I'll introduce you to my mates, and we'll play some cards after dinner, okay?'

Against her will, Tiffany warmed to the offer, the kindest she had received since her arrival. 'Okay,' she said carefully, 'I think I'd like that.'

'Good.' Georgie's expression changed slightly; became more earnest. 'And I'd really like you as a friend.' She reached out and rested her hand on Tiffany's thigh, the fingers curved towards her sex and moving slowly closer. 'I think you're beautiful, Tiff.'

With a wail of disgust Tiffany pushed Georgie away and surged to her feet. 'Keep your hands to yourself, you little pervert!'

'Oh, would you listen to her?' Georgie sounded more amused than offended. 'She wasn't so high and mighty crawling on the floor last night. Hey, where are you going?'

Tiffany did not answer, but strode into the woods until she was out of everyone's sight. Then she began to run.

CHAPTER FIVE

Tiffany found herself moving through more densely packed trees than grew around the footpaths. Here the sun's rays were blocked by high leaves and branches and had to struggle to reach the dark, mossy ground and lichen covered rocks. An abundance of life thrived in the luxuriant undergrowth, and some small trees had even taken root in the moss festooning the larger trunks, and the soil trapped in tangled roots became flowerpots for ferns, bright begonias and elegant orchids all scrabbling for the shifting rafters of light. Mosquitoes buzzed lazily and were easily caught by lime-green, bronze-eyed tree frogs and chameleons, while further up in the trees birds attacked papery yellow wasp's nests hanging from the branches like Chinese lanterns. But Tiffany was blind to the beauty around her as only thoughts of escape filled her mind.

Before she knew it she had reached another section of the perimeter wall. The ground between the wall and the trees, perhaps two or three metres wide, was bare; nothing grew on it to help her scale the barrier. Then she saw the gates; elaborate wrought iron gates that looked freshly painted an impenetrable black and teased her with the promise of the winding dirt road beyond them. She went and stood before them, grasping the bars as if she could bend them like

Superman, and stared forlornly towards freedom.

'Tiffany?'

She turned. Remy was standing at the edge of the forest with a beautiful black Alsatian on a lead. The dog barked and snarled, and she felt panic rising inside her.

'Stop it, Jarita,' Remy admonished the animal, jerking on the lead to emphasise his words, before turning his attention back to Tiffany. 'What the hell are you doing here, girl?'

'I - I just—'

The radio clipped to his belt chirped like a mechanical bird, and raising a finger to his lips, he answered the call. 'This is Remy. I'm at the gates and there's nobody here. It must have been a false alarm. I'm heading over to the north field to check on Kemp's team.' Switching off the radio, he nodded to her. 'There are hidden sensors on the property. You were lucky I was nearby to investigate.'

Tiffany suddenly felt like a child running away from her first day at school, and she did not like the feeling. Besides, she was still sore at him for turning her into Rache at assembly. 'Why so generous, Remy?' she challenged, sticking out her chin. 'Earned enough bootlicking points this morning?'

'If I hadn't caught you in Kemp's office, someone else would have,' he countered. 'Come on.'

'Wait.' She changed her tone. 'Remy, I'm sorry, please help me get out of here.'

He shook his head. 'I can't.'

'Sure you can, just open the gates and then close them again. No one will know it was you who helped me.'

'The keys I have only open my locker and the key box in reception. I have no direct access to the outside world. I told you that last night, Tiffany.'

'Then give me the telephone access code, at least,' she persisted.

He shook his head again. 'No, out of the question.'

'You... you can fuck me if you want to,' she suddenly blurted, surprising herself probably more than she surprised him.

Silence hung between them for a moment, then he motioned towards the woods. 'Come on,' he said, 'let's go.'

They walked between the trees in silence. Tiffany realised she had insulted him and embarrassed herself at the same time. She could not blame herself after all she had been through lately, but finally she managed to say softly, 'I'm sorry, Remy.'

'Forget it,' he said equably. 'It takes getting used to, being here.'

'But at least you can walk away whenever you want to.'

'No I can't, not even if I want to.'

She stopped in her tracks.

'I'm on parole,' he elaborated, 'like the other guards here, on parole to Rache. We're like the subjects, only we get paid. We're indebted to him.'

'And that's why you let him switch you last night?'

'No... I enjoyed that,' he revealed candidly.

His answer repelled and intrigued her at the same time, but she pressed on. 'So, you're a criminal?' she asked.

'I was. Gang fights.' He shrugged. 'I was young and thought I had something to prove. And I did, I proved what an idiot I could be. Rache put me on a different path, a better path, one you'll be travelling soon.'

'I thought someone with a criminal record couldn't be allowed to work in a prison,' Tiffany puzzled.

'Rache has influence beyond these walls, and you shouldn't forget that.' He looked around anxiously as if the doctor himself might appear from behind a tree. Then he took Tiffany by the elbow. 'Let's get you back. Kemp won't report you missing right away to save face, but he won't wait forever.'

Tiffany pulled away from his grasp, but kept up with him.

Back at the north field, Kemp and the girls watched her return. 'Good work locating my missing mare, Remy,' Kemp said.

Remy let her walk ahead of him. 'Try not to be too hard on her, Mr Kemp. It's a natural instinct for a new horse to bolt.'

'Thank you, Remy, I'll keep that mind.' Kemp did not sound terribly convinced, however, as he grabbed her by the wrist. 'And you, little mare, follow me.'

The interior of the shed was hot and humid, and flies buzzed in the background. She could see cubicles where horses might have been kept which were now filled with tools and other equipment. She made out chairs, a table strewn with magazines the groundskeeper amused himself with while his 'mares' worked, and hanging on one wall was a collection of bits, leather cords and feedbags.

Tiffany took all this in just before Kemp bent her over the table and struck her on the bottom with his crop so hard the blow nearly knocked the breath out of her. The fiery glow from the previous evening's chastisement re-ignited in her buttocks, and she yelped in pain.

'Face me on your knees,' he ordered.

She obeyed him slowly, and her bottom cheeks throbbed against the back of her heels as she watched him pacing before her.

'Did you think you could get away, my proud little mare?' he asked. 'I should report you to the doctor. Would you like that?'

'No, sir, I wouldn't like that,' she admitted meekly.

He reached out, removed her sunhat, and flung it aside. Then he stroked her hair almost gently. 'I don't want to see you hurt, Tiffany,' he spoke quietly, 'except by my own hand, of course, and only if it gives us both pleasure.' Despite her spinning confusion, Tiffany trembled with a feeling disturbingly akin to desire. 'I've offered to overlook this incident, Tiffany. What do you offer me in return?'

She understood, and stared at his crotch, the material tenting as his penis stiffened within. Tentatively, not sure she was doing the sensible thing, she reached out with both hands, pulled his zipper down, and watched the long length of his cock spring from his trousers. When she saw her first erection, years ago, she was amazed by the resonant strength of the male organ as it stood erect, an unavoidable materialisation of its possessor's desire. That she was the object of desire had not gone unappreciated by her, and she found the sight still affected her now in much the same way.

She reached up slowly and curled her fingers around Kemp's pulsing, waiting shaft. She began stroking it, gently and sheepishly at first, hypnotised by the way the foreskin smoothed back from his bulbous glans. Then as the warm glow from her bottom spread to her pussy, she pulled at him with more vigour, and licked her lips as his helmet grew purplish and moist. She could smell him as she worked his velvety skin up and down his rod until he moaned and closed his eyes, and then she knew she had power over him even though she was only a helpless subject.

'Good... good...' he murmured, and his gloved hands reached out to gently cup the sides of her head. Tiffany relished his touch, a man's touch, and looked up at him questioningly. He looked down at her, the hint of a smile on his slightly parted lips, his eyes expectant.

He would come soon, she could sense it, and her pussy cried out for relief. She wanted him inside her. 'Do you want to fuck me, sir?' she asked sweetly, amazed by her bluntness; and even more amazed by his shockingly cruel reply.

'Fuck you?' he mused scornfully. 'Fuck you? You presumptuous little mare. You'll have to be especially well behaved before you receive that privilege.'

The arrogance of his words was like a physical blow, and she stopped masturbating him.

'Don't stop,' he said fiercely, and his tone frightened her into instant compliance. After a few moments he moaned, and his whole body tensed as a stream of sperm arched into the air before her and spattered her face.

She blinked wildly to keep his spunk out of her eyes, and instinctively licked her lips to savour it as he baptised her face, her hand still clamped around the base of his pulsing organ directing the flow of his pleasure straight towards her.

'Now you can stop,' he sighed.

She released him and sat back on her heels, reaching up to wipe his seed off her face as curious, multifaceted feelings were flowing through her. Having serviced him despite his arrogant insults and his denial of her needs had left her feeling oddly satisfied.

He tucked his penis away. 'Okay, my little mare, back to work,' he said.

The afternoon proceeded much as the morning had, with Tiffany harnessed to the plough under Jude's direction. Jude was not as vocal as before, but Tiffany's mind was elsewhere, anyway. She thought she could somehow manipulate Kemp into making life easier for her, but he was obviously an experienced dominant, and would not allow himself to be led around by the nose like one of her erstwhile beaux's back in England.

She had just finished eating dinner when Singh appeared and summoned her outside. Anxious as to the reason why he should want to see her, she nearly tripped over her own feet as she followed him out of the dining room.

Evening came quickly to Cascara, with none of the interim hours of twilight more northerly and southerly countries enjoy; it was as if the sun knew its shift was over and left without fanfare or sentimental goodbyes. And with it went all the small, vulnerable creatures of the forest, back into their burrows to hide from the nocturnal predators.

Tiffany felt as vulnerable as prey in the presence of a predator despite his affected casualness as he motioned for her to take a seat on one of the benches on the porch. Then he sat down close beside her and stared out at the garden as if admiring it. 'Young Remy has approached me with the idea of taking you onto my team,' he announced.

Intrigue mingled with her trepidation. 'Has he?' she asked tentatively.

'Yes, he has. He seems to think it would be better for you than Kemp's team.' He glanced at her. 'What do you think?'

She paused as the words caught in her throat. 'I - I don't know.'

'Do you enjoy working in the fields like a peasant?'

She wondered if it was a trick question even as she answered candidly enough, 'No.'

'I didn't think so. I wouldn't either. And the rest?'

She knew what he meant, and blushed. 'I can handle that part,' she muttered, staring down at her feet to avoid his eyes.

If he recognised her unconscious double entendre, he did not acknowledge it. 'I'm sure you can. But the physical work's still a bitch, and a waste of your superior talents and breeding. Of course, I understand Nuala Quinn's looking for girls with athletic abilities.'

Her heart jumpstarted again beneath a charge of hope. 'Yes, she mentioned it to me.'

He leaned closer, and added in an almost conspiratorial whisper, 'Of course, with Nuala's particular kinks, her girls would have to be athletic, if you get my meaning.'

Tiffany thought she did, and it made her stomach turn. She felt as if she were on a roller coaster with all these ups and downs coming at her out of nowhere all the time.

She should not have expected any better from the place, and yet she felt betrayed, and increasingly miserable. 'It looks like I have little choice,' she said finally, but the cicadas filled the silence when he did not respond. 'Could there be a place for me on your crew?' she heard herself ask humbly, as she finally dared to look at him.

He smiled. 'Your actions yesterday and this morning do not speak well of your discipline,' he said frankly. 'You're to report to the doctor's office at eight o'clock tonight, by the way, for that little stunt with the phone, but I trust Remy's opinion. I won't promise you an easy time under my authority, but I will promise that the... *personal* compensations will be worthwhile. I want you to think about what I've said, however, before you ask me again if you can be part of my crew.'

'But I know now,' she insisted, 'I—'

'Don't argue with me,' he said shortly. 'Just do as you're told.'

For some reason his intense arrogance excited her, but more importantly, he could somehow be her ticket out of there. He was chief of security, after all. If she could win his confidence and learn his secrets, the keys to the gates could be hers... but at what price? How far would he take her under his mastery?

Back inside the house Quinn approached her in the TV room, smiling brightly. 'And how are we feeling tonight, Welborne?'

Tiffany reminded herself that disrespect would not be appreciated. So steeling herself, she drew breath and replied politely, 'Fine, thank you, Ms Quinn.'

The sports manager did not seem to feel the chill in the air between them. 'I was wondering if you had given any thought to my offer of joining the crew? We have a football match next month with another house, and a player of your calibre would be invaluable.'

'No thanks,' Tiffany said.

Quinn frowned, and then shrugged. 'Fine. But if you change your mind, I—'

'Is that all, Ms Quinn?' Tiffany said respectfully but abruptly.

The woman's eyes hardened. 'Yes, Welborne, but my offer still stands,' she said, and then left the room.

Tiffany relaxed somewhat; Quinn's offer could stand forever, as far as she was concerned.

She spent her free time channel surfing and watching other girls polish their boots. No one spoke to her, whereas everyone struck up a conversation with Jude.

At eight o'clock Tiffany was outside Rache's office. She was the only one there, and he took his time calling her inside.

'Well, Welborne, any comment about this morning?' he asked urbanely.

Now that she was in his presence, she found herself wondering why she found it so difficult to stand up to him. Was it a helpless emotional reaction to his authority over her? Was it desire? He displayed the confidence that only came with age and experience, and yet he possessed the strength and vitality of a man half his age. As with Kemp, only more so, she was torn between hating him and longing to please him. 'I - I'm sorry about that, sir,' she said humbly. 'You see, Shazza and the other girls... well, they attacked me last night, and—'

'The welcoming?' he mused. 'Oh yes, I know about it, unofficially, of course. Officially, only my staff and myself are permitted to order and discipline subjects. Were you physically harmed?'

'No,' she admitted, 'not really.'

'I would hope not. And did you not participate in similar initiations back in boarding school in England?'

'No,' she lied, unconvincingly, she knew. In fact, new arrivals at the academy were often stripped down to their panties, tied to the hockey goalposts and pelted with eggs and flour. But that was good, clean, harmless fun. Last night had been strangely, disturbingly, different...

Rache glanced at the file on his desk. 'It usually takes a week before a subject starts a record of infractions,' he stated. 'You, however, now have two on your record in a little over twenty-four hours. First trafficking with Baptiste, and now breaking into Mr Kemp's office and attempting to use his phone.'

'I wasn't trying to use the phone,' she lied again in desperation. 'Remy lied about that. I just got lost.'

He stared at her coldly. 'He never mentioned the phone. He didn't have to. Any attempted access of the communication lines without the proper access codes is recorded by security.'

Mortification that her feeble effort to avoid punishment by blaming someone else had so easily been seen through made her feel nauseous.

'You're quite an honourable young lady,' he said with undisguised contempt. 'A credit to your breeding.' He leaned back in his chair. 'The choice of punishment is yours. Fifteen by tawse, here and now, or an additional thirty days added to your sentence.'

Her jaw dropped. 'You can't do that!' she gasped. 'I was sentenced to three years, you can't—'

'Three years under my authority, and like any prison authority anywhere in the world, I have the right to extend the amount of time served by a prisoner, dependent upon his or her behaviour during their sentence.'

Her breathing quickened as she felt herself being cornered. 'And that's my choice, is it?'

He shrugged. 'Normally for an offence of this nature there would also be the option of forfeiture of work credits, except you've only earned a day's worth so far, and confinement in solitary, but you're needed in the fields.'

'I'll take my punishment now.' She felt the words threatening to stick in her throat, so she said them quickly.

He nodded, and rose. 'I thought you might. Push your uniform and your panties down to your knees and kiss the desk, if you please.'

Tiffany obeyed him reluctantly, peeling her panties off her perspiring skin. The air in the office was cool and dry, and suddenly she craved the sensual pleasure of the long hot bath she was accustomed to taking at this time of night.

Rache stepped behind her.

She reminded herself he was a doctor, and that he had seen her naked and touched her intimately already. This was just a procedure, nothing more. Leaning over the desk, she glanced at him over her shoulder, and saw him holding a strange black leather paddle as long as his forearm with three extensions and studs running along one side.

'Eyes down!' he barked.

She obeyed, focusing on the swirling patterns in the desk's wooden surface.

The first blow sent a sharp stab of pain through her buttocks as the smacking sound filled her stunned head. She winced and cried out beneath each subsequent blow, and yet as the beating progressed she began to feel strangely invigorated, as if she was awakening from a lifelong exhaustion and realising what it was like to feel really alive for the first time. The pain was metamorphosing into a sweet fire, concentrating itself between her thighs as her libido fully surfaced from the depths of her subconscious into her rational awareness for the first time.

After the fifteenth allotted blow, Rache returned the tawse to its place and sat down behind his desk again. 'Pull up your clothes,' he said shortly.

Tiffany fought back tears of pain and humiliation as she obeyed him, wincing even at the soft caress of cloth across her beaten flesh. 'How can you be so sadistic?' she whispered faintly.

'It takes years of practice,' he replied matter-of-factly.

'You don't give a damn about anyone, do you?'

He chuckled, but his eyes did not look amused. 'I was right; you're beginning to enjoy it already, aren't you? The beatings excite you, don't they?'

Arousal as much as embarrassment made her face burn. 'I don't know what you're talking about.'

'Liar.' He leaned forward towards her over the desk. 'Your head might not understand the truth,' he said quietly, his tone seductive, 'but your cunt does. Be careful, though; don't make the mistake of being a deliberate troublemaker. If you're obedient and respectful, you'll learn the difference between being beaten for punishment and beaten as a reward.' He leaned back in his chair again. 'Now you may go.'

Back out in the corridor, Tiffany struggled to ignore her aches and the shameful way her pussy was smouldering for attention. *Beaten as a reward?* Was that why no one rebelled and what Remy had been hinting at? Had Rache brainwashed and seduced everyone?

Tiffany was determined not to let the same thing happen to her, no matter how tempting the prospect might be.

It was nearing lights out as Tiffany showered and readied herself for bed. Furtively, she studied the marks on other girls' buttocks and thighs, some red and fresh, some fading to a gentle pink. It was bizarre to see such marks on so many bodies. Then she looked at her own welts, Rache's legacy, in the basin mirror. It reminded her of the morning after her arrest, when she returned to her suite at daddy's estate and stripped to study the glowing souvenirs of the night's spanking in the catacombs on her supple flesh.

Except on special occasions such as welcoming parties, the normal procedure immediately preceding lights out was for the girls to stand at attention before their beds while Colbert, and her assistant Bonnie, walked down the centre aisle like a country lady inspecting her house staff. There were always some girls missing, and where they were Tiffany did not dare to wonder.

Colbert stopped before her, and smiled. 'So, how was your first full day at *Rache House*, Welborne?'

'It wasn't what I expected,' she replied vaguely.

'Life would be boring if everything went as expected,' Colbert remarked philosophically, and continued her inspection, with Bonnie at her heels. Then the housekeeper said loudly, 'Good night, girls.'

The night outside the dorm was a soothing hypnotic concert of chirping cicada disturbed only by the occasional squeak of a fruit bat and the stir of the wind rustling through the trees.

The night inside the dorm was filled with more intimate sounds; soft cries and secret giggles. For a long time Tiffany resisted the urge to touch herself while listening to them, which would be too much like endorsing such deviant behaviour, but her hand irresistibly found its way into her panties.

CHAPTER SIX

Tiffany's body ached all over. Her muscles were tight and sore from the morning exercises, followed by toiling behind the plough all day, and then performing whatever additional chores Colbert assigned to her. There were no days of rest at *Rache House*; Tiffany had never worked so hard in her life.

And what was worse, the increasing demands of her pussy were driving her to distraction. Masturbation, her usual outlet, was no longer enough when she thought of the times she spent in harness under Kemp's authority, even though he had not shown much direct interest in her since that first day. She wondered what it would take to get his full attention again, and recalled Rache's warning about being a deliberate troublemaker. Her carnal hungers were becoming a dull, continuous ache that gnawed at her spirit even more remorselessly than the constant work, and she was finding it more and more difficult to focus on a viable means of escape.

Every morning was the same, followed by lunch behind the stables. Jude joined the other girls beneath the makeshift shower and always looked to be genuinely enjoying herself.

The afternoon work was about to begin, and the 'mares' were preparing to get back in their harnesses, when Kemp unexpectedly blew his whistle and called everyone to attention. He had removed his gloves and tucked them into his belt. 'You'll all be glad to know we're ahead of schedule,' he announced. 'Which means you've earned yourselves an afternoon off. And for those of you who have been here long enough, you know what that means. It's derby time!'

A cheer rose from the veteran subjects, but Tiffany was more wary.

'We have some new mares in my stables,' he went on, 'and at least one of them shows promise. Of course, they couldn't possibly surpass my more experienced fillies. Or could they?' He smiled as he approached Morrow, and reaching up playfully he cupped her chin. 'I know you wouldn't let me down, my proud mare. Still, we must give the new girls a chance, mustn't we? Morrow, Forrester, Welborne, and...' he looked around, and then pointed to Nadine Fairfax, a broad-shouldered blonde with piercing blue eyes and full breasts, 'and Fairfax for balance. Get undressed.'

All but Tiffany moved to obey him.

'Is there a problem, Welborne?' he asked. 'Don't you want to participate in the derby and show the others what you're made of?'

She did, at least a part of her did, but she held back. 'What's going to happen?' she asked.

Kemp took a step forward and spoke slowly and deliberately, as if addressing a particularly dim-witted child. 'I want to conduct a race among four of my mares,' he explained simply. 'The winner gets, among other things, a week's worth of work credits and an afternoon off work. Now, you don't have to participate if you don't want to, but I need an answer now, because I'm certain there's no shortage of volunteers to take your place.' He looked to the other girls. 'Is there?'

To her surprise, Tiffany saw several girls raising their hands like eager schoolchildren. Afraid, angry and excited all at once, she unbuckled her boots and began unbuttoning her uniform by way of response. It would not be the first time she had been naked in public, and the thought of Kemp seeing her that way deepened her modesty and made her feel almost faint with desire.

When her clothes were lying in a pile on the ground, she stood beside the other three girls, vainly attempting to conceal her pubes with one hand and her breasts with her other arm, blushing to her roots.

Kemp smiled, seemingly amused by her demure stance, and his hands, once more hidden inside his gloves, gripped both ends of his riding crop. 'Is there a problem, Welborne?' he goaded. 'Is there something special about your private parts that require you to keep them covered? Look at your fellow horses... I said look!'

Trembling, Tiffany looked to either side of her. The other naked girls were standing with their arms at their sides, appearing as relaxed and casual as if they had been walking around naked all their lives.

'Or maybe it's not pride?' Kemp took a step closer. 'Maybe it's shame?'

His words had the desired effect. Angrily, Tiffany pulled her hands away, challenging him with her eyes to look her over all he liked.

'More of a pony than a mare,' he said, accepting the challenge, 'judging from the size of the tits.' As all the girls laughed, he moved on to Jude. 'Now this is a proud mare.' He reached out and weighed one of Jude's breasts, mauling and squeezing it. Then he tapped one of her thighs with the tip of the crop. 'Sturdy limbs, fine promise.' He disappeared behind the quartet as the appraisal continued. 'Of course, I know all about my other mares. Their performances in, as well as out, of the stables are near legendary.'

Tiffany heard the sounds of flesh being slapped appreciatively.

He stepped before them again. 'But appearance isn't everything. There's performance, too. I need to see how they canter. Morrow, take the lead. You others watch and follow. Giddy up!'

Morrow dutifully began jogging around the other girls, her head held high. Fairfax, Jude and Tiffany followed behind her. To the cheers of the spectators they trotted around in a wide circle, Morrow always leading them near Kemp, who made a show of admiring their figures as they passed.

'Right, my mares, line up here and get down on your knees,' Kemp at last commanded, drawing a line in the dust with his boot.

They did so, perspiration making their flesh glisten as Kemp walked before them, scrutinising them again.

'Fine forms, all of you,' he said. 'But as the veterans know from experience, the ultimate test is whether or not you can handle riders. Holbert, the reins.'

From the corner of her eye, Tiffany saw Georgie Holbert run towards the cottage.

'For those of you who might cry foul,' Kemp went on, 'as if you'd dare, I try to match riders with the sizes of their mounts to keep things fair.' He looked to the spectators behind the mares and pointed to each in turn. 'Jowett, you take Forrester. Rosenberg, you have Morrow. Young, you're on Fairfax. And Holbert, sorry, but you'll have to take the pony.'

The four riders appeared before their prospective mounts, each carrying simple ropes of orange twine.

Georgie stood before Tiffany, holding the ends of the rope in both hands. 'It's like the bit,' she explained. 'Open up.'

'Don't do this to me,' Tiffany begged in a whisper.

'Oh, stop whining,' Georgie said. 'As a rider I have a chance at the credits and the afternoon off, too.' She let go of one end of the rein to grab her by the hair. 'Open up.'

Unsettled, Tiffany obeyed, remembering to keep her tongue down like she did with the bit on the harness as the rough rope was inserted between her teeth.

Georgie circled behind her holding the other end of the rein, and pulling on it, she drew Tiffany back. 'On all fours,' she ordered, brooking no defiance and showing no sympathy.

Tiffany obeyed her rider, feeling her palms sinking into the soft earth as Georgie straddled her, putting her full weight on her back. To their left, the other mares were also being mounted, and all bore their riders with varying degrees of difficulty.

'Lovely,' Kemp declared, enthusiastically cutting the air with his crop. His boots kicked up clumps of dust as he strode about twenty metres away from them, and stabbed the tip of his crop into the earth. 'The first horse to capture this wins,' he declared. 'Now get going!'

The mares set off beneath encouraging slaps and kicks from their riders. Georgie's boots dug into the sides of Tiffany's thighs again and again as she urged her mount onward. Groaning, Tiffany tried to ignore her aching limbs and the deadweight on her back as she struggled forward, making an effort to at least match, if not surpass, the progress of the others. And she found it was not all that difficult. Kemp had been true to his word and matched each horse with a rider of suitable weight to make it an interesting race. Even so, she stumbled a few times, rising again when Georgie kicked her and pulled her head back with the reins. She was gaining on Jude, who with an almost subliminal motion kicked out, and knocked her and her rider over. Tiffany coughed and spluttered through her rein, spitting dirt from her mouth mixed with tears as Georgie half helped, half struck her, back onto all fours.

The riders' cries filled the air as the mares struggled not only with the burdens on their back but with the abuse they received. Then, without warning, Tiffany's last reserves gave way and she collapsed in a heap, oblivious to Georgie still tugging at her reins and swearing in her ear.

Amidst distant cries and cheers of congratulations, she looked up from the dirt as she felt Georgie lift her weight off her, and spat out the rein. She crawled back to her clothes as everyone else gathered around Jude, who was beaming as she held the riding crop high in triumph.

Kemp retrieved it. 'Very good, Forrester,' he said. 'I never thought anyone would beat Morrow. The credits and the afternoon off are yours. And, as a special treat, you can spend your afternoon off serving me in the stables.' He reached up and stroked her breasts. 'If you like, that is.'

Her eyes met his. 'Yes, sir, I would,' she panted.

He nodded, and looked around at the other girls. 'Take an hour's break,' he said magnanimously, and wrapping an almost protective arm around Jude, he led her towards the stable house, pausing beside Tiffany where she lay sprawled on the grass in her bra and panties. 'Your performance was pathetic,' he said, 'but I suppose you'll improve with practice.'

Rache leaned against the front of his desk as Tiffany knelt on the floor before him, shivering, but not from the air-conditioning. Her wrists were cuffed behind her, and she was hanging her head wishing her hair was long enough to cover the front of her body. After Kemp disappeared into the barn with Jude, she picked herself up off the ground, and attempted to escape again. And again she had been caught at the gates and brought back to the house by a grim-faced Remy.

'Raise your head,' Rache said. She obeyed, and found him staring at the birthmark on her breast, which was just visible over the cup of her bra. 'Local superstition maintains that such star-shaped blemishes indicate the bearer was blessed by the gods,' he informed her. 'How blessed do you feel now? By the way, your father's written to you.'

'Daddy?' she cried in hope.

'Yes, *daddy*, well, his solicitors actually. They hope you're keeping well.' He lifted a slip of powder-blue notepaper from his desk. 'You are.'

She thought he was showing her the letter from her father's solicitors, but it was handwritten and addressed to Zak Welborne. Then she realised it was her handwriting. 'How...?'

'We have an abundance of talented people staying here.' He returned the letter to the desk. 'Although they're more accustomed to forging welfare agency documents than personal letters. When you've proven yourself trustworthy, you'll be able to write your own letters. Not that I expect your father will notice the difference.'

'You've thought of everything, haven't you?' she accused bitterly.

'Everything except how to deal with you. Attempted escape is a serious offence. It could mean an addition to your sentence of an extra three months.'

'What?' she gasped in disbelief.

He nodded. 'Or more.'

'Instead of a beating?'

'No, including a beating. Nor would you have any right of appeal, especially with all the freedom given you here.'

'You really think that, don't you?' She ignored his white cat as it strolled around her curiously. 'Twisting innocent women into becoming sexually submissive slaves is your idea of freedom? Making them do perverted things with each other is freedom?'

He smiled. 'Very melodramatically put, but "twisted" implies changing something from its proper form into an improper one, which is not the case. We seek those for whom submission comes naturally, those for whom submission is, deep down, their *raison d'être* but who don't know it yet as a result of circumstances or self-denial. These people engage in petty crimes and usually get themselves easily caught in an unconscious effort to fulfil their unspoken need to be dominated through the criminal justice system, the only system made available to them by society. But their need is never really satisfied that way. Look at yourself and all the crimes you committed. Did they satisfy you?'

'I - I don't know what you mean.'

'Yes you do.' He reached for an armless, hard-backed wooden chair, and pulled it over to the centre of the office. Then he reached down and grasped her bound wrists, lifting her to her feet as he sat on the chair and spread her facedown across his lap. 'You're the textbook definition of a spoiled brat, Tiffany,' he told her in the quiet, seductive voice that frightened her by exciting her so much. 'You're a lying, undisciplined girl.' She flinched as he cupped her left buttock. 'Aren't you, Tiffany?'

Part of her wanted to protest, to tell him she was an eighteen-year-old woman who deserved some respect, but her deepest self whispered, 'Yes, sir.'

He stroked the soft flesh of her bottom before suddenly spanking her hard, bringing his hand down again, and again. 'As the Americans say,' he remarked casually over her cries, 'no pain no gain.'

She kicked her legs feebly, gasping and sobbing as he chuckled. Her bottom was radiating heat, and after a while this acted as a kind of mysterious shield against the sharp pain of his blows, softening them even as the intense warmth spread distractingly to her pussy, and she began to ache for something more than the jarring of his continued spanking.

He caressed her burning bottom, gently massaging her wounded flesh. 'Tell me how this makes you feel, Tiffany,' he crooned.

'Sore...' she whimpered.

'You know what I mean.' His voice was harsh, unsympathetic, even as he continued gently caressing her throbbing cheeks. Then his hand slipped down and stroked her inner thigh before swiping softly across her pussy. She gasped, and raised her head as a thrill of delicious sexual energy shot through her body. Then she realised he could feel how moist she was, and flushed in embarrassment.

'Tell me how excited you are,' he commanded.

'I - I'm not—'

'You're not being honest with me, or with yourself, Tiffany. Are you?' Again he lightly stroked her labia. She moaned. 'Was that a "no"?'

'No... I mean, yes... I mean... I don't know!'

'Tiffany...'

'I - I've forgotten the question.'

Abruptly, he slid a finger between her bottom cheeks and touched the tight opening into her rear passage.

'No...' she gasped.

'Feeling a little excited, Tiffany?'

'No,' she cried, her face scarlet.

'I think you're lying, Tiffany. What do you think, Stuart?'

'I think you're right, sir.'

She looked up in horror. Stuart Knowles, one of the house guards, had walked silently into the office while she was being spanked, and was standing by the door, watching. Shame twisted her insides, and then an entirely different feeling flooded her as Rache's hand abruptly slipped between her thighs and cupped and squeezed her mound. Her legs jerked as he palmed her sensitive flesh, and she groaned as his fingers parted her sex lips, sliding between them and into her wet pussy.

'You're such a responsive creature,' he noted, moving his fingers slowly in and out of her as she instinctively pushed her buttocks up to his hand.

She moaned in rapture, but then forced herself to gasp, 'Let me go.'

'As you wish.' He shoved her to the floor as he stood up. 'Stuart, put Welborne in solitary.' Knowles moved behind Tiffany, lifted her up to her feet, and drew her towards the door.

Rage, disbelief and a profound frustration ignited inside her. 'You fucking bastard!' she shrieked. 'If daddy knew about all this he'd have you killed!'

'What makes you think he doesn't already know, Tiffany?' The doctor asked her calmly. 'What makes you think he didn't arrange to have you sent to a place where you'd be properly punished in an effort to make up for a lifetime of selfish indulgence? Take her away.'

CHAPTER SEVEN

Solitary was little more than a closet-sized room, windowless and bare except for a mattress and a blanket laid directly on the stone floor, a chamber pot, and a naked bulb hanging from the ceiling, out of reach.

Knowles would not get her clothes, but at least he removed her cuffs. There was precious little to do but pace the cell, and think. Tiffany was haunted by the possibility that Rache had been telling the truth. Had daddy sent her deliberately, eschewing the under-the-table deals and plea-bargaining his solicitors had employed before whenever she got into trouble?

Her pussy still felt warm and tight with need, but she deliberately ignored it. To give in to desire now would be giving in to Rache and his perverse ideas, and she had no intention of doing that, tempting as they were. She had to be strong...

What felt like hours later all her strength, physical and emotional, had left her. She sat on the mattress with her knees up and spread, her panties discarded beside her. Then she leaned back against the wall and began comforting her clitoris, stimulating it with earnest circular motions of her fingertips while her free hand kneaded her breasts. Images and sensations danced in her mind's eye like the twisting colours in a kaleidoscope... the hard slaps of the masked man in the catacombs, a lifetime ago, across her bottom... Singh's firm hand... the girls' wet towels and shirts beating her during the initiation... kneeling before Kemp and before Rache's expert hand...

Panting, Tiffany slipped one, then two fingers into her tight vagina while continuing to tease her clitoris with her thumb, and she climaxed remembering the feel of Rache's hand cupping her mound and squeezing her pussy as she desperately wished her fingers were his...

Time dragged, and dragged, and then the door of the small cell jerked open and Remy entered carrying a sandwich on a plate, and a water bottle. 'Hello,' he said soberly.

'Oh, erm, what time is it?' she asked, surprised by the sudden intrusion, sitting up against the wall.

'Dinner time.' He closed the door behind him with his boot, and set the food and drink on the floor beside the mattress. 'Do you need your pot emptied?'

'No, but you know what I do need, Remy,' she said, getting stiffly to her feet.

He looked her naked body up and down slowly. 'I can't get you out of here, Tiffany,' he told her.

'I know.' She smiled. 'But you still want the best for me, don't you?'

He looked at her affectionately and cupped her face in his hands. 'Of course I do,' he said honestly.

His touch was warm and firm and sent shivers of delight through her body. She flung her arms around his neck and kissed him greedily. He kissed her back, and almost at once she could feel his erection pressing into her tummy through his trousers.

He pulled away. 'I have to get back,' he gasped. 'We'll have to hurry.' She pulled him down to the mattress. 'It's against the rules,' he protested weakly, but began kissing her again as he squeezed her breasts. Then he thrust a hand between her legs and cupped her sex hungrily for a moment before piercing her with one finger.

She pulled back and moaned as she fumbled with his trousers, desperate to get them off him, and quickly she had them, along with his briefs, down to his ankles.

He pushed her back and spread himself over her, his cock jabbing blindly between her thighs, hungrily seeking to penetrate her fully. Eventually his engorged tip eased inside, he paused for a second, and then impaled her with one powerful thrust of his hips.

Tiffany gasped as her pussy enveloped him and clung to him as they became one in a mutual hunger and urgency. They fell into a rapid rhythm with each other. He drove into her as if his life depended on it, and within moments she was crying out beneath him in the throes of a wonderful orgasm. He came with her, ejaculating deep inside her as he buried his face against her neck.

He lay still for a moment, breathing deeply, filling his lungs as his heartbeat and pulse slowed, but then he quickly pushed himself away and rose unsteadily to his feet, pulling up his underwear and trousers.

Tiffany watched him contentedly, satisfied for the moment, which was all that mattered. She was content to recline on the mattress letting the waves of pleasure slowly ebb away.

'You won't say anything, will you?' he asked anxiously.

'Say anything about what?' she said with mock innocence, her eyes sparkling.

He smiled a smile of relief. 'I really enjoyed that, Tiffany.' He opened the door.

'Will you be back, Remy?'

'Not tonight,' he said. 'Maybe for breakfast tomorrow, though.'

'I'll be here,' she teased.

He regarded her soberly for a long moment, and then the door closed and locked behind him. She sighed, closed her eyes, and went to sleep, a pretty smile on her lips.

Tiffany was fast asleep when the door opened again. She almost called Remy's name, before she heard Singh's voice. 'Get up and follow me,' he commanded brusquely.

He led her to the security room. In contrast to its austere look during processing, the room was now filled with an array of objects - tables, posts, boxes and barrels - that all had manacles fitted into them in various places. There were even chains and trapeze-like devices hanging from the ceiling. Bizarrely, the room had been transformed into a dungeon. One long table at the far end of the space was covered with a display of instruments made of metal, wood and leather, and they were all arranged as if in a museum exhibit.

It alarmed her, and she sleepily asked what the time was, drawing the blanket she had brought protectively around her.

'It's late, but at least we won't be disturbed. Have you given any thought to joining my team?'

'You mean, I might still be allowed to?' she asked.

'That depends upon tonight. Follow me.' He guided her to the other end of the room, where she got a closer look at the table and all the instruments of bondage and discipline laid across it. There were canes, switches, paddles, clamps, cuffs, manacles, harnesses and iron bars with leather restraints. 'Head-hunting between teams is frowned upon,' he added, 'but I could argue with Rache for your transfer.'

She struggled to get her sleep-sodden brain working again. 'Why would you do that?'

'Maybe it's pity.' He looked at her. 'Or maybe it's desire. Does it matter?'

'I suppose not,' she sighed, and then nodded. 'Okay, yes, I want to serve under you.'

Smiling, he reached out and tugged away the blanket, leaving her naked. She trembled, but kept her arms at her sides.

'Address me as master,' he instructed quietly.

She knew now this was part of his game. 'Yes... master,' she said obediently.

In moments her wrists were manacled to a trapeze bar that pulled her arms straight up over her head. Then he attached a spreader bar to her ankles, parting her feet an uneasy distance from each other, so that she was now effectively spread-eagled and had to concentrate to keep her balance. She watched him return to the table, where his fingers drifted over various items.

'We employ a wide variety of instruments here,' he informed her with a note a pride, 'from the exotic, like this Malaysian rattan.' He lifted a long, slender cane resembling a bamboo shoot, and cut the air between them with it before setting it back down. 'To the basic, like this paddle. Each instrument has its own strengths and weaknesses, its own optimum method of employment, its own flavours. In time, you may taste them all.'

Her eyes glazed slightly as she took in each sinister item, her breaths quickening. Both her mouth and her pussy were open and moist as her belly tightened again with the familiar mixture of dread and excitement.

Singh selected an instrument she had only ever seen in films, a frightening black object of multiple cords made of various materials all attached to a long black handle that made her think of the heads of the mythical hydra.

'This is a cat o' nine tails, Tiffany, and my personal favourite, a holdover from my piratical ancestors, who were the first to settle on Cascara.' He walked slowly behind her, and she started beneath the delicate touch of the cat's tails on the small of her back, tickling her as they ran lightly down her body like water before reaching the firm roundness of her bottom cheeks. He leaned close to her ear and whispered, 'Do you like the touch of my cat, Welborne?'

'Yes,' she admitted softly, surprising herself.

He replaced the trailing tails with the thick handle, running its tip in the valley of her cheeks down to the puffed outer lips of her sex. 'Do you want to join my team, Welborne?'

'Um, yes...' she sighed.

'I don't believe you.' He stroked her labia with the firm handle. 'You'll have to convince me.' He stepped back, and she gasped as a pain more intense than any she had ever felt before shot through her flesh when the cat's tails viciously licked her back as he struck her. 'This room is soundproofed, Tiffany. Yell all you want.'

She accepted his invitation, crying out and sobbing as each subsequent blow burned into the tender skin of her back and buttocks. And whenever he paused to tease her soaking pussy with the handle, her cries deepened to oscillating moans as she writhed in her bonds, desperate for release of any kind. Then it all began again, and as he alternately beat her and teased her, she felt herself getting closer and closer to an orgasm that threatened to completely dissolve her. But he always stopped just before driving her over the edge, tormenting her.

'Do you want to join my team, Welborne?' he asked again, squeezing her hot, aching buttocks with his free hand.

'Yes,' she gasped. 'Yes, please...'

Apparently satisfied with the passionate sincerity of her response, he finally let her climax, thrusting the cat's handle fully into her yearning sex. An orgasm exploded inside her the instant he penetrated her, her body bucking wildly in its restraints as she screamed, because the pleasure was so intense it was almost harder for her to bear than the pain.

He withdrew the handle, and held it up before her so she could see how it was covered in her own glistening juices. 'Kiss it,' he ordered. 'Thank it for the gift of punishment.'

She did not hesitate to obey; she kissed the handle, her gesture inspired by a genuine awe for the object of her pain and pleasure, and somewhere in the distance she heard Singh whisper, 'Good girl.'

Chapter Eight

Singh may not have promised her an easier life, but the weeks following release from solitary were certainly sweeter for Tiffany. She had more freedom than the other prisoners whilst on duty. She could walk outside unattended, for instance, and was even allowed to wear a watch. And the work she did was far less strenuous than the work she had done under Kemp. During the day she patrolled forty-six acres of the property, performed safety and security inspections of the various buildings surrounding the main house, and tended to Almira and Jarita, Singh's two Alsatian patrol dogs. After lights out she monitored the grounds from reception, and kept the security areas within the house spotless, which included cleaning and polishing the various tools of bondage and discipline.

Another bonus of the transfer was her increased time alone with Remy. Their relationship was probably one of the worst kept secrets in the house, and after her transfer she feared Singh would arrange things to keep them apart. But he did not do so, and although she and Remy sometimes operated on separate shifts, more often than not they were together, and more often than not they used their time alone to get to know each other better, and more and more intimately.

'Ah, lovely,' Remy sighed, writhing beneath her and lifting his hips slightly to meet hers as his hands reached up to knead her breasts.

'No, no, no,' she scolded gently, grasping his wrists and pinning them down on the ground, glad for his lack of resistance to her control. She enjoyed her breasts being fondled, but feared it would make her climax too quickly and she wanted to enjoy herself. She glanced at the copper-black Almira, the dog they had taken with them into the woods to this makeshift grotto of shadows and fallen trees. The dog was tied to a nearby branch, and watching the two humans copulating with panting interest. 'Ah, lovely...' she sighed, letting another climax spark inside and begin spreading through her tummy, making her pussy tighten reflexively around his erection. Maintaining a slow, steady rhythm, the crunch of twigs and leaves beneath their bodies the only sound in the world, she let the waves of pleasure flow through her like a river in flood. Remy's control was admirable, and she took full advantage of it to indulge in a marathon bout of multiple orgasms.

Then their radios chirped simultaneously where they lay in the grass, and she released his wrists and pounded against him in urgent frustration, seeking a final release.

He reached for his radio. 'Yes, Hannah?' he said breathlessly.

'What's your location?' Hannah demanded. 'Is Tiffany still with you?'

'Of course...'

'You haven't checked in yet. What's up?'

Remy smiled up at Tiffany. 'Oh, we... well, we put the radios down while we went to look for Almira. She'd come off her lead.'

Tiffany leaned down and said into the radio, 'He's talking bollocks, Hannah. He stopped for a pee and dropped his radio along the way. We only just found it.'

'Hmm. Well, tell Almira and Remy to stop dawdling. You were supposed to have completed your sweep five minutes ago. And don't forget your own appointment with Singh in twenty minutes. No more stopping for a pee.' She cut the transmission.

'Roger that, mummy, patrol out.' Remy set aside the radio, glaring up at her. 'Silly cow, you shouldn't mess about like that. What if Singh was listening? One wrong move could ruin both of us.'

'Yeah, yeah, I know.' She began rocking back and forth on his softening cock. 'Come on, one more quick one.'

'No, we have to go.'

'One more,' she insisted, arching her back and grinding her clit against his firm body. 'And slap my bum.'

He ground his teeth, but did as he was bid. His hand was callused from hard labour, and his slaps were suitably firm and sharp. She started coming again, and as her grip on his organ tightened he began thrusting rapidly upwards beneath her, easily raising her off the ground with him until he came, too, with a strangled cry. Then she fell over him, and rained grateful kisses on his face and neck. But she had learned to resist the urge to relax after lovemaking; she quickly lifted herself up so he could slide out from beneath her. They both cleaned themselves off and dressed with efficient speed, dusting dirt and leaves off their uniforms. They were soon on the path again, with Almira eagerly leading the way.

'We're going to get caught someday,' he warned, sounding glum.

'Aren't I worth the risk?' she teased.

'Yes.' He smiled. 'Am I?'

'Sure,' she said, even as the unspoken truth gnawed at her insides - if she had run into Remy at a club or a concert in the outside world, she would not have given him a second glance.

He shrugged. 'I suppose I should be thankful for small favours.'

She nudged him with her elbow. 'Small favours?'

'I don't mean that. I'm just thankful you've given up the idea of escaping.'

Tiffany blinked innocently. 'I have?'

He nodded as they stepped out from beneath the trees into the open. 'I'm guessing you have, since you haven't talked about it for days now.'

She frowned, and searched her recent memory. He was right, not only had she not talked about escaping, she had not even thought about it, although initially it had been one of her major reasons for wanting to join Singh's group, to learn as much as she could about the house's security and exploit her knowledge when the time was right.

Kemp's team was working in the north field. She stopped and squinted to watch Jude, stripped down to her bra and panties, pulling one of the ploughs.

'You're still mad at her,' Remy observed.

She continued on her way, letting Almira pull her along. 'You didn't see her that day. You weren't there.' The memory of that race was still fresh and bitter in her mind.

'You can't blame her, Tiffany. A submissive's ultimate loyalty must be to her master or mistress, not her fellow slaves.'

She quickened her pace as if to escape his words; she did not like to hear him talking like that. 'Then she's fully embraced the philosophies of *Rache House*.'

Remy did not try to keep pace, but instead called after her. 'So, the only difference between Jude and you is that it didn't take her as long to give in?'

Tiffany froze in her tracks. 'Hurry up,' she said, unable to look him in the eye as he caught up with her.

It was a half-hour before lights out and Quinn's team had not returned from evening practice. This was not unusual, particularly with the upcoming inter-house match, and Tiffany had been sent out to remind the sports manager of the time.

The team was not on the pitch, floodlit and eerie in the darkness, but she heard noises from near the sports bunker and followed them to their source. Tiffany was annoyed; she was supposed to be off tonight playing cards with Hannah, Eva and Shazza.

There was a rough clearing behind the bunker, a grove of wild grass and cicadas, and as the noise suggested, Quinn and her team of twelve core players were there. The core players were the only ones under her direct authority, although other subjects also played on a part-time basis.

'You were bloody pathetic today,' Quinn was saying loudly. 'Practice is supposed to improve one's performance, but all I see is a sorry bunch of amateurs making fools of themselves on the pitch. Desiree!'

Desiree reminded Tiffany of Jude, with her big bone structure, baby face and upturned nose, which made her look even younger and more vulnerable than she was. She was lined up with the other girls, standing to attention in military fashion, but at the sound of her name she somehow managed to straighten up even more. 'Yes, coach?'

'Desiree, correct me if I'm wrong, but I was led to believe that the main chore of the goalkeeper was to keep the goal, as in keep the fucking ball from getting past you! But after the ball got past you the second time tonight you just seemed to give up.'

'Coach, I—'

'And I didn't hear you speak out once. As a goalie you're the only player who can see the entire field of play. You should have been continually providing your teammates with advice. You can't expect me to be on the pitch with you during the match pointing out the bloody obvious. And you, Tara, where were you when Kamesha needed cover? And as for you, Kamesha, what exactly were you doing with the ball, anyway? I've seen drunks in Shaftesbury Square with better footwork than what I saw from you tonight.'

Kamesha, a striking girl, tall and slender with rich dark skin and earnest brown eyes, was the team captain, a responsibility that meant little at times like this, and in fact became a burden when she was asked by the others to speak up on their behalf, like now. 'Coach, we...'

'Yes, Kamesha?'

The girl took a deep breath, and blurted, 'We're tired. We've been working twice as hard this past week.'

'You're tired? None of you know the meaning of the word. Everybody strip. Everything off, now!'

Tiffany had been about to speak up, but kept silent as she watched the team undress, and then return to standing at attention in a neat row. She leaned against the wall of the bunker, enjoying her voyeuristic position. She noticed that all the permanent members of Quinn's team were shaved between their legs, so that the lips of their sex were enticingly visible.

'You think you know what being tired means?' Quinn demanded. 'I doubt it, not yet, anyway. But you will. Start running on the spot, and don't stop until I tell you to. The first one to fall gets a punishment, the last one gets a reward.'

'Some reward,' whispered a voice from behind Tiffany, and she turned to see Eric Kemp, a cigarette dangling from one corner of his mouth. He offered it to her, but she declined by shaking her head silently. 'It helps keep the bugs away,' he urged.

Shrugging, she accepted the cigarette, unsettled by the presence of her ex-supervisor. Had he come looking for her? Or perhaps he made a hobby of observing Quinn's special exercise routine.

Together they watched the group of girls running on the spot, their breasts - some small and firm, some luscious and full - bobbing up and down. Their laboured breathing was clearly audible in the still night air as Quinn orbited them slowly, clearly enjoying the view of unfettered flesh from every conceivable angle.

'She does love her work,' Kemp commented, retrieving his smoke.

The girls were now gleaming with perspiration, their mouths gaping as they struggled to catch their breath, yet none of them stopped running. Desiree was slowing down, however, until she felt Quinn's firm hand come down on her bottom, and then she sped up again.

From behind, Kemp surreptitiously pressed closer to Tiffany until she could feel his erection through their clothes, its buried tip poking between her buttocks.

A part of her wanted to pull away, but that part of her weakened as he tossed away the butt of his smoke and slipped his arms around her waist.

'Are you turned on, too?' His face was near her throat, his breath hot and his voice croaky.

She did not answer, except with an involuntary gasp as, in the clearing, Desiree fell heavily onto the grass. She seemed dazed and confused as she tried to get up, but found it impossible because Quinn planted a foot on her back.

Kemp's fingers were working on the buttons of Tiffany's uniform, and she was tempted to help him, but she remained content to let him handle the task. His right hand snaked inside the opening, and slipped down to the waistband of her panties. He cupped her pubic mound and squeezed it gently, making her gasp again and then bite her lip, as she did not want to interrupt the scene in the clearing by alerting Quinn of their presence. Other girls were quickly joining Desiree on the ground, and it was a strangely erotic sight.

'I want you,' Kemp hissed, sending chills down her spine as he licked and nibbled on her earlobe. 'I want you back, I mean.'

She was barely listening, her attention riveted on the girls still running on the spot, their legs pumping like steam pistons, their nipples erect and red as their breasts bounced painfully up and down, perspiration glistening over their firm young bodies. Their exhausted teammates were sitting up and also watching them.

'I didn't treat you right,' Kemp whispered fervently. 'I can change that.'

She found his words almost as distracting as his fingers working inside her panties, tracing the moist furrow of her sex lips, teasing before one of them penetrated her. She parted her thighs a little more to accommodate the invader, and bit her lip to keep from crying out as two more fingers joined it in plumbing her tight depths. Meanwhile his thumb efficiently massaged her stiffening clitoris with a circular motion, heightening the sweet torture that just made her more and more desperate for his rigid cock.

In the clearing only one girl, Kamesha, remained standing, yet she continued running, not yet having received permission to stop. When Quinn finally gave the command she fell gratefully onto all fours, gasping for breath.

'Will you return to my crew, Tiffany?' Kemp pressed huskily. 'I can arrange it—'

'I'm sure you can.' The voice from behind them was loud and clear, totally unexpected and instantly recognisable.

Kemp quickly pulled his hand from her uniform and stepped back. 'Armin!' he exclaimed. 'What a surprise.'

Singh stepped forward. 'Obviously.' He glanced at the undone buttons on Tiffany's uniform, but continued to address Kemp. 'You had your chance with her. She belongs to me now.'

Tiffany did up her uniform, fighting back her frustration. She had been so close, both to her own climax and to seeing what Quinn was about to offer her girls as punishment and reward.

The sports manager appeared on the scene. 'What's going on here?' she demanded.

Singh looked at her. 'It's fifteen minutes to lights out,' he said simply.

'And it takes three of you to come out here to tell me that?' Quinn demanded.

'I thought it would only take one.' The security chief glared at Tiffany. 'I seem to have been mistaken.' He reached out and gripped her shoulder. 'Get back to the house.' He shoved her towards it. She obeyed him, practically running all the way. Her pussy still ached for attention, and her mind was reeling from the delicious experience of being fought over by two men.

CHAPTER NINE

Singh and Tiffany circled each other on the thick blue dojo mat, never taking their eyes off each other. She felt it sink with a sigh beneath her each time she moved her bare feet, but she refused to let it distract her. Singh, stripped to reveal a lean chest with dark nipples and a washboard stomach grounded with a clump of curly hair descending into his trousers, would sense the distraction, take advantage of it, and she would be on her back yet again.

He smiled. 'Well, Welborne, I'm waiting.'

Tiffany gulped. 'Yes, master...' She rushed forward, arms out to tackle him, but with his usual contemptuous ease he caught her and flipped her over his shoulder so that she landed hard on her back with a loud *splat!* He was on her in a flash, pressing down on her middle as if to make it even more difficult for her to catch her breath. 'Never attack when your opponent asks for it,' he instructed her mildly. 'Always do the unexpected.'

'Yes, master,' she gasped.

He held her eyes. 'Undress,' he said.

'Yes, master.' She sat up as soon as he released her, and standing up herself, she quickly stripped off her clothes and dropped them aside. 'May I ask you a question, master?'

He was by the table now, selecting items with as much relish as a starving man standing at a gourmet buffet. 'You may,' he replied absently.

Naked, she sank to her knees, her thighs apart, her bottom resting on her heels, the flats of her hands on her knees, her head bowed in the manner he preferred. 'Why do you teach subjects how to fight? I mean, isn't that like teaching burglars how to pick locks?'

He chuckled. 'I'm not teaching you how to fight, Welborne, I'm teaching you how to defend yourself. There's a difference. I've found that the most aggressive people often turn out to be the most insecure. They're so afraid of losing a fight that they start one in order to seek some perceived advantage in striking first, or in order to prove themselves. Often those with the skills to defend themselves have the confidence not to abuse those skills. It's a well-founded theory in reformation.'

'Then how do you reconcile trying to build self-confidence in your subjects while simultaneously trying to turn them into submissive slaves?'

'I gave you permission to ask one question,' he said bluntly. 'You've abused that privilege, and must now pay the price. Look up.'

She did, and saw the items he would use to collect that price; his favourite cat o' nine tails, an ankle spreader bar, and a whipping post; a metre-high wooden cylinder as thick as a man's thigh, dotted with chrome studs and mounted onto a leather covered board adorned with two short wrist manacles.

He dropped the cat and the post on the mat. 'Assume the position,' he commanded.

She obeyed him, climbing onto the board until she was almost straddling the post while he fed her wrists into the manacles. Her nipples rose to attention, and she was achingly aware of how wide her thighs were parted. Her sex felt hungry for more and more attention.

Singh's touch was businesslike, as he attached the spreader to her ankles, forcing her to lean forward as her vulva pressed even more firmly into the post. Then he removed the rest of his clothes, revealing his erection, which was long and thick, rising from an ebony cluster of curls at his groin. He circled, prowling, scrutinising her, before retrieving the cat, which hung lazily at his side as he smiled. 'Have you been a good girl, Tiffany?'

'As good as I can be, master,' she said meekly.

'That tells me nothing.' The cat's tail slashed down. 'Let me rephrase my question. Have you been naughty, Tiffany?'

She averted her eyes. 'I fear so, master,' she admitted honestly.

'I see. And how have you been naughty?'

'I - I let Mr Kemp touch me the other night.'

'Yes, I remember, and I've been meaning to do something about that. I fear you must be punished for your indiscretion.'

'I understand, master,' she whispered, her pussy tightening. 'I'm ready, master.'

'I hope so.'

She heard the swish of the cat through the air, and then felt the stinging blow across her clenched buttocks. She gasped, her hands reflexively pulling at their bonds as her nipples hardened and her pussy clenched almost painfully. And as her master beat her, Tiffany shifted her position until her clitoris was pressed against the whipping pole, relishing the additional stimulation as the fire building within her sex spread through her whole body. Her bottom felt as hot as an oven, but her approaching orgasm felt mysteriously hotter. She rubbed her magic button hard and fast against the post, further encouraging the pressure building up inside her as the whip sliced through the air with increasing speed and force.

Sheer bliss blinded her as an orgasm carried all her thoughts away. Her back arched and she flung her head back, her breasts rising and falling as she cried, 'Oh yes... oh yes... ooooh yes! *Yes!*'

Gradually she became aware that Singh was releasing her ankles, not to free her entirely, of course, but to make the following minutes easier for him. She knew what was coming, and mustered her dwindling strength to move her body into position, rising to present him with a view of her rounded bottom decorated with the fresh red stripes he had just cruelly painted on her. She wanted nothing more than to lie down and rest, but then she heard his zipper lowering and suddenly she longed to feel him inside her, to feel the tangle of hair at his groin pressed against her wounded cheeks, scratching and adding to her delicious torment.

Gripping her hips he mounted her, his cock pressing urgently between her legs. He moaned as he rubbed his bloated helmet up and down between her wet folds before plunging between them, and she climaxed again as his body pressed against her red-hot cheeks, re-igniting the intense pain and pleasure. She braced herself on the post as wave after wave of searing joy crashed through her blood beneath his deep, generous thrusts. She wished they would go on forever, but even her master was just a man, and in what seemed like no time at all he ejaculated with a strangled groan as she used her inner muscles to milk every last drop of sperm from his pulsing erection.

Eventually he pulled out of her, and she listened to him closing his trousers before releasing her wrists. Sliding off the post she slumped on the floor, looking up at him in happy exhaustion. 'Thank you, master,' she sighed.

He nodded. 'That was almost as good as my time with Shazza and Olivia yesterday,' he remarked hurtfully. His insulting comment made her feel humiliated in a way the chains and beatings never did, and she suddenly saw him for what he was, and in seeing through him, she saw through herself.

And she did not like it one little bit.

Tiffany stood beside Shazza, brushes in hand, listening to Singh next door ordering the newcomers to undress and step forward to be inspected.

Shazza nudged her again. 'I hope there's some pretty ones today,' she said eagerly.

'Yeah...' Tiffany replied absently. It was something she still could not quite get used to, having Shazza addressing her as an equal now that they were on the same team. It disturbed her that she wanted to be there, that she wanted to be a part of all this, to see other girls naked and humiliated and subject to her intimate touching.

The first of the new arrivals came through the doorway, a tall, well-built black woman with short chestnut hair, pert breasts and firm buttocks. As briefed beforehand, Tiffany followed Shazza's lead, soaking her sponge in the trough of disinfectant and scrubbing the newcomer from head to toe. Then Shazza sent the unfortunate new recruit to the showers with a slap on her tight bottom.

Next, a much shorter Oriental woman entered the showers. She had full breasts and a plump rear ripe for beating, Tiffany noted as she proceeded with her work trying not to think about it or enjoy it too much.

Then came the last new subject, a girl with honey-blonde hair, deep blue eyes, pink cheeks, pale skin, pert breasts, and boyishly tight buttocks. Tiffany took her in, wondering what it was about her she found so oddly attractive. Was it the lost look on her face, perhaps?

After she had been scrubbed down with disinfectant, the girl reached out to her. 'Please, please help me, I shouldn't be here,' she pleaded, but Tiffany shoved her towards the showers and turned away, unable to meet her eyes.

Shazza grinned. 'I think she wanted to be your friend, Tiff,' she chuckled.

Tiffany wiped suds off herself with her gloved hands - the hands of someone who participated in the degradation of other human beings. She helped reduce others to her own level of submissiveness, and loved it. What would she be like in three years' time? It was a frightening question.

Processing went smoothly. After they had dressed and left their possessions with Colbert, the new girls were ordered into the TV room until dinner, and Tiffany was instructed to baby-sit them. They sat quietly on the battered old couches, most of them staring as if hypnotised at the television screen. They wore their crisp new uniforms, and the astringent smell of soap still clung to their fresh skin.

Tiffany sat by herself, absently flipping through a magazine, trying not to look over at her charges, particularly at the blonde, who looked as miserable as she had been on her first day. But then the girl looked up, their eyes met, and neither seemed able to look away, each waiting for the other to say something.

'I - I'm sorry for... for...' the newcomer finally stammered.

'Forget it,' Tiffany said dismissively. 'The first day's always the worst.'

The girl smiled tremulously. 'Thank you.'

Tiffany refrained from adding that the first day was also only the beginning. She set aside her magazine and moved to sit beside the newcomer on the couch. 'My name's Tiffany Welborne,' she said warmly.

'Wendy Howard.' Her accent was English and her eyes had a distant, haunted look. 'I didn't... I didn't think I could be degraded like that. They treated us like animals today. I thought I would die.'

'We all went through it and survived, as you will.'

But Wendy did not seem to be listening. 'The way that man touched me... I thought only female wardens were allowed to do that.'

'This isn't England,' Tiffany pointed out.

'You're British, too?'

'Yes, and I've not been here long. What are you in for?'

'Drugs. I'm... I was a student at Cascara City University. It was only a little cannabis... What's going to happen to me?'

Tiffany held her initial response in check. She could not explain the sexual conditioning regime of *Rache House* without terrifying the girl, so she deflected her question with one of her own. 'What was your sentence?'

Wendy choked back a sob. 'Three months.'

'Well then, you're going to spend the next three months here with no contact with the outside world except through vetted letters. Whether or not your sentence is increased or decreased depends on you, and if you provide the staff with what it expects of you.'

'And what do they expect of me?' she asked anxiously.

'Obedience, as the director told you today. Full, unadulterated obedience. Obey the regime, obey us, and you'll attain fulfilment such as you've never known before. Disobey, and you'll soon learn the true meaning of the phrase "hell on..."' Tiffany's reply drifted away as she realised she was echoing Rache's first words to her.

'But this is wrong,' Wendy gasped. 'I have to get out of here. I shouldn't be here!'

Suddenly Tiffany's sympathy evaporated. 'No one made you come here,' she snapped, three chimes of the dinner bell punctuating her rebuke, and she stood up. 'Come on,' she said to all the girls, 'I'll show you the procedure for meals. And pay attention, because you won't be excused for ignorance if you foul up the next time.'

Rache was behind his desk, reclining in as casual a manner as Tiffany, standing to attention before him, had ever seen. Another surprise was the music coming from speakers hidden behind one of his glass-fronted bookcases. But she said nothing, allowing him to initiate the conversation.

'I was a fan of your father's music before you were born, Miss Welborne, though I never cared for his later work. Somewhere in the attic of my mind, if not in my residence, lies a treasured pair of flares.' He indicated the source of the music. 'You've heard the particular song now playing before, haven't you?'

She nodded. '*Colette*, the piece he wrote for my mother.' She remembered the summer of her fourteenth birthday, the summer her parents had divorced, when the local stations played the damned song over and over again while the news of their separation made the headlines for weeks.

Rache smiled ineffably. 'She must have been flattered he'd written a song for her, particularly when it made the top ten before they married. Some men pay tributes to women through paint and canvas, pen or photographs, but there must be something about a song...' He sat up abruptly, and used a remote control to lower the volume. 'Mr Singh claims your progress has been exceptional,' he went on, abruptly changing the subject. 'Are you learning much from him?'

She felt herself blushing. 'I hope so, doctor,' she said.

'Good.' He smiled and stood up. 'Would you care for some cognac? Someone of your... breeding... would surely appreciate my particular favourite.'

The mention of cognac made her mouth water, and she realised it had been nearly three weeks since she'd had anything to drink besides water or skimmed milk. 'Oh yes, please,' she said enthusiastically.

'Then take a seat.' He walked over to his drinks cabinet while Tiffany moved to the single chair before the desk, where she found his cat reclining. She reached out and lifted the heavy bundle of fur up in her arms, set it down on the floor and took its place.

Rache, having poured one snifter, was staring at her in what looked like sheer disbelief. 'What did you just do?' he asked, his voice dangerously quiet.

'Nothing, sir, that I know of,' she replied, a bit bemused.

Disbelief turned to indignation. 'Don't "nothing, sir" me. You moved Chairman out of his seat, didn't you?'

'Um, yes sir, I did,' Tiffany admitted the obvious, somewhat confused, 'but you told me to take a seat...'

'And if the only seat in the room had been occupied by Mr Kemp or Mr Singh, would you have lifted them off to take their place?'

The intensity of his anger chilled her. 'I-I'm sorry, but - but it's only cat,' she stammered, shifting uncomfortably.

'Only a cat, Miss Welborne?' He stepped close to her, his eyes blazing. 'Only a cat? Let me tell you, young lady, that I value Chairman more than I do a brainless, feckless, pampered scapegrace such as yourself. Get up and get undressed. Now!'

Bewildered by the alarmingly swift change of atmosphere in the office, Tiffany hurried to obey, feeling more rattled than she had in a long time. The sessions of chastisement and pleasure she underwent with Singh were organised, prepared, expected - and they had obviously made her complacent. Now, however, she felt as she had on her first day. She even tried to cover herself once she was naked in an act of modesty she thought had been exorcised from her forever.

Rache walked behind his desk, disappeared momentarily as he knelt down, and rose with Chairman in his arms. Then stroking the cat affectionately, he took the seat both his pet and his subject had occupied moments before. 'So, Miss Welborne,' he regarded her with contempt, 'you think you're better than my cat, do you?'

'No, doctor, I just—'

'Silence!' Such was the force of his command that Chairman nearly leapt out of his arms, but Rache restrained and stroked him until he relaxed again. Calmer himself then, but no less angry, the director ordered, 'Get down on your hands and knees but don't look away from me.'

Tiffany obeyed him, her stomach churning as she kept her eyes fixed on his cold stare.

'Cats have a well-developed sense of hierarchy and protocol when it comes to territory,' the director went on. 'Some cats may encroach upon another's patch, but they had better be assured of their superiority over the original resident. And as I've already stated your inferiority to Chairman, you may now ask his forgiveness for your effrontery.'

Tiffany could not believe what she was hearing. All the humiliation she had endured up until now seemed to pale in significance compared to what she was about to do. She was expected to abase herself before a cat?

Rache lifted and pointed a clearly uninterested Chairman at her. 'Well?'

Tiffany realised then that her pride, which she thought had been scoured away, was merely buried, and when it resurrected, alive and kicking, it stuck in her throat. She tried to swallow it. 'I'm... I'm sorry, Chairman,' she managed.

Rache held the cat up until his own face was concealed behind it. 'And what are you sorry for?' he persisted.

Once more Tiffany swallowed the restless ghost of her pride. 'I'm sorry for removing you from your seat,' she said.

'And why are you sorry?'

She looked down, her tone a blend of false repentance and barely contained anger. 'Because... because I had no right.'

'And why not?'

Her jaw tightened, and she spoke through clenched teeth. 'Because I'm... I'm inferior to you.'

'Repeat, please, I'm a bit deaf at my age.'

'Because I'm inferior to you, Chairman.'

'Raise your eyes.'

She did so, and saw Rache looking at his cat as he asked, 'What do you think? Does that satisfy you?' He brought Chairman's face to his ear as if the cat was actually whispering to him, and his expression when he heard the mock reply was one of horror. 'Oh dear, Miss Welborne, I'm afraid Chairman and I are much alike - very unforgiving. Kiss the floor.'

Tiffany lowered her forehead until it touched the carpet, which raised her bottom as high as possible. She looked between her hanging breasts at the soft tuft of her bush and at the office wall behind her, waiting. She heard Rache rise and walk around her, and listened with trepidation as he rustled though the umbrella stand by his desk - which contained everything but umbrellas.

He selected the bamboo cane, and she realised why as soon as the first blow struck her buttocks; she clenched her cheeks and brought her thighs together reflexively.

'Keep them spread!' he commanded. 'Wider... and keep still.'

Tiffany clenched her jaw and clawed at the burgundy carpet beneath her fingers as she fought to hold still and not scream as the assault continued, the pain and trauma inflicted by the cane preventing any segue way into pleasure. She was sobbing when the ordeal finally ended, and had to struggle to obey when the doctor ordered her to her feet. She was shaking uncontrollably as he circled her slowly, cane still in hand as if threatening to renew its attack, anger still blazing in his eyes.

'Presumptuous little animal,' he spat, 'believing a few weeks here could change her so much. How little she knows. How much she has yet to learn.' He stopped and stabbed the cane in her direction. 'What you've just undergone is nothing. Nothing. Every time you think you've settled down, every time you think you've gone as far as you can go, I'll take you one step further. Now pick up your clothes.'

Tiffany reached for her panties first, and was slipping them on when he barked, 'No! Don't waste my time, get dressed outside.'

She let the tears flow unchecked as she gathered the rest of her clothing and stumbled out into the corridor. Thankfully there was no one there, and she hurried to get dressed again. Her head was spinning. He was insane and sadistic beyond belief, she knew that now. And he was in total command of her mind and body.

Tiffany was upstairs watching Colbert and Bonnie put Wendy and the other new girls through their paces, teaching them how to properly maintain their beds and lockers. But her mind was busy elsewhere, dwelling on schedules, layouts, routines; all the information she had picked up during her time in Singh's group. The security layout at night was simple, relying on the cooperation of the subjects. The outer buildings, including the garage containing the house vans, were locked and alarms set. After lights out, the alarms would activate even if someone used the right keys to unlock any doors. The alarms and gate controls were monitored at reception. The keys to the outside buildings and the vehicles were kept there, too. Of course, the subjects on duty could not switch off the alarms themselves - the system automatically activated at nine o'clock - but if Tiffany timed it right, she would not have to. All she needed was fifteen minutes' luck, and a key to the key box. The luck would have to provide itself, but the key...

'Remy, could you help me?'

He was suspicious, though Tiffany guessed it was for other reasons. Still, he followed her as obediently as a puppy to the sports bunker, a former servants' bungalow converted for Quinn and her team's use. The door was, thankfully, unlocked; Quinn sometimes forgot to lock it on her way out, as Tiffany had learned on previous patrols.

The smell of perspiration hung heavy in the still air. Tall green lockers and benches dominated one part of the interior, while another part was taken up by the showers and benches used for massage. Quinn's office sat in the far corner beside the exercise and storage rooms, but the place was dark and deserted.

'Why are we here, Tiff?' he asked.

'Because you live with the other two guards, so we can't use your room.' She left the lights off, content to gaze at him in the meagre illumination from the main house seeping through the bunker's high windows; she was almost afraid her guilt would show. 'Remy, Rache punished me today,' she disclosed.

'What did you do this time?'

'Does it matter? What's important is that it got me hot.' She embraced him, squeezing him tightly. He hugged her back and they stood there, rocking gently together. Then she felt his erection pressing against her, and her smile became an eager grin. She started nibbling on his earlobe, making him squirm in her grasp as his hands dove down to knead her buttocks.

'You have to hurry,' he warned. 'It's not long before lights out.'

'I know,' she whispered; more than he expected it had to be timed right, not so soon that he discovered her deception, and not so late that the activities preceding lights out would overtake them. There was not time for both of them to strip and have intercourse, so she backed away from him and whispered, 'Force me down.'

He looked puzzled.

'Force me down to my knees and make me take you in my mouth.'

It sounded odd, her forceful and dominant voice ordering him to make her submissive. It was a strange contradiction, but it worked. With both hands on her shoulders, he exerted an insistent pressure and made her sink to her knees before him until she was eye-level with the bulge in his trousers. Her hands reached up to tentatively caress him as he undid them, and she promptly lowered them along with his briefs to his ankles. A flaring helmet, glistening with moisture, tipped the firm damask stem of his cock as she inhaled his familiar musky scent. Then she closed her eyes, parted her lips and slid him in between them, taking his full length into her mouth. He groaned above her as she ran her tongue around the rim of his glans, tasting and relishing him. Blindly she reached out, found his hands, and placed them on her head, urging him to direct her.

As he moved her selfishly back and forth her nipples pressed against the inside of her bra and her pussy grew hotter and wetter by the second, soaking the gusset of her panties. That she was not being directly satisfied did not matter; she was thoroughly excited and enjoying herself. She continued working her mouth up and down his full length, loving the taste and feel of his cock, loving the control and domination expressed by the hands gripping her head. With a sucking motion she manipulated the skin insulating his erection, drawing it up to the swollen head, and then relieving the pressure before repeating the cycle over and over again. His moans grew urgent, and it was not long before she tasted his salty pre-come.

When he finally climaxed with a cry, jerking against her, she welcomed the full rush of his sperm, swallowing each spurt hungry for the next one. His nails dug into her scalp, a discomfort she also welcomed as an indelible ingredient of her excitement.

As surprised as Tiffany was when Quinn abruptly entered the bungalow, part of her was not too surprised, just embarrassed. The sports manager was dressed in baggy black cotton sweatpants and a matching T-shirt and trainers, and she appeared to be alone.

Remy quickly pulled up his trousers as Quinn closed the door behind her and switched on the overhead fluorescent lights, which revealed that her expression was more amused than censorious. 'Didn't get enough at dinner, Welborne?' she said.

Tiffany blushed as she rose to her feet. 'We weren't expecting you.'

'No kidding. I remembered I'd forgotten to lock the door again, and then I heard sounds coming from inside... very interesting sounds.' She leaned back against the lockers, folding her arms across her chest. 'Guys, I may not be as big a stickler for the rules as the others are, but even I have to admit that this is pushing the boat a little too far, don't you think?'

Remy took charge. 'We're both very sorry about this, Ms Quinn,' he apologised. 'If there's anything I can do to make it up to you...'

'You can't, but Welborne can.'

Tiffany instinctively stepped behind Remy, her arms wrapped protectively around herself.

Quinn rolled her eyes. 'Calm down, Welborne, I'm not about to punish you, but I do want you to try out for the football team tomorrow. Promise me you will, and we'll forget about this little incident.'

Tiffany almost refused, but then she realised that, if all went well tonight, she would not even be there tomorrow. So she drew breath and said, 'Okay, Ms Quinn.'

'Good. I'll arrange a work break for you in the afternoon.' She nodded towards the door. 'It's half-eight; let's all get back to the house before lights out.'

Dutifully the two subjects complied, Tiffany walking behind Remy and Quinn so that neither of them could see her pocket the key she had taken from Remy's trousers; the key to the key box in reception. Everything was falling into place. The staff would be busy with their newcomer placement meeting, the subjects busy with the welcoming, and Remy would be off-duty and hopefully not notice the missing key until it was too late. Hannah Greer was first on duty at reception, from eight o'clock to twelve o'clock, but she would be easily persuaded to let Tiffany take her place so she did not have to miss the welcoming. In fifteen minutes Tiffany could be driving a van down the road outside the walls. She had friends on the outside besides daddy. Yes, everything was falling into place. And yet her stomach felt queasy with anxiety.

The first floor was dark and deserted except for reception. Hannah, a dark-skinned girl with long burgundy hair was sitting with her feet up on the countertop thumbing through a magazine when Tiffany appeared, smiling.

'Hi,' Tiffany beamed.

Hannah smiled back. 'Hi yourself. Did you forget you weren't taking over until midnight?'

'Actually, I wondered if you wanted to switch shifts so you wouldn't miss the newcomers' welcoming.'

'Oh, thanks,' she returned to her magazine, 'but that's okay. You shouldn't miss your first.'

Tiffany froze, unable to believe she had heard her correctly. 'No really, Hannah, you go on. It doesn't interest me.'

'Yeah, right.'

She tried to control her accelerating pulse as her plans began resembling a house of cards in the wind. 'Look, I'll be honest with you...' she said, thinking quickly, 'Shazza's been... she's been making advances, and I was hoping if I took this shift she'd be asleep when it was over.'

Hannah seemed to consider this, raising Tiffany's hopes before dashing them again. 'Look, Tiff, I know she can be bitchier than most, but she's not totally unreasonable. You have to confront her. Avoiding the issue won't make it go away.' She looked back down at her magazine. 'You should get back to the dorm. You've no reason being here now.'

'Yes, you're right...' The frustration welling up inside Tiffany made the moments that followed seem distant, surreal, as if they were happening to someone else. She found herself sidling right up to Hannah, and punching her in the mouth with a clenched fist. It was a totally unexpected action - as Singh had taught her - and the girl toppled over in her chair, her magazine fluttering from her grasp like a wounded bird. Tiffany's hand then reached out for the roll of masking tape lying on the counter, and in moments the stunned guard's hands were bound behind her, as were her ankles. Her mouth was already filled with a handkerchief, and taped shut.

Tiffany paused to stare down at the young woman, feeling terribly guilty. But the dye had been cast, and she would have plenty of time later for remorse. She turned to the red key box mounted on the wall above the filing cabinet, withdrew Remy's key from the pocket in her uniform, inserted it into the lock... and found it did not work.

Chapter Ten

Tiffany stared at the key in utter disbelief. She tried it again, and then again, the last time putting all her effort into it - and the key broke.

Panic almost had her hyperventilating. What was she to do now? Oh, God, what was she to do now? Oh, God. Oh, God...

Jude! Jude had stolen cars in Cascara City. She could hotwire one of the prison vans and they could crash through the gates.

Tiffany had to struggle to keep her boots from pounding loudly down the dark, empty corridors as she ran towards the dorm, and skidded to a halt just outside it. The veteran girls were hurrying around, getting ready for the welcoming, while all the newcomers were out of sight. She forced the butterflies in her stomach to settle down long enough to scan the faces for Jude's. There she was, sitting amongst her new friends.

'Jude!' she called urgently. 'The director wants you to serve tonight.'

The last three weeks had not been unkind to Jude. She was as tanned as Tiffany, and she had lost some, if not all, of her body fat, so that she looked very appealing in her T-shirt and panties. And there was more, an invigoration of her spirit, the same spirit Tiffany had felt in the van when they first met, but tempered now, polished by experience. And while she looked disappointed about missing the welcoming, she also sounded excited. 'Really?' she squealed. 'He wants me?'

The thought only occurred to Tiffany then and there that Jude was not exactly dressed for an escape, but there was no time to spare. 'Yes, come on, he's impatient tonight.'

For a moment there was only the sound of their contrasting footfalls, boots and bare feet, down the hall and then down the stairs, where Jude paused when Tiffany opened the front door. 'What's going on?' she asked suspiciously. 'Is he outside?' She glanced at reception. 'Shouldn't someone be—?'

'No questions,' Tiffany hissed, grabbing Jude by the wrist. 'Come on!'

Jude allowed herself to be led outside. The clearing between the main house and the garage was unlit. She winced as her bare feet touched the gravel path, and snatched her wrist from Tiffany's grasp. 'Tiff, what the hell is going on?' she demanded.

'We're escaping, that's what's going on,' Tiffany told her. 'Come on, we've got less than five minutes.'

'Escaping? Are you serious? I can't escape looking like this!'

'Don't worry about it, I've got it all worked out,' Tiffany lied desperately, glancing around them. The grounds outside would be deserted this soon to the execution of lights out protocols, but she felt as if she were being watched. 'I'll break the window to the garage and open the door. All you have to do is hotwire one of the vans.'

'What? I can't do that!'

Tiffany froze in her tracks, knowing the girl's denial could be read any number of ways, but suspecting she meant the worst possible way. 'But you said you were arrested for stealing cars.'

'Yeah, me and some of my friends, but they did all the work. I just tagged along.'

'What?!'

Further explanation was lost in the cacophony of the escape alarm blaring from speakers mounted on the roof of the house, and immediately all lights within and without, even the floodlights surrounding the exercise field, came to blinding life.

Tiffany glanced at her watch. She had three minutes left. What had gone wrong? Had someone discovered Hannah, or had they happened to glance out of a window and seen them? Then she asked herself why she bothered questioning what had happened, and bolted down the winding road towards the front gate, not knowing whether Jude would follow her, and not caring.

The drive wound out of direct view of the house and the lights, becoming a dark track lined by trees and only faintly illuminated by starlight. And then lights appeared behind her dancing like errant fireflies rapidly overtaken by scrabbling feet... the dogs! Immediately she skidded to a halt, knowing enough about Almira and Jarita not to run in their presence. The twin Alsatians easily caught up with her, circling and barking but keeping well back as they had been trained to do while Tiffany fought her fear and remained absolutely still, breath rasping in her lungs - waiting.

The first to arrive was Stuart. During the evenings one guard would remain on duty patrolling the upper floors and occasionally checking in on the subject minding reception. Stuart was obviously on first shift, and he had probably found Hannah and set off the alarm. He was just a silhouette in the white lights from the house as he, too, skidded to a halt. 'Okay, Tiffany, get down on your knees, cross your ankles, and lock your hands behind your head.'

She knew the drill already - make the attempted escapees immobilise themselves while awaiting assistance from the house. The gravel road felt rough through her uniform as she watched additional flashlight beams darting closer, and then heard another familiar voice as someone in the house silenced the alarms. 'Good work, Stuart.'

'There was no struggle, Mr Singh.'

'Pity.' Singh moved behind Tiffany, clasped a fistful of her hair, and pulled her back to her feet. She yelped and struggled, but he hissed, 'Shut up and keep your hands where they are.' Still gripping her, he twisted her to face the other guard, Keith Osbourne, a slim, wiry specimen with shocking red hair. He approached her, not meeting her eyes, carrying a bar and chains. In moments her wrists were bound behind her back with an arm spreader, and a collar and lead was attached to her throat, with Singh holding the other end. 'March back to the house, Welborne,' he commanded angrily. 'Move it!'

In front of the house Tiffany saw Jude on her knees, her arms bound like hers, and she could not bring herself to meet her eyes.

She was marched into Rache's office, and the director's expression was stony. 'How far?' he asked abruptly.

'Forrester was still outside the front door,' Singh reported. 'Welborne was about a hundred metres down the path.'

The doctor nodded, and then motioned to her with his forefinger. Tiffany did not understand the gesture, and then found she did not have to; Singh forced her down to her knees again, and made her bow her head.

She was breathing heavily as anxiety made her stomach ache. She could only see the director's boots as he walked around her, and she feared he might kick her at any moment.

'How's Greer?' Rache asked quietly.

Behind her, Keith answered. 'Apart from the cut and swelling to her lip and a bruised arm when she fell,' he informed the director, 'she seems fine.'

'I'll check on her afterwards.' The doctor paused for a tense heartbeat, during which Tiffany thought her own would stop with terror, and then kept pacing around her. 'Welborne, you've a choice; thirty with the cane, plus three days in the kennels and forfeiture of all work credits to date, or an extra six months added to your sentence. Don't keep me waiting for your answer.'

She did not keep him waiting. 'The first punishment, sir,' she blurted hastily.

'Take her to security, Keith. Hannah will have the privilege of beating her.'

'Yes, doctor. What about Forrester?'

'Bring her in after you've moved Welborne.'

Keith pulled her to her feet again, and led her to security, where Singh and Hannah Greer were waiting. Tiffany saw the shiny bruise on the left side of the girl's mouth and looked away, thoroughly ashamed at having been the cause of it.

But Hannah would not let her off so lightly. She stood face-to-face with her, grabbed her by the chin, and forced Tiffany to look her in the eye. 'Don't look away, you traitorous bitch,' she hissed venomously. 'See what you did? Have a good fucking look at what you did to me.'

'I'm sorry,' she mumbled, tears welling up into her eyes.

'Not yet you're not.'

'That's enough, Greer,' Singh said firmly. 'You're allowed to give her thirty with the cane if you want to.'

Hannah grinned. 'Oh, I want to.' Tiffany's stomach plummeted towards her boots.

'Remove her arm restraints and lead,' Singh instructed, 'but leave the collar on.

The director's expecting me back after this.'

Tiffany barely had time to flex and move her arms before Hannah commanded, 'Strip, you bitch. Move it!'

She struggled to comply as quickly as possible, her eyes looking for the cane that would soon be used on her flesh. Trembling, she dropped her clothes aside and let Hannah drag her to the centre of the room.

'Where will you bind her?' Singh asked, handing Hannah a long and slender bamboo cane.

'I won't, I want her to be able to move about.' She cut the air with the cane. 'I'm going to enjoy this.'

'Not more than thirty, Greer, and no blows to the head or neck.'

'I'll try to remember that.'

'You will remember,' Singh warned her. 'Or you'll receive thirty yourself.'

Hannah gave Tiffany's arm a spiteful squeeze before stepping back and looking her over, making a malicious show of choosing her first target. 'Where to begin...' she mused. 'Where to begin...'

'Just get on with it.' Singh's annoyance was discernible, and growing. 'The privilege granted you tonight is under the director's and my sufferance, so don't try my patience.'

For a heartbeat Tiffany believed he was protecting her, and then she realised he was probably angry he could not beat her himself.

Hannah's eyes narrowed. 'Bend over and grip your ankles, bitch,' she ordered with evident relish.

Tiffany obeyed miserably, and did not have to wait long for the first agonising blow. Pain cut into her as never before, swiftly followed by another searing flash of agony, and then another, and another. She found herself gasping like a fish out of water and struggling to keep herself steady as the scalding torment sent the blood rushing to her head. There was nothing stimulating or sexually arousing about this punishment; Hannah wanted her to suffer without the balm of an orgasm. She did not concentrate merely on her buttocks but alternated cruelly between her bottom and her back, and even the tender backs of her thighs.

Tiffany tried counting the strokes, but she could not focus beyond her body's growing anguish. Then, to her surprise, she heard Hannah snap, 'Straighten up!' and did so gratefully.

Hannah stabbed the tip of the cane at her. 'You're only halfway there, bitch,' she spat. 'Lift your arms over your head.'

Tiffany winced as she did so, and tensed as she watched Hannah raise the cane again. This was even worse, to see the blows coming. The first one struck her directly across her breasts, and she instinctively lowered her arms to cover them as she wailed in shock at the excruciating pain. Hannah said nothing as she lashed her victim's stomach next, and then moved down to the front of her thighs, before moving unexpectedly and viciously back up to her pubic mound. Pure pain overwhelmed Tiffany, coupled with the terrible conviction that it would never end.

Hannah raised the cane once more, her ire unabashed, her eyes burning, but

Singh's voice halted her. 'That's it, Greer,' he barked.

Cuffed and leashed once more, Tiffany was led back outside. She walked stiffly, her eyes glazed, barely feeling the harsh gravel beneath her bare soles as she relished the cool caress of the night air on her flaming flesh.

Only two dogs were employed at *Rache Correction House*, yet the kennels, another converted servants' bungalow, were large enough for an entire pack, and her time in security - for it was surely over now - had taught her why. She was led to an enclosure that had once served as the bungalow's kitchen. It was now a stark area furnished with shredded newspapers, a slop bucket, old blankets, water bottles, a hole in the floor where the sink was mounted, and numerous iron rings bolted into the walls at varying heights.

Singh freed her hands, and then attached her collar's chain to one of the wall rings. 'You'll be checked on regularly,' he said shortly.

Tiffany sank to the floor, ignoring the protests from her back and buttocks, and pulled one of the blankets over herself. The chain was long enough to enable her to lie down. She looked up at Singh where he stood looming over her, and felt the tears streaming down her face. 'Please, master, don't do this to me. I can't stay in—'

'You should have thought of that before you betrayed my trust,' he interrupted her coldly. There was not a trace of sympathy in his demeanour. 'You've made your bed, now lie in it.' He turned on his heels and headed for the door, ignoring the eagerly barking dogs. Seconds later the lights went out, the door was slammed shut, and locked. The dogs fell silent at once, and were apparently asleep within minutes.

It took Tiffany longer to slip into the peace of oblivion. In the half-light filtering in through the high windows from the main house, she fidgeted uncomfortably, every part of her body aching. Hannah had done a thorough job of caning her, and it was difficult to find a position to settle in that did not aggravate her stiffening welts. And yet a perverse delight was blended in with her pain. She imagined how she looked now, naked and beaten, collared and leashed to the wall of a kennel like a beast, the ultimate degradation. She fought to ignore the response in her sex, and wiped the tears from her face as she did her best to make herself comfortable.

The night was not kind to Tiffany. Naked and cold beneath the thin blanket, the leash and collar and her tightening welts kept her awake, as did a gnawing hunger. She slept only fitfully, starting every now and then at the screech of fruit bats outside. At one point she woke up so quickly that she banged her head against the wall behind her, an additional and unnecessary pain that sent her into a fit of sobbing. She had never felt so alone and so sorry for herself in her life.

It was daylight, and well after assembly and exercise judging by what she could hear outside, before Stuart and Hannah, the latter carrying a tray, visited her. Her assaulted mouth had bloomed even more overnight, and she looked and sounded as if her anger had also grown, developing from a potent raw fury to a cool, controlled sadism. 'Breakfast, bitch,' she snarled.

Tiffany sat up eagerly, her welt-covered nakedness forgotten even as she winced unconsciously. She thought her first week in *Rache House* had been an ordeal, but it was nothing compared with the last nine or ten hours. The smell of the food - traditional English sausages, bacon, eggs and toast - hung in the air and made her stomach growl ravenously.

She reached for the tray, but Hannah stepped back out of her reach. 'No, no, no,' she scolded. 'You're in the kennels, and animals live in kennels. Animals don't reach for their food with hands.'

'Apes do,' Stuart pointed out.

'Canines live in kennels.' Hannah ignored his input. 'And dogs beg for their food.'

Tiffany glared at her, her stomach rumbling uncomfortably at the delay, and sank down onto her hands and knees.

Hannah's face adopted a look of mock disappointment. 'I don't hear you barking, and I don't see any paws in the air,' she derided. 'You must be sick, and sick animals shouldn't be fed.'

Swallowing her pride, Tiffany raised her hands to chest level and began making little barking sounds.

Hannah laughed, and Stuart stepped forward. 'That's enough,' he said. 'Feed her.'

Tiffany stopped barking. Hannah glared at the guard, but said nothing - he had authority over her, after all - and finally set the tray down.

Tiffany greedily helped herself to the food, finding it easier than she had expected to lift the meat up with just her lips and her teeth. The eggs were a bit messier, but she enjoyed lapping up the runny yolks and sucking up the whites with a lusty slurp.

Stuart turned away in disgust. 'I'll be outside,' he said.

'Hey, you're supposed to stay here with me,' Hannah protested.

'You'll be fine, I'm sure.'

Tiffany saw the sudden look of alarm on the girl's face. Had she thought her attacker might overpower her again while they were alone, even though she was chained and helpless? Tiffany rejoiced in the ephemeral victory, because in truth she was too hurt and tired to try anything. She finished her breakfast, literally licking the plate clean, and Hannah snatched up the tray and took it away without saying another word. The sneer on her face was eloquent enough.

The subsequent hours were unpleasantly tedious. Occasionally the sense of her confinement would overcome her, and she would pull on the chain in frustration. Then Wendy arrived carrying a small pot of moisturising cream. She stood there, not quite knowing what to say.

Tiffany sat up. 'Can I help you?' she asked testily.

The question sounded so imperiously polite that, under the circumstances, the new girl could not help but giggle. 'I'm sorry...'

Tiffany smiled grudgingly. 'What brings you here, Wendy?' she asked.

'Ms Colbert sent me with this salve to treat your wounds.'

'Colbert?'

The girl nodded as she knelt down before her, and unscrewed the lid of the jar. 'Yes, you'll be working for her now, and she wanted me to take care of you.'

'Awfully decent of her,' Tiffany said dryly. But she stretched out gratefully and allowed the pretty girl to see the extent of her welts, which covered both the back and front of her body.

'Oh my...' Wendy whispered in awe.

'Your bedside manner needs improving.'

'Sorry.' She soothed the white cream, with its rich fragrance, into Tiffany's sore limbs, and gently massaged her flesh, at first gently and then with increasing strength. The cream warmed up as it was worked deep, its heat penetrating her aching muscles, and she moaned gratefully.

'Enjoying it?' Wendy asked hopefully.

'Mm, yes...' Tiffany turned and stretched out on her stomach. 'How did your welcoming go?'

'I - I tried to get it over with as quickly and as painlessly as possible,' Wendy confessed.

The penetrating heat was soothing and relaxing Tiffany's mind as well as her body. 'I resisted on my first night,' she admitted lazily. 'You were right to submit.'

'I've been talking with some of the other girls,' Wendy's tone became conspiratorial. 'They say you've tried to escape before. Is that true?'

'Yes.' A sound that was not quite a laugh escaped her lips. 'A testament to my courage or my stupidity, take your pick.'

'I believe it's courage,' Wendy stated emphatically. 'I'm done with your back.'

Tiffany rolled over, too relaxed to be concerned about anything much at the moment. Her breasts were striped with candy-red welts.

Wendy carefully smoothed more salve into each tender mound. 'I have to make a confession,' she said quietly. 'When I first saw you yesterday, I thought... I thought you were like the rest of them, part of the system here.'

'Oh?' Tiffany's voice sounded distant even to herself, and she felt both detached and perfectly at one with her body. It was someone else's thighs that parted slightly... someone else's pussy that warmed in response to another female's touch...

'Yes, I did.' Wendy moved down to Tiffany's stomach, working the salve in lovingly. 'But now I understand. You're a fighter. You're going to get out of here.'

'Am I?' Her senses focused on Wendy's hands as they ventured closer... closer... she parted her thighs instinctively, offering easier access...

Wendy's cream-slick fingers slipped smoothly into Tiffany's warm pussy, stirring up a sweet sensation as they slowly explored its soft satin walls. Then she bent down and pressed her mouth against Tiffany's, invading it with her tongue.

The hand between her legs was no longer gentle, but she did not mind. Already Tiffany could feel her arousal rolling in like the tide, ready to drown her as the expert fingers teased and stroked. She sighed into Wendy's mouth and gave herself up to the rhythm of thrusting fingers as a climax swelled deep inside, and then burst, flooding her with bliss. She moaned softly, feeling as though she was dissolving.

Wendy sat back and smiled as she gently withdrew her fingers. Tiffany lifted her hands to her face and covered her eyes as she tried to make sense of her feelings. Another girl had touched her sexually, and not only had she permitted the contact, she had enjoyed it.

'Consider it a gesture of thanks,' Wendy whispered.

Tiffany lowered her hands and looked up at her. 'Thanks?'

'For giving me hope; hope that we can get out of here. Tiffany, I have a confession to make.'

Tiffany reached up and took Wendy's hands. 'Another one?' she teased.

'Tiffany... I'm not a foreign student in Cascara,' the lovely girl said carefully. 'I'm a foreign reporter.'

Tiffany's eyes widened. 'You're a what?' she gasped.

'I'm a reporter,' Wendy confessed again. 'A journalist, on assignment.'

'Are you serious?' Tiffany paused to absorb what she was being told. 'Then what are you doing here? What story are you covering?'

Wendy glanced over her shoulder. 'I was a secretary,' she divulged, 'but I always wanted to see my work in print, and I practically had to blackmail the publisher I worked for so he'd give me an assignment, and this is the one I got. I'm undercover here to either confirm or deny rumours about improprieties in the Cascaran penal system. And I guess they're true.'

Tiffany felt as though the proverbial chair had just been kicked out from under her. She sat up, her discomfort and pleasure forgotten as she clung to Wendy's hands. 'Then the drug charge—'

'Was a set up, just like my student identity.'

'Do you mean to tell me that you purposely had yourself imprisoned here just to get a story?' Tiffany was shocked.

'An exclusive story with global multimedia coverage,' Wendy corrected her soberly.

'You're mad.'

'I'm ambitious.' But then ambition transformed into anxiety. 'Tiffany, please, please promise me you won't tell anyone.'

'Of course I promise, but you're wasting your time; Rache has too much power—'

'You believe that? Power enough to silence the entire world media?' Her tone suggested what she thought of such a ridiculous notion. 'No, more than likely the Cascaran government will disavow any knowledge of his actions to cover their own tracks if he's exposed.'

Tiffany struggled to keep still as her mind and senses reawakened and reeled with hope. 'Why are you telling me this now?' she asked suspiciously.

Wendy moved her lips close to Tiffany's ear. 'Because I trust you,' she whispered. 'You've already tried to escape, and I think you're going to try again soon, and I want to come along.'

'But why? You've only a few months to serve—'

'Why hasn't anyone spoken out before now? This place...' The young reporter looked around again as if the atmosphere was poisonous. 'I can feel myself... responding to this place, to it's perverse coercion, and I've only been here a day. They're brainwashing us.'

'It's not brainwashing,' Tiffany said quickly, and then wondered why she felt so defensive.

'Whatever. All I know is that I can't finish my sentence here if I want to keep my objectivity.'

'Then get yourself transferred to Cascara state prison. At least you'll have access to the outside world there.'

Wendy shook her head. 'I can't, Rache won't let me. I've asked. He gave me a cock-and-bull story about the shortness of my sentence and administrative restrictions.' She sighed. 'I have to leave here!'

'No.' Tiffany shook her head determinedly. 'I couldn't face the media, Wendy. They'd tear me to shreds.'

'But I don't have to specifically include you in the story,' Wendy pointed out. 'There'll be enough subjects and ex-subjects willing to come forth to make money with their stories once the whistle's blown.' She suddenly kissed Tiffany on the cheek. 'I promise to keep your name out of it. No one will ever have to know. Just promise me you'll think about it when you work on your next escape, okay?'

After Wendy left Tiffany tried in vain to get some more sleep. She was exhausted. So much had happened she felt as disoriented as on her first day during processing, and she had no idea what would happen next.

There is an expectant pause in the atmosphere on Cascara just before a storm when nature seems to hold its breath. Tiffany knew the feeling, she had experienced it many times, but it seemed far more eerie in her present circumstances. She received no more visitors, apart from the subjects who came to take out the dogs. Then Remy appeared with a lead and a cuffed, naked Jude at the other end of it.

Tiffany sat up at once. 'What's going on?' she asked. 'Jude, why are you here?'

Remy was uncuffing the girl, but he spared a glance in Tiffany's direction. 'There's no talking allowed in here,' he said.

Tiffany bit back further words, watching silently as he motioned for Jude - whose back and buttocks were also criss-crossed with red welts - to the opposite wall.

'Remy, please, put her nearer to me,' Tiffany requested humbly. He stared at her a long moment, and then attached Jude's lead to a ring on the same wall. Then he turned to go. 'Remy, I'm... I'm sorry,' Tiffany said truthfully.

He paused on his way out, but did not look back at her. 'We're through, Tiff,' he said coldly.

That was it and she could not even protest; she had no right to. Silence hung in the air after he departed, then eventually she asked, unable to face the unexpected pain of losing him, 'What's going on, Jude?'

The other girl was silent for a moment, her face turned away. 'Singh had me talking for most of the night,' she said finally, 'about the escape attempt, for a security review.'

Guilt tore at Tiffany's insides. 'They didn't believe you? I'm so sorry, Jude, so sorry.'

'Don't be. I lied to him. I told him I was in on it from the start.'

'But - but why?'

Jude sighed, and looked at her. 'He wanted to hear you planned it all yourself so you'd get extra punishment. And I didn't like what that implied, that I was too stupid, or frightened, or tame, to have had a hand in it.' She shrugged. 'Besides, you're my friend.'

Tiffany felt another pang of guilt. 'Thank you,' she said humbly. 'I'm beginning to realise what friendship means.'

Jude smiled. 'Will you be trying to escape again?'

Tiffany hesitated before answering. This was the second time someone had asked her that in one day. Her last attempt had been an abysmal failure. Now they were all in the big house having a good laugh at the 'princess' naked and chained in the kennel for her troubles. 'Bastards!' she hissed.

'Pardon?'

'Yes, I will be trying to escape again,' she vowed, 'and I'll succeed next time, with your help. Are you interested?'

Jude's smile broadened. 'You can count me in, Tiff,' she said enthusiastically.

They talked for a long while after that, and unlike during their first conversation in the prison van that delivered them, Tiffany actually listened. Time lost its meaning, the passing of the hours marked only by the disappearing light and the growing heat and humidity inside the building as the storm brewed outside.

Finally the two girls fell silent and the only sound came from the cicadas chirping outside. Then a sudden flash of lightning briefly illuminated their faces, and the rumble of thunder that followed immediately afterwards shook the very foundations of the building.

They shuffled as close together as their collars and leashes would permit. 'Jude,' Tiffany began quietly, 'I'm sorry.'

'Sorry for what?'

'For being a bitch to you from the beginning.'

Jude shrugged. 'You were frightened. I understand.'

Outside the lightning and thunder continued erratically, like an air raid in an old war film. Then a particularly close thunderclap made the windows rattle.

Jude shrieked and nearly climbed on top of Tiffany. They held on to each other, and suddenly their lips were pressed together. Tiffany felt her stomach do somersaults as Jude's tongue caressed hers deeply and urgently, then she pulled her mouth away to lower her head and engulf one of her nipples. Tiffany gasped, and arched her back as Jude's hand found its way between her thighs.

She closed her eyes, and let her own hands reach up to squeeze and knead

Jude's breasts, which were deliciously full and heavy. Waves of exquisite pleasure flowed through her as she spread her legs and let Jude's fingers begin fucking her.

Her climax was as inevitable as the rain outside, which began pounding against the roof just as her pleasure peaked and overflowed the banks of her veins.

'There, there,' Jude cooed gently as she withdrew her fingers and held Tiffany's face in both hands so she could plant kisses all over it. 'Now lie down and rest.'

Tiffany obeyed as the storm commenced in earnest, the driving rain beating against the building swiftly lowering the temperature enough to make her shiver.

Chapter Eleven

It was morning when Shazza, wielding a long and resilient black cane, surprised the captives by tapping the tops of their heads with it. 'Wakey, wakey, ladies, rise and shine!'

Following her lovemaking with Jude, Tiffany had fallen into a relaxing stupor, and from there into a deep sleep which blessedly lasted the whole night, restoring her vital energies as her body healed itself. Her eyes still closed, she wet her lips and asked a little hoarsely what was going on.

Shazza knelt down and removed Tiffany's collar. 'You won't believe it, but somehow the outside world has heard of your plight.'

Tiffany's eyes opened. 'What?'

'There was an emergency United Nations meeting about the poor girls locked up in here,' Shazza said. 'The director and the staff have been arrested, and we've all been given unconditional pardons.'

The news made Tiffany's head spin, and her eyes opened even wider in sheer disbelief. Then she saw Shazza's expression and her heart sank. 'That isn't funny!' she sulked.

Shazza laughed, and moved over to free Jude. 'Kennel time's up, Lassie. You and Spot here can return to the main house, as long as you promise to stay off the furniture.'

'You're still not funny.' Tiffany struggled to her feet, reflecting Jude's equally stiff attempts and echoing her moans. Stretching her limbs was agony. She was so stiff it was as if the blood in her veins had been replaced with embalming fluid.

Shazza was not the patient type. 'Let's go, bitches, assembly in ten minutes,' she bullied.

Tiffany ignored her as she worked to get her body moving smoothly again. The air outside was cool and refreshing. The dorm was still quiet, though many of the girls were up and dressing to beat the assembly klaxon.

Then it was outside again for exercise following the warm-ups. Tiffany was called away from the main group by Quinn, who was surrounded by several of the girls on her football team. 'Yes, *Miss* Quinn?' Tiffany asked.

The coach looked none too amused by the display of attitude. 'Here's a ball, there's the goal, and there's Kamesha between the posts. I assume you know what to do?' She kicked one of the footballs towards Tiffany, who instinctively trapped it beneath one foot.

'I'm not interested in joining your team, Miss Quinn,' Tiffany told her.

'Then you shouldn't have promised to try out.'

That's what this was about - the promise Tiffany made the night she attempted to escape. She had not meant it, and they both knew it. But Quinn was going to hold her to it anyway.

'I understand you have a decent kick as a left inside,' the coach said. 'Prove it.'

The rest of the subjects were still jogging around the track, and Tiffany wished she was one of them. This was a waste of time.

'Well, Welborne?' Quinn was losing her patience.

Tiffany scowled at her, and then stepped back and kicked the ball towards the goal, sending it a total of ten feet. It was a pathetic display, one that could have been surpassed by a six-year-old, but it had the intended result.

'Get back with the group, Welborne,' Quinn said in disgust.

'Yes, Miss Quinn.' Tiffany could not help but smile; she may have to exercise each morning for Quinn, but that was where her obligations to the woman ended.

Later in the showers - a time when Tiffany always indulged herself in a good long soak - she was startled from her repose by a pair of hands encircling her waist from behind. 'Hi!' Jude's face appeared at her shoulder, smiling.

'Hi yourself.' With both their bodies slick and smooth from the water, the intimate contact was most welcome, as was the feel of soft breasts pressing against her back.

'I'm working on an escape plan.' Jude's voice was barely audible over the showers running around them. 'I'll visit you tonight to talk it over. In the meantime, we have to act as if we've finally given in to their regime, as if they've broken us. Whatever they want done, we have to do, no questions asked. Agreed?'

Tiffany's pussy warmed with desire, and she pushed her bottom back against Jude's soft bush. 'That won't be too difficult,' she said.

Jude chuckled, and her tongue darted out to lick the outer rim of Tiffany's ear, sending electric tingles through her, then she left the showers. Tiffany watched her depart, and caught the other girls in the showers watching her, no doubt ready to spread the word about Tiffany's unexpected change of heart regarding sex with women. She did not care, caught up as she was in the excitement of attempting to escape again, and the behaviour this would entail in the meantime.

Following her shower she was preparing to dress until Bonnie, Colbert's second, approached her. 'Follow me,' the girl said peremptorily.

Tiffany indicated the towel wrapped around her body. Bonnie was in a similar state. 'As we are?'

'Yes,' Bonnie confirmed. 'Madam's in one of her moods today.'

Moments later they were in the prop room, which was filled to bursting with wall-mounted and freestanding shelves containing labelled boxes of all sizes.

There was a coeval mirror in one corner, and the crowded space was thick with the unmistakable odour of must and mothballs. Here the dozen other girls on Colbert's staff, including Wendy, dressed every day, fitting themselves into starched black-and-white maid's uniforms, including white caps, stockings and high-heels. Or they slipped into equally antiquated butlers' outfits complete with ties and tails. Tiffany had seen them dressed like this on several occasions during her day shifts with Singh.

Bonnie dried herself off quickly, and stepped into a pair of slinky black bikini panties and a matching bra. 'Your clothes have been picked out for you,' she informed Tiffany. 'They're in that box at your feet. Hurry.'

Tiffany tried to comply, but she was feeling very relaxed after her shower. She had been given a maid's outfit. The panties and stockings were a sheer caress to her skin, a satiny reminder of all the finer things she had enjoyed, seemingly a lifetime ago. The heels were less a reminder than an embarrassment as she tried to walk in them, a task made even more difficult after nearly a month wearing nothing but boots and comfortable trainers.

Bonnie was pinning her hair back. 'You will address her as madam like always, and curtsey whenever she addresses us, individually or as a group. Got it?'

As she dressed, Tiffany noticed how it was usually the less curvaceous of the women who were dressed as butlers. They wore no make-up, of course; that luxury was permitted only to those in feminine attire, who applied modest amounts of lipstick to each other. Then they all assembled in the TV room just as they had done nearly two hours earlier for Rache. Anne-Marie Colbert stood before them now, her hands clasped behind her, acting very much like the director himself. 'Good morning, staff,' she said formally.

The maids curtseyed as one and the butlers bowed as they chorused, 'Good morning, madam.'

Colbert walked around her staff, and Tiffany noticed the longer, deeper stares she gave those girls dressed as men. 'We have someone new with us as of this morning,' she announced. 'Tiffany is our new recruit. Having been raised in a fine household, she will certainly be aware of what is expected of her here. Won't you, Tiffany?'

Tiffany bit back her initial reply - that she was more accustomed to ordering servants about than behaving like one - and curtseyed again prettily as she instead said, 'I hope so *madam*.'

'Good.' Colbert addressed the whole team again. 'Continue as yesterday. Tiffany will assist Dorothy in the dusting and cleaning of this room, for a start.' She clapped her hands twice, and the girls dispersed.

Dorothy took Tiffany by the arm. 'Follow me,' she said. 'We'll go get the dust cloths.'

They worked for a while with no furniture polish, just elbow grease. Tiffany was not comfortable in her new clothes, particularly the stockings, after the relative freedom and comfort afforded by the uniforms. She ran a bare forearm across her brow. 'It's hot in here, isn't it?'

Dorothy shushed her. 'No talking,' she whispered.

Tiffany frowned, accustomed to the more relaxed regime under Singh, and understanding now why it was always quiet in the house during the day.

After about half-an-hour Colbert returned. 'And how are my young ladies progressing?' she enquired civilly.

Dorothy straightened up upon her supervisor's appearance and curtseyed, saying nothing. Tiffany simply reflected her actions, still feeling the aches in her limbs after her ordeal. They watched Colbert move about the room, stopping at the mahogany bookcases and peering at them closely before extracting a white cotton handkerchief from her trouser pocket and running it over the surface of one of the shelves. She stepped back and studied the minuscule amount of dust collected on the handkerchief, and disappointment darkened her face. 'Oh my, young Tiffany, I'm afraid this simply will not do.'

'What?' In her exhaustion, Tiffany forgot her place. 'But I did my best.'

Colbert arched an eyebrow in her direction. 'Did I ask for a response, young lady?' She strode up to her and gave her a light smack on the bottom. Then she sighed like a woman burdened with the most hopeless of tasks. 'I will not warn you again, Tiffany. Return to your work and redouble your efforts.'

Tiffany, remembering Jude's caution, obeyed as Colbert left, going painstakingly back over her work. She pressed so hard against the wood as she polished that soon her arm ached.

'Tiff,' Wendy whispered even though they had been left alone in the second floor classroom they were cleaning.

Tiffany looked up, and watched the girl move over to the door and glance up and down the corridor before she closed it, shutting them off from the rest of the house. She then moved to the floor-to-ceiling bookshelves lining one wall. 'Come here,' she said urgently. 'I want to show you what I've started.'

Infinitely curious, Tiffany watched as the undercover journalist removed a particular book from a shelf at the level of her knees. It was, ironically enough, a copy of Dostoyevsky's *Crime and Punishment*. Opening it, Wendy revealed a thin cardboard-bound notebook like the kind used by subjects in class. 'All note-taking material is monitored,' Wendy explained proudly, 'but I rescued this one from the incinerator and have been writing in it with whatever pens and pencils I could lift from offices. I'll have a detailed account of my experiences here when I escape.'

'Are you sure you should be keeping this record?' Tiffany asked nervously. 'What if it's found?'

'It's a risk I'm willing to take. Having notes, precise details, times and names, is ten times better than relying on one's memory alone. Also,' her expression grew even more grave, 'if for some reason I can't escape with you, I want you to get this out. My publisher's name and address are inside. Promise me you'll get this to him.'

'I promise,' Tiffany vowed.

Wendy looked visibly relieved as she closed the cover of the novel over the notebook. 'Have you any ideas how to get out?' she asked.

'Not yet, but...' She stopped in mid-sentence. Her back was to the classroom door but she heard it open.

Wendy, looking beyond her, suddenly drew her into a kiss, pressing the book between their breasts.

Tiffany froze, confused and terrified, and then, as understanding dawned, she began kissing Wendy back passionately.

The voice behind them was laced with indignation. 'What is this?'

Wendy pulled back, and surreptitiously managed to slip the book back on the shelf as she said in a flustered voice, 'Oh, madam! Um, we didn't mean—'

'You two are supposed to be working,' Colbert strode towards them, 'not indulging in your carnal lusts.'

'Forgive us, madam,' Tiffany begged hastily, hoping the woman's focus would remain on them and not on the book Wendy had been holding. 'We... we couldn't help ourselves.'

'Then we must teach you both a little something about self-control, mustn't we?'

Back in Colbert's office, the subjects stood to attention as the housekeeper moved behind her desk and retrieved a formidable looking black leather paddle hanging on the wall beside the work chart. It sat well within her grip as she eyed her subjects. 'Howard, raise the hem of your skirt and drop your panties to your ankles, if you please.'

Tiffany's hands moved to her own clothes before she realised she had not been included in the command. So she stood by uneasily as she watched Wendy obey, revealing her pale bottom cheeks and blonde bush.

'Now, Howard, bend over and grip the edge of the desk.'

Wordlessly the girl complied as Tiffany stood by, confused at not being included, her expression taut as she watched Colbert step out from behind the desk, and lightly tap Wendy on the buttocks with the paddle.

'Spread them wider, Howard... wider. That's it.' The woman smiled enigmatically at Tiffany, and motioned for her to move closer. 'I said you'd both learn about control,' she went on in a purring voice, 'and so you will, but in different ways.' She handed Tiffany the paddle. 'You will administer correction, and Howard will receive. It might help you to know that she'll enjoy it. And, of course, she will thank you after each blow.' She stepped back, and indicated for Tiffany to proceed. 'Now you will begin, and you will continue to paddle her until I tell you to stop. Only I will know beforehand how many blows she is to receive. And if you don't use your full strength, I shall add more blows to the amount I have already decided upon. Now proceed.'

Tiffany held the paddle, a heavy, alien thing. The idea of inflicting pain on Wendy unnerved her, and perhaps Colbert knew it and that was her punishment.

'Hesitation means more blows,' Colbert warned.

Tiffany stared at her intended target, a pair of tight, pale cheeks waiting for her abuse, waiting for her to raise the paddle and lash out. She watched the black leather board streak through the air, and heard it strike Wendy's buttocks with a loud smack that filled the office.

Wendy shuddered, and had to catch her breath in order to say, 'Thank you!' as instructed.

'Good.' Colbert sounded pleased. 'Keep it up.'

And Tiffany did, shifting slightly to deliver the next blow. Working out a perverse rhythm to the chastisement, her incipient unease gave way to an unexpected excitement, and she watched with grim satisfaction as her handiwork painted dark-red patches across Wendy's delicious little bottom.

'Enough,' Colbert finally said. 'Straighten up, Howard.'

Tiffany dropped her arm, exhausted, as she watched Wendy straighten up, her face flushed, her nipples erect and her hand resting almost subconsciously between her thighs, her fingers cupped as if to protect or comfort her sex. She was breathing heavily - as heavily as Tiffany.

If Colbert had enjoyed the show in her own way, she did not show it. 'Howard, pull down your skirt and return to work,' she ordered. 'Welborne, you remain here.'

Once Wendy was gone, the housekeeper's expression softened. 'You can put that down now and take a seat on the couch,' she said almost gently.

Tiffany, still confused and now also aroused, carefully placed the paddle on the desk and approached the plush leather couch, sinking into the cushioned seat gratefully. She watched as Colbert extracted two soft drink tins from the refrigerator.

'You have questions,' the housekeeper observed, offering her one of the tins.

'Yes.' She cradled the can for a moment, relishing its wet chill against her hot hand. 'Why did you have me do that? I was as guilty as she was.'

Colbert's upper lip curled with amusement. 'Don't you think you've been beaten enough already here?'

Tiffany opened the tin with a brisk snap. 'What I think hardly matters, does it?'

'It does to me.' She opened her own tin while keeping her eyes fixed on Tiffany. Then she raised her drink in a salute. 'Here's to power, the ultimate aphrodisiac.' They both took a sip. 'You've just had your first taste of some. How was it?'

'What makes you think I don't know about power?' Tiffany demanded mildly. 'You know who I am.'

Colbert waved her drink dismissively. 'I know who you were. And I know that money, influence and titles, even though they all wield a power of their own, are nothing compared with the power of pain and pleasure over another human being. To have them squirming beneath your touch, a slave to their own hungers and your whims, gives you an ineffable joy.' She regarded Tiffany seriously. 'You understand what I mean.' The housekeeper's breasts were full and heavy inside the black cotton of her button-down shirt.

Tiffany needed to regain some control of herself, deep inside the enemy camp. 'Are you trying to seduce me?' she asked casually.

Colbert chuckled softly. 'You arrogant bitch,' she mused. 'You've lost little of your original fire. But if you had, you'd be of no use to me.'

'What are you talking about?' Tiffany asked suspiciously.

'I want you as my assistant,' Colbert announced. 'Bonnie has lost her appeal for me. Out there I have to treat you as I do the others, but as my assistant you won't have to perform chores like the other girls. You'll have a far easier time of it here, and earn double the usual work credits.'

Tiffany continued to eye her warily; the woman was up to something. 'And what do I have to do in return?' she asked tentatively.

'You have to behave. I want to show Rache and the others how obedient and compliant you've become under my authority.'

'Why?'

'That's my business. Well, what's your answer?'

Since her arrival, all the supervisors had shown an interest in having her serve under them, and Tiffany wondered why. Then she shrugged mentally. She had nothing to lose that she had not already lost. Besides, being so close to the housekeeper could come in handy for her next escape attempt. 'Okay,' she finally agreed. 'I accept, madam.'

Colbert smiled. 'I knew you would.' She reached out and took the drink from her new assistant's hand, and then set her own aside as well.

Tiffany trembled slightly as their fingertips touched. Her senses focused and grew sharper, more vivid. She found herself breathing heavily and feeling strangely passive. Then the housekeeper pulled her up into a kiss before she realised what was happening. Her mouth opened in surprise, allowing Colbert to snake her tongue deep between her lips. She struggled a little to pull away, but it was only a token gesture of resistance.

It was the older woman who finally pulled back and, still holding Tiffany's blouse with both hands, fixed an inescapable magnetic gaze on her face. 'When we're alone you can call me Anne-Marie.' Her voice was husky, thick with wanton passion.

'Yes, madam...' Tiffany whispered. 'I mean, yes, Anne-Marie.'

Jude leaned closer to Tiffany where they sat on a couch in the TV room. 'She made you her assistant?' she enthused. 'That's brilliant! It makes what we have to do so much easier.'

Tiffany held a magazine up in front of her face to reinforce the illusion that she was reading it. 'How so?' she whispered.

'Colbert's the key. She leaves the house every now and then to go into Cascara City for supplies, and she always takes someone with her. If we can find out when she goes, we can—' She stopped talking abruptly as she saw the rapidly approaching figure of Bonnie, her face flushed with fury, her hands balled into fists, heading straight for Tiffany.

Bonnie's tone was as loud and incensed as Tiffany had ever heard it. 'You bitch!' she cried. 'What did you do? Why has she taken you? I belonged to her!'

Tiffany was nonplussed, at a complete loss for words, but Jude spoke up. 'Shouldn't you ask Miss Colbert that?'

'Stay out of this!' Bonnie hissed, and redirected the force of her emotions back towards Tiffany. 'Everything was fine until you showed up!' She seemed ready to burst into tears. 'The whole house has been turned upside down because of you! I wish you were dead!'

Jude made a move to rise. 'Now wait a moment—'

Bonnie turned and stormed from the room while everyone's eyes followed her. Tiffany was dumbstruck by the ferocity of the verbal barrage against her, so much so that she hardly registered Shazza rising from an adjacent table, and following Bonnie out as she commented, 'You sure know how to make yourself popular, don't you, Welborne?'

Jude wrapped a protective arm around Tiffany's shoulders. 'We'll talk later in bed,' she said soothingly. She drew closer and nibbled Tiffany's earlobe, helping take her mind off the unpleasant encounter.

Tiffany wore only a T-shirt and panties to bed, and the oppressive evening humidity made her question even these scant items of clothing. She would probably peel them off following Colbert's walk through before lights out, when Jude joined her in bed.

The housekeeper's tour was quick tonight, though she paused long enough to smile at Tiffany and remark, 'Regrettably, I'm busy tonight. Otherwise I'd invite you to my quarters for a drink. Perhaps tomorrow night.'

Tiffany blushed, aware of the eyes of the other girls upon her. She had not expected, or wanted, to be the focus of so much attention. 'As you wish, madam,' she said humbly.

Once Colbert departed, Tiffany turned to Jude and smiled at her from across the room. Jude smiled back and got up, but Shazza abruptly blocked her passage. 'Forrester, you'll be sleeping with me tonight,' the bully announced.

Tiffany's eyes widened in shock, and her feelings were reflected in Jude's face.

Shazza looked at Tiffany. 'I hope you don't have a problem with that, teacher's pet?'

She had challenged Tiffany, but it was Jude who answered sullenly, 'No, Shazza, she doesn't have a problem with that.'

Tiffany was dismayed by her friend's acquiescence, and traded a questioning look with her. But then she understood. *Show no rebellion*, Jude had said. They had to act as though they'd been broken by the regime of *Rache House*.

'Glad to hear it,' Shazza said with a gloating smile. Her eyes still on Tiffany, she reached out, hooked her fingers into the waistband of Jude's panties, and drew her along behind her like an unruly child. 'Come along, sweetie,' she urged condescendingly.

Tiffany watched them depart. *Damn the bitch! She did it on purpose!* How she longed for the opportunity to beat Shazza Dewitt to a writhing, whining pulp. Then the lights were out and everyone had gone to bed, their own or someone else's. She slipped beneath her own sheet trying to ignore the soft sounds around her, a taunting reminder of what she was missing.

A short while later Tiffany was disturbed from her doze of self-pity when a silhouette suddenly knelt by her cot.

'Tiffany?' Both the figure and the voice were familiar. 'Can I join you tonight?

'Yes, Wendy,' she sighed, longing for some comfort, and shifted over slightly.

Wendy cuddled close to her. She was naked, and her skin was warm. 'I'm sorry about Jude and Shazza,' she whispered.

Tiffany tried to ignore the sounds she heard coming from the far end of the room, where Shazza was being deliberately loud and obvious just to infuriate her. 'It's not your fault,' she whispered, and then added, 'I'm sorry I was made to beat you today.'

'I'm glad it was you and not her. That made it more... tolerable.' They kissed for a tender moment. 'Have you come up with an escape plan yet?' Wendy asked.

'We're still working on it.'

'Don't forget about me, okay?' Wendy moved her hands around to cup Tiffany's bottom, and gently squeezed each cheek in turn.

Tiffany smiled in the darkness. 'It would be impossible to forget about you, Wendy.'

'We need to talk, Cyrus.'

Rache looked up from where he was reclining on the bench on the second floor balcony just outside his quarters. It was early morning, just after breakfast, and the sun was behind the house. Soon the day would grow uncomfortably hot and the mosquitoes would emerge from the forest. Nearby, Chairman made half-hearted attempts to chase after slower flying insects as if to recapture the glorious hunting days of his youth. Rache set aside his book - Victor Hugo could wait another few moments - and offered the place beside him on the bench to his visitor. 'I think it's going to rain, don't you?' he pondered.

'I'm here to talk about Welborne, not the weather,' Quinn stated.

Rache smiled. 'Really? She's quite a popular character, at least amongst the staff.'

Quinn remained standing. 'And who's made her that way?'

The doctor reached for his tomato juice, shooing away the more eager flies; bugs were one of the less pleasant aspects of life in the tropical climes. 'You sound upset,' he observed mildly.

'I'm concerned. There's a difference.'

'But what's there to be concerned about? She finally appears to be settling in under Anne-Marie's authority.'

'My girls have been saying that Welborne's been getting a hard time of it amongst them now that she's taken Bonnie's place as Colbert's assistant. She hardly has any friends, except for Forrester, and that new girl, Howard.'

Rache shrugged. 'That's more than many young people have. We can't all be overwhelmingly popular.'

'I don't get the feeling that she's truly fitting in here,' Quinn insisted.

The director smiled his cold, calculating smile. 'Are you an expert in psychology now as well as sports?'

Quinn was neither amused nor intimidated. 'I'd like to see her psych profile.'

Rache continued idly waving away obstinate flies. 'You know that's not routine, Nuala.'

'Hah! As if anything we did here was routine. What does she mean to you? Why did you make her the object of your persecution as part of this ridiculous competition to find your replacement? Why are you retiring now, anyway? You made no mention of it until a few weeks back.'

Still looking away, Rache shrugged. 'Time takes its toll on all of us,' he said philosophically. 'The mind fades. The vision dims. I find I'm just not as sadistic as I used to be.'

Quinn smirked.

He turned his head so their eyes met, and his expression was insultingly dismissive. 'If it makes you feel any better, I swear to you that I cannot recall ever having seen or spoken to the young woman before her arrival here. And as for the alleged competition, why should you care? You've expressed no interest in becoming the new director.'

'I care about who might end up being my next employer,' Quinn pointed out reasonably. 'Eric Kemp is young and inexperienced, and—'

'Jealous, are we?' he teased.

'Colbert's a fawning, untrustworthy sycophant,' she continued her assessment, undaunted by his attitude. 'And Singh's a bloody criminal.'

The doctor sighed. 'It would be both foolish and hypocritical to be overly fastidious in our recruitment practices as long as my supervisors abide by my principal standards against violence and the use of force.' Then his shoulders sagged for a moment and his face took on an almost pained looked. 'None of us are perfect, Nuala. Even you have your skeletons in the cupboard.'

Quinn drew herself up to full height, which was considerable. 'I'm well aware of my past, Cyrus.' She refused to concede anything to him. 'But we're talking about Welborne—'

'No, we're not.' He set aside his glass and rose, his face taut. 'It's a closed subject as far as I'm concerned. If you were that concerned about her, you should have taken her under your authority last week when you had the chance. I'll not entertain any more talk about her. Is that understood?'

Quinn's sarcasm was bitter. 'Yes sir, Dr Rache, sir. Whatever you say, sir.' She even gave a little bow as she stormed back into the house.

Rache sat down again and picked up his book, but he found his interest in it had departed along with the sports instructor.

As if sensing his melancholy, Chairman approached and hopped up onto his lap, purring. Rache absently stroked his oldest and dearest friend. Nuala could not understand. None of them could understand. They were amateurs when it came to punishment.

In the distance, more thunder rumbled menacingly.

The heavens had opened up as if it was the last day on earth, and the storm showed no signs of abating. The rain drumming on the roof was almost deafening, and the sound became a hypnotic drone broken only by sporadic rumbles of thunder that deepened the dark tension permeating *Rache House*.

Kemp's, Quinn's and Singh's teams, the majority of whose work was conducted outside, was under nature's enforced house arrest. They were working with Colbert's crew, which was conducting spring-cleaning.

Tiffany watched guiltily as Wendy, crouched on all fours, polished the floor of one of the corridors on the second floor near the staff quarters. As Colbert's assistant, she did not have any manual work assigned to her, but served only in a supervisory capacity. The position was easier on her physically, but it hardly made her any more popular amongst the girls. Still, with another escape attempt imminent, that hardly seemed to matter.

'From what you've told me, your last plan was sound,' Wendy said as she scrubbed away dutifully. 'You were just tripped up by the key box. If we could get around that...'

Tiffany squatted beside her, and kept her voice low even though there was no one else around. 'It won't work now,' she said conspiratorially. 'They've changed the security routine. You're still too new to have noticed the changes.' She felt a sudden surge of despair; she would never be able to leave before her time.

Her despair must have shown on her face, because it prompted Wendy to reach out and squeeze her arm with encouraging warmth that was matched by her words. 'Don't worry, girl, we'll be back in England before you know it.'

Tiffany gratefully accepted the gesture. 'I'm hammering out a plan with Jude now that—' She stopped herself in mid-sentence when she heard the click of boot heels approaching.

'Welborne?' It was Shazza. 'Follow me!'

Tiffany followed the king girl up to the prop room. Shazza glanced at the slip of paper in her hand and began selecting boxes, dropping them carelessly on the floor. 'I'd start stripping if I were you,' she grunted. 'You're on in ten minutes.'

'On? As in, on stage?'

Shazza's smile did not reach her eyes. 'Very good, Welborne, but then rumour has it you did some sort of theatre workshop at your posh academy. The staff are bored because they can't go out and play, so Colbert's arranged to entertain them with a drama.'

'How kind,' Tiffany quipped, kneeling to unbuckle her boots. 'And is it going to be a one woman show?'

'Oh no, Welborne, that would be boring, especially if it involved you. No, the other cast members are already dressed and waiting in the staff room. I suppose I should have collected and briefed you at the same time I did them. I guess I'm getting old.'

Tiffany set aside her uniform. 'And did you forget to bring the script with you as well, old woman?'

Shazza, thoroughly enjoying the situation and presumably the one to come, took the barb with another cold smile. 'It's all improvisational.' She dropped one more box on the floor. 'There's your costume. All you need to know is that the drama is set during the *Hammer Bay Uprising* of eighteen-two. Do you know it?'

'Yes, I do.'

'Good. It's set in... oh, let's call it *Welborne Manor*, when the...'

She paused as if to recall the exact words of the premise she had been given.

'It's set when the continental spirit of republican revolution infects the staff and they turn the tables on the lady of the house.'

She stopped to rub her chin in a theatrical display of contemplation.

'Now who can we get to play the pampered, bratty aristocrat, I wonder?'

Tiffany did not respond.

'For the sake of the skin on your fat ass, I suggest you give an Oscar-winning performance. Unless, of course, you refuse to perform. You can, you know.' The king girl grinned as if hoping Tiffany would spurn the opportunity to appear in the limelight.

'Not a chance,' Tiffany said stiffly.

'Good. You've got ten minutes. Enter through the left door, the stage will be there.' She marched out of the prop room, adding over her shoulder, 'Break a leg, sweetie.'

Tiffany's dress was an effective prop. Like the maid's outfit Colbert had made her wear earlier in the week, it helped put her in the right frame of mind for the impending drama. It felt strange against her skin after wearing the same clothes for nearly a month. She was distracted by the sound and feel of the long skirt swishing around her legs, and the click of the high-heels on the polished floor. The make-up, too, was a welcome novelty, and she enjoyed piling her hair up elaborately.

How strange, she mused, that she wanted her performance to be a success. Perhaps it was just her sense of pride, but she wanted her jailers and masters to see how good she could be at whatever task they set her.

A tall curtain divided the staff drawing room. In the section Tiffany entered, some of the room's old-fashioned furniture had been arranged to face the rest of the room behind the curtain.

Bonnie was there looking bizarre but undeniably attractive in one of Colbert's antiquated black-and- white maid's outfits. Her hair, like Tiffany's, was pinned up and gathered beneath a frilly white cap.

Beside her stood Stuart Knowles dressed in a simple gardener's outfit complete with cap and braces.

Remy Baptiste was also one of the designated players, and he looked decidedly uncomfortable in an Edwardian gentleman's tie and tails. 'Tiff,' he said, staring at her uneasily.

'Remy...' A week before she would have had so much to say to him. Now, face-to-face, words failed her completely.

Bonnie, however, was not having that same problem. 'At last the *prima donna* has arrived.' She looked Tiffany straight in the eye defiantly.

Tiffany, taken aback by seeing Remy again and finding it hard to express herself, was suddenly filled with a resolution that dominated all her negative emotions. She was about to perform - in every sense of the word - before an audience, and if she viewed the situation in the proper light, she found the prospect enticing, almost thrilling. Also, she'd had no say in Bonnie losing her post of assistant to Colbert, so the girl had no right to try and intimidate her now. 'A *prima donna* is the principal singer in an opera,' she corrected her, 'not an actress in a play, you idiot.'

Bonnie stuck her chin up indignantly. 'I may not know the difference, Welborne, but I do know who'll soon be going down on me in submission. Well, smart mouth, what have you got to say about that?'

Tiffany's eyes narrowed. 'I hope you're ready for me,' she warned.

The staff, Rache included, entered the room from the right door, taking their places in the chairs facing the curtain. Some were leading subjects in various stages of undress on leads, subjects who knelt silently beside their master or mistress as everyone waited for the show to begin.

Colbert had a very willing Dorothy Carver beside her, stripped down to her bra and panties and crouched on all fours to serve as a table for the housekeeper's wineglass. The mistress looked to Singh, who had one of his own girls in a similar position for his vodka glass. 'You should enjoy this, Armin,' she said. 'Young Tiffany has a talent for role-playing.'

'Don't we all?' Singh responded out of forced politeness, only because the director was watching him. Colbert had been crowing about her progress with the Welborne girl, the most wilful and difficult subject ever to enter *Rache House*, which of course meant that the post of director would probably go to her as a result of her success.

Behind them, Rache and Quinn sat together without any subservient company. Quinn looked fidgety, perhaps even uneasy. 'Is this mandatory, Cyrus?' she asked quietly.

The director lit a small cigar. 'Mere courtesy, dear Nuala,' he said, the silvery smoke drifting up from his lips as he spoke. 'Our colleague, Anne-Marie, generously arranged this *divertissement erotique* for our amusement. Don't tell me you've lost your appetite for seeing beautiful young women humiliated, dominated and chastised?' He smiled at her playfully, leaning closer. 'Or are you so smitten with young Welborne that you can't bear to see her hurt?'

'Look who's talking.' With one hand she wafted away the smoke hanging between them. 'Do you mind pointing that cancer log in the direction of the sea, please?' she added tartly.

Rache laughed, and obliged her. At a subsequent nod from him, Shazza, standing in a corner of the room, switched on the CD player. Harpsichord music tinkled over the audience's heads, just barely audible over of the drumming of the rain on the roof. Then, peeking behind the curtain to ensure the players were ready, Shazza drew it open.

Tiffany, in her role as the lady of the house, sat in a large leather-bound chair pretending to read a book, while Stuart, Remy and Bonnie entered the room by walking on stage.

'Milady,' Bonnie took the lead, 'we wish to speak with you on a most urgent matter.'

Tiffany looked up. 'What are you servants doing away from your posts?' she snapped. 'Be gone at once!'

Bonnie held her head high. 'No, milady, the spirit of revolution has ignited the world and the flames have reached your very doorstep. Your days of ordering us about are over.'

'You think so?' Tiffany sneered, and flung her book aside. She found herself fully immersed in her role, her inspiration fed by the knowledge that truly enjoying herself would rob her tormentors of their victory... or perhaps she was just enjoying her own talent. 'Feckless illiterate peasants!' she cried. 'You're lower than the dung in the streets. None of you are fit to clean my shoes with your tongues.' She pointed towards the door. 'Leave, all of you, before Lord Cyrus returns and sets the hounds on you.' It was a flamboyant performance on her part, perhaps a little over-the-top, she acknowledged, but suitably melodramatic. And the potency of her acting seemed to throw Bonnie off; she had perhaps expected a more hesitant, anxious milady.

'We, uh... we will not leave, milady. Today is the day of revolution!' To Remy and Stuart, Bonnie cried theatrically, 'Take her, men!'

And they did, each man grabbing one of Tiffany's arms and easily subduing her token struggles while Bonnie approached her, a mixture of fear and triumph in her eyes that was not an act. 'Peasants, are we, milady?' She reached up and tore the bodice of Tiffany's dress with a sickening rip, revealing a portion of her cleavage. 'Lower than the dung in the streets, are we?' She tore at the dress again, and then again as Tiffany, quickly recovering from the initial shock of having her clothes ruined just for a play, returned to her role and began struggling. Bonnie sneered at her efforts. 'We'll see who's fit to clean whose shoes with her tongue, won't we?'

When Bonnie was finished, Tiffany's dress hung in tatters over her arms and around her waist, revealing her heaving breasts and shapely legs, lovely in sheer white stockings. The violated aristocrat spared a glance at her audience, and shifted her position to offer them a better view of her breasts even as she remained in character. 'Filthy louts!' she gasped. 'You'll pay for this indignity!'

'No, milady,' Bonnie said triumphantly, 'you'll pay for the indignities you've heaped upon us all these years. Make her assume the posture of one of her husband's hounds.'

Stuart and Remy manipulated Tiffany down onto all fours, facing her away from the audience, as expected, and she could not help but feel her face warming up as Bonnie lifted the ragged pieces of her dress, exposing her bottom to a dozen pairs of eyes. And yet with the embarrassment came the welcome twinge of pleasure at being forced into a thoroughly humiliating position. She parted her thighs slightly, as if accidentally, to let her captive audience glimpse the shadowy valley between her buttocks.

'Welborne is certainly showing more cheek than usual,' Rache murmured. 'I wonder who's responsible for that?'

'Why, thank you, Cyrus.' Colbert looked across at him, ready and willing to accept responsibility for the girl's progress. 'You're too kind.'

'Yes,' Singh agreed darkly, his eyes fixed on Tiffany's sweet young bottom, 'you are.'

Tiffany heard none of this, enveloped as she was in the sensual tension of her predicament.

Bonnie strolled around her, sounding genuinely pleased with herself. 'Yes, how lovely to see the mighty fallen, but our vengeance has just begun,' she announced grandly. 'Mellors, your belt, please.'

It took a moment for Stuart to realise he was being addressed. With an uneasy start he drew the brown leather belt with its stout brass buckle from his trousers.

Bonnie accepted the belt, doubling it up and making it snap like the jaws of a trap. 'Oh yes, milady, prepare to feel the same treatment you generously meted out upon us. Prepare to taste the sting of our retribution and to hear the sounds—'

'Are you going to beat me to death,' Tiffany looked up in mocking annoyance, 'or are you planning to bore me to death?'

The audience guffawed, and even Remy and Stuart tittered appreciatively. Before Bonnie could reply Colbert called out, 'She's right, girl, stop talking and start belting!'

Bonnie frowned, but she knew better than to argue with her real mistress. 'This is for all the orders you've dished out over the years,' she said, and began striking Tiffany's buttocks with the belt, over and over again, raining down blows on the tender white flesh at her disposal as the rain drummed passionately on the roof and the harpsichord music wove delicately between each cruel smack of leather upon flesh.

Tiffany held herself still, expelling the expected cries as she relished the rapid moistening of her pussy. Her bottom was radiating like an open furnace when Bonnie finally stopped after ten lashes and handed the belt to Remy, who took her place. Silent until now, when he spoke it was with the conviction of either a fine actor, or of someone whose words could be interpreted as having meaning outside the play's context. 'This is for your deceit,' he whipped the belt across her cheeks. 'This is for using me for your own ends.' He lashed her again even more viciously. 'And this is for your selfishness!' His blows were harder than Bonnie's, and his ferocity seemed to cut into her very soul because she knew she deserved this punishment from him.

Then it was Stuart's turn. 'And this...' he froze in mid-sentence. 'And this is...' A pregnant silence hung over the room. 'This is for no reason I can think of right now,' he concluded breathlessly, and his blows rained down on Tiffany's smouldering buttocks amidst laughter from the audience.

When Stuart was finished Bonnie stepped in again. Grabbing Tiffany by the hair, she forced her back up onto her feet. The tattered remains of her dress teased the hot flesh of her bottom before Bonnie ripped them away, leaving the lady only her stockings and shoes.

'Treacherous creatures,' Tiffany cursed ruefully, nearly naked but still defiant. 'Lord Cyrus will flay you all to within an inch of your lives when he sees what you have done to me.'

Bonnie's eyes boldly scrutinised Tiffany's body before she raised the back of her hand and slapped her. 'Stand to attention, hands on your head,' she commanded.

Tiffany obeyed, feeling herself blushing uncontrollably as her breasts, with peaked nipples, and her bare pubic mound and pouting sex lips were opened up to examination. Bonnie circled, inspecting her like a beast at market. She trembled as the maid's fingers ran lightly over every part of her body, from her head down to her ankles, and closed her eyes when she felt the girl's fingers near her pubis.

'Now bend over and spread your cheeks,' Bonnie snapped.

Barely able to suppress the thrill shooting through her and making her kneels feel weak, Tiffany complied. The blood rushing to her head, she warily watched Bonnie loiter behind her, and then stop to squeeze her taut cheeks before she inserted one finger, and then two, into her hot wet channel. Tiffany moaned, tightening her pussy around the intruders.

'Quiet, servant,' Bonnie admonished, and Tiffany stifled a groan of frustration as she withdrew her fingers and licked them. 'Mm, tasty,' she purred. 'Now rise.'

Tiffany did so, caressing loose strands of hair away from her face and affecting modesty by covering her breasts and pussy with her hands.

Bonnie smiled at this futile display of defiance. 'Not a bad purchase, but can she fuck?' She nodded towards Stuart and Remy. 'Let's find out.'

Swiftly, eagerly, the two men advanced on an equally determined Tiffany, using the belt to bind her wrists before her. Then Remy lay down, undoing his trousers and pulling them down to his knees to reveal his erection, straining for attention from where it jutted straight up out of a clump of wiry black hair.

Meanwhile, Stuart guided Tiffany down on all fours between Remy's thighs, and her hands supporting her just beneath his balls, she took his cock in her mouth. He tasted salty, familiar, and she could feel him tightening as her head rose and fell, her breasts swinging beneath her, the hot moisture of her arousal trickling down her inner thighs from her yearning sex. She arched her back and presented the audience with a view of her alluring bottom, decorated with the pink stripes of her punishment.

Then Stuart was kneeling behind her and unzipping his trousers. She could only imagine his cock springing into view as she lifted her buttocks higher to meet it, wriggling her hips until he found her pussy. He plunged into her without ceremony and made her cry out with her mouth full of cock. He gripped her hips, forcing her to adopt his rhythm while servicing the other man.

Beneath her, Tiffany felt Remy tense, and readied herself for his ejaculation, swallowing deeply and confidently when it began erupting into her mouth. And then, with her lips still enveloping him, her attention was captured by the waves of pleasure washing through her courtesy of Stuart's hard thrusts. As she climaxed she used her muscles to milk Stuart's cock of every pleasure it could provide her. Then as he pulled out of her she closed her eyes and collapsed across Remy, but her head was abruptly pulled up by the hair.

'No rest yet, milady,' Bonnie snapped. 'Crawl over here.' Tiffany obeyed her. 'Worship me,' Bonnie said simply, raising her skirt to expose her pussy, buried in the golden triangle of hair crowning it. It opened as she parted her thighs and arched her pelvis, an exquisite oval shape of flesh with a deep pink inner lining, moist with milky dew, her clitoris peeping from the folds encasing it. She looked down, seeking a look of discomfort on Tiffany's face, and found none as Tiffany rose and leaned closer, taking in the overpowering musky scent of an aroused pussy before burying her face in it, tasting and sucking and wishing her hands were unbound so she could caress her new lover, her new mistress, forgetting all the bad blood between them. Bonnie moaned and trembled beneath her ministrations, digging her nails into Tiffany's scalp as she gasped, 'Help me... help me lie down...'

Remy and Stuart, once again fully dressed, assisted Bonnie, never allowing Tiffany's mouth to leave her succulent purse as they helped her lie down. Tiffany used her tongue to pry apart the swollen lips, which were deliciously silky and warm and emitting an even more luscious perfume now. She was intoxicated by the taste of Bonnie's juices, and even though she was too close to see it properly, she felt the rise of her new mistress's protruding clitoris as it emerged from its hood, and once she had a hold of that nub between her lips, Bonnie elevated her buttocks further, until it seemed as if she would smother Tiffany between her thighs.

In the audience, Rache leaned closer to Quinn. 'She's learned a few tricks since her arrival,' he observed.

Quinn's arms remained folded, yet she could not help being affected by the scene before her. 'I doubt if any of her supervisors were responsible,' she replied testily.

Mockingly miffed by her attitude, he handed her Chairman. 'Here, stroke my pussy for a while.' Quinn rolled her eyes at the tired old joke, but complied.

Meanwhile, on stage, someone was moving their body closer between Tiffany's thighs, their skin bare against her own. Was it Remy, or was it Stuart, up and ready for another round? She felt lost, swallowed up by the terrible ferocity of the sexual need that made her pussy ache and her clitoris throb with expectation. The erection prodded its way further between her legs, until quickly and unceremoniously its notable length impaled her. Now she knew it was Stuart inside her as she kept her mouth fixed on Bonnie's sex, emitting muffled cries of delight as he bored through her tight folds to the hilt, then slid back out again, all at a leisurely pace which threatened to drive Tiffany mad.

The room was hushed, expectant, and Tiffany could feel all eyes fixed on her as she struggled to please her captors. She wondered where Remy was, but then put the thought of him aside, tapping all her available sources of energy to keep performing, allotting just enough strength to reaching another fulfilling orgasm. Meanwhile, below her, Bonnie began bucking her hips with increased vigour, pressing her labia against Tiffany's face as her orgasm broke free, her tight channel embracing Tiffany's weary tongue passionately.

It seemed to take ages, but Bonnie finally collapsed away from Tiffany's exhausted mouth, and edged herself away as she pulled her dress down staring at Tiffany, who was wiping the moisture from her lips and face with her bound hands. Bonnie had clearly not expected such a performance from her.

Then Stuart came a second time, and pulled out of her at once, completely spent.

'"Lord Cyrus"?' Quinn scoffed in the audience. 'Does she see you as a husband figure?'

Rache frowned. 'If she does,' he snorted, 'then she's a bigger fool than I imagined.'

Chapter Twelve

Tiffany changed back into her uniform in the prop room. Remy, Stuart and Bonnie had dressed more quickly, and once again in their real uniforms, they left without saying a word to her. She had wanted to say something to Remy, but exhaustion kept her words in check. What could she say to him, anyway? It was better to simply concentrate on her plans for escape.

She was buttoning up her uniform when Colbert appeared with a broad smile on her face. 'Tiff, come with me,' she said.

The housekeeper led her to her quarters, and Tiffany had the distinct impression that work was not on Colbert's mind. 'Madam—' she started, but the woman interrupted her.

'When we're alone, it's Anne-Marie.' She began to kiss Tiffany gently, her tongue tracing a path over the girl's lower lip. 'You did exceptionally well back there,' she breathed huskily, 'and I want to reward you.'

Tiffany closed her eyes and began drifting into renewed ecstasy, arching her back as Anne-Marie's hands began playing with her breasts through her clothes, and then gently undressing her. She helped the woman, feeling as though she should not have bothered getting dressed again in the first place. She was partly naked before Anne-Marie clamped her mouth over one of her nipples and began tonguing it, closing her teeth around the firm pink bud as she began removing her own clothes.

Tiffany stood there feeling exquisitely exposed before her mistress as Anne-Marie's hands ran down her body, pausing at the curve of her hips, by which she pushed her gently but firmly towards the bed, attached to the frame of which were metal manacles. Anne-Marie drew Tiffany's wrists up and secured them, then looked down on her subject with a cunning smile on her face. 'I've tamed you,' she said huskily. 'I've conquered you. I've won.'

Tiffany parted her thighs, inviting her. 'You've won what?' she asked dreamily.

'Never mind.' Anne-Marie slid one hand up the inside of her thigh, letting it graze her pussy, which was gratifyingly wet. Tiffany whimpered softly as her mistress began toying with her, teasing apart her sex lips and nudging her erect clitoris, making her spread her legs even wider. She slipped a finger inside her, and Tiffany gasped as she felt it penetrating, finding her inner moisture. And despite her recent exertions her carnal hungers were fully awake again and she tugged at her bonds, wanting to embrace her mistress.

Anne-Marie withdrew her hand, making Tiffany gasp with disappointment. 'Wait here,' she said with a secretive smile, as if the bound girl had any choice in the matter.

'What are you doing?' Tiffany's voice was soft yet hoarse with arousal.

'It's a surprise,' Anne-Marie teased. 'Close your eyes, and keep them closed.'

Tiffany obeyed, her imagination running riot as she heard her mistress rummaging through a drawer. 'Very well, you can open your eyes now,' Anne-Marie said.

Tiffany opened her eyes, and exclaimed, 'Good Lord!' Anne-Marie was standing beside the bed wearing a black leather harness strapped around her hips and waist. The device seemed to enhance the strong beauty of her curves, but what made it truly special was the realistic rubber cock rearing up from it. The artificial phallus was large, impressive both in length and girth, with a slight upward curve from base to tip.

Anne-Marie was clearly pleased by Tiffany's reaction as with one hand she reached down to stroke the length of the shaft. 'Frightening, isn't it?' she mused. 'I have dozens of them in all sizes, shapes and colours. I love nothing more than to fuck a begging submissive, to turn her inside out and leave her craving more. Now spread your legs wide for me.'

'Yes, mistress.' Tiffany obeyed, growing more and more aroused by the sight of Anne-Marie stroking the dildo with increased vigour, as if she was a man masturbating before her. Then the housekeeper crawled onto the bed between Tiffany's parted thighs. 'Yes... oh yes...' Tiffany panted as she felt the head of the dildo nudging open her pussy lips. The size of the plastic shaft had alarmed her at first - it was certainly bigger than any real penis she had ever seen - but her desire to meet the challenge and sate her curiosity along with her appetite overrode any concerns she had about the erection's demanding dimensions. She relished the sensations as the bulbous head stretched her open, gently but insistently, as its wearer eased her hips slowly forward.

The older woman's breasts pressed against Tiffany's as her mouth opened in an ecstatic cry when the shaft impaled her and her mistress began fucking her just like a man. The feel and stretch of the dildo in her tight sex was enough to make her come almost immediately. But Anne-Marie was taking her time, starting with gradual strokes as Tiffany squirmed beneath her. Vaguely, Tiffany wondered what it was like to thrust into another woman like a man, and then all such musings were drowned out in a torrent of pleasure. Tossing her head from side to side, she let out a long wail of joy as a climax dissolved her.

Anne-Marie's hips ground to a halt, leaving the shaft buried deep inside the girl as she nuzzled her throat and ear and whispered warmly, 'Did you enjoy that, darling?'

'Yes!' Tiffany gasped. 'Oh, yes...'

'And do you love your mistress?'

'Mmmm...' Tiffany nodded wearily; barely able to speak any more, so replete did she feel.

'And who is your mistress?'

'You are,' Tiffany mumbled, and she meant it. 'You are, Anne-Marie.' Colbert was different from the others; it was so obvious to her now.

'Did you enjoy that, darling?'
'Yes! Oh, yes...'
'And do you love your mistress?'
'Mmmm...'
'And who is your mistress?'
'You are. You are, Anne-Marie.'

'I've seen enough,' Rache said dismissively, and Colbert switched off the videotape she'd made of her time with Tiffany.

'Well?' she asked expectantly.

Rache leaned back in his chair. 'Well, what?'

The housekeeper extracted the tape from Rache's video player, and held it in her hand like some courtroom drama prop. 'Do you need further proof regarding my conditioning of Welborne?'

The director lit another cigar. 'Today's play more than sufficed, but it's always good to see you in action with others, dear Anne-Marie. And it would appear you have succeeded where the male supervisors failed.'

Colbert's triumphant grin softened to a satisfied smile as she moved around the desk to sit on his lap. Caressing him, her tongue snaked out to lick the curves of his ear. 'So, when will you announce that I am to replace you?'

His body stiffened beneath hers, and not in the way she preferred. 'When I am ready,' he said coldly.

She pulled back to meet his eye. 'But you said whomever broke Welborne—'

'Whomever broke Welborne might have an influence on my choice of successor,' he finished for her, clarifying any confusion there may exist over the matter. He unbuttoned her blouse to the waist, exposing her full breasts to the light. 'It was never meant to be the only factor.'

She scrutinised his expression, seeking the humour she was certain was driving his revelation, but he appeared to be perfectly serious.

She fought to contain her sudden surge of rage; she had controlled her temper for so long with that Welborne bitch in order to win her confidence and make her appear conditioned and compliant that she thought she might blow her top now in frustration. But anger would be useless, so she pouted sweetly instead. 'But Cyrus, you promised.'

'Nobody likes a whiner, old girl,' he said patronisingly, as he stroked her nipples to firmness and pinched one, making her wince on his lap. Yet instead of pulling away she slumped against him, breathing heavily, and he chuckled. 'Perhaps you've forgotten how you started out as a submissive?' he went on. 'And perhaps it's time you returned to that role.'

'No, Cyrus, I—'

'Call me master.' He pinched her nipple again.

'Master, I... please, I didn't mean...'

'Then stop annoying me,' he snapped bluntly. 'All of you will learn soon enough who is to succeed me. Is that clear? You will all learn soon enough.'

'Yes,' she gasped contritely. 'Yes, that's perfectly clear, master. I'm truly sorry for annoying you.'

Normal exercise routines had been suspended during the storms, so Quinn's team could not be properly put through their paces the fortnight before the match with *Farrell House*. Tiffany did not want to participate, but she had been given little choice. She was surprised when she was made centre forward of the opposition; Quinn had obviously read her school records and knew she had played in that position at the academy. She was even more surprised at how quickly she fell back into the game.

It was less of a surprise to find that the first practice matches were a shambles. They could have been better if Tiffany had been given time to put her side through a few practices of its own, and they would definitely have been better if a conscripted Shazza could manage to remember she was on Tiffany's team. When they first stepped onto the pitch, the king girl assured her that she was going to kick her ass more than the other side's, and she continually leaned on Tiffany to prove it, 'accidentally' stepping on her toes and tripping her up.

Quinn, acting as referee, seemed not to notice, so wrapped up was she with verbally murdering her crew. 'You pack of gutless cowards!' she yelled. 'You've forgotten everything I coached into you! I see no combination, no teamwork! Watch out for each other, and work for each other, for crying out loud!'

'Send them home!' Shazza called out, ignoring the glare Tiffany shot ather. The ironic thing was that the king girl showed potential on the pitch, she just never bothered to take the game seriously.

Quinn's team definitely took the game more seriously, and as a consequence they scored the most goals.

At one point Tiffany lurched and stumbled forward onto the ground, shielding her face with her forearms as she curled up and rolled painfully onto her side, the breath knocked from her lungs. Shazza had tripped her again, and she gratefully let herself be helped back to her feet, until she realised Quinn was the helping crutch.

'There's a difference between toeing the line and letting anyone and everyone trample all over you,' the coach said to her. She left it at that, but the words lingered in Tiffany's head long after the match.

Shazza approached her after dinner that evening. 'Hey, teacher's pet,' she sneered, 'we want you to do something for us.'

Tiffany looked up, determined to show no signs of intimidation as she remembered what Quinn had said to her earlier. 'What do you want?'

A slight smile crossed the king girl's lips. 'We're throwing a little private party tonight, and we want you to get us some food and drinks from the kitchen. And since you've taken Bonnie's job—'

'I get it,' Tiffany cut in. As Colbert's assistant she had access to the kitchen keys, which would be necessary since the kitchen door and pantry were locked up after dinner. She sat back. 'I suppose I could manage to get you a few scraps.'

If Shazza noticed how calm and nonchalant Tiffany was acting, she did not acknowledge it. 'Wait until five minutes after lights out,' she told the recipient of her abuse, 'then the guards will have started their first patrol.'

'I know the drill,' Tiffany said obstinately.

Shazza's mouth curled in amusement. 'You do this and you can have Jude in bed with you tonight,' she said magnanimously.

'That won't be necessary,' Tiffany declined the offer, 'since I'll be at your party tonight.'

Shazza sniggered. 'Oh, you will? And who says you're invited?'

Tiffany got to her feet. 'I say I'm invited, if you want your illicit food and drink, that is.'

The king girl regarded her soberly for a moment. 'You might not like it,' she said finally, her eyes dull. 'We do all sorts of bad things at my parties. We might shock you.'

Tiffany remembered the last 'private party' she had witnessed soon after her arrival at *Rache House*, during which she had seen Lynn's head buried between Shazza's thighs. The sight had shocked her at the time, but she was a different girl now. 'Maybe I won't,' she acknowledged easily. 'Or maybe I might just shock you.'

The ice cream - mint chocolate chip - was a luscious repast in the warm and humid evening, especially in the washroom away from the open windows of the main dorm. It was after lights out, so just a few candles illuminated the venue, and Tiffany sat in her bra and panties with the other girls, listening to the dirty jokes and limericks. In attendance were mostly Shazza's closest mates and allies, who accepted Tiffany's presence, but just barely.

After a particularly raucous story involving Singh and some of his crew, a story Tiffany was able to believe having literally served under him, Shazza called for silence. 'Okay, okay, we're here for a reason,' she called. 'One of our new arrivals, Ling, here,' she put a friendly arm around Ling Tai, a diminutive Oriental girl with braided hair, one of the three newcomers Tiffany had helped process when she worked for Singh, 'thinks she has what it takes to become the new king girl.'

There were the expected 'oohs' and 'ahs' of sarcasm from the circle of girls. Ling blushed, and Shazza quietened her subjects down, laughing. 'Now, now, we can't blame her for being ambitious, can we?' She looked at Ling as she continued. 'But she understands the rules, and the penalties for losing.'

'So what are the rules?' Tiffany asked, the first time she had spoken up since the party began.

The warm mirth in the room subsided into a sudden chill. Shazza regarded Tiffany as if debating whether or not to answer her, and then she said as though addressing an inquisitive child, 'Ling will try to make me orgasm. If she succeeds, she becomes king girl. If she fails, or stops trying, even for a moment, she becomes my private personal slave for a week and forfeits a week's work credits, unofficially, of course.' She looked around with a conspiratorial smile. 'We wouldn't want to break the trafficking rules, now would we, girls?'

'And that's it?' Tiffany asked further, once all the laughter had died down again. 'She has to make you come?'

An evil gleam burnished Shazza's dark gaze. 'The trick's not only to make me come, teacher's pet. The trick is to make me lose control, to have me thrashing and screaming and begging for mercy.' She went into a mock climax of moans and groans and exaggerated writhing motions that had all the girls in stitches again.

Except for Tiffany, whose mind was focused on confirming the rules of the game. 'Like Singh would do?'

Shazza frowned as if annoyed at being reminded that she had a master above her. 'Yes, like Singh would do,' she confirmed. 'Now, if you're finished with all the tiresome questions...'

Tiffany opened her arms magnanimously. 'Yep, go right ahead,' she said.

The circle of girls expanded slightly, like an inflating balloon, as Shazza slipped out of her bra and panties and lay back on the mattress that had been dragged into the centre of the ring of onlookers. 'Do whatever you like, Ling, just don't be offended if I nod off,' she scoffed.

Ling took the gibe good-naturedly, accepting pats on her back from those around her like a fighter going into the ring. Then she removed her own panties. She was as beautiful as Tiffany remembered her during processing, and she bore her stripes well. She fell upon Shazza at once, touching and stroking. The circle of girls fell silent, watching raptly as Ling kissed their leader. Tiffany could see her opening her pretty mouth, and imagined her tongue slipping between the king girl's lips. Some of her subjects already had their hands down the front of their panties, or inside the panties of the girl beside them. Tiffany's own body was tense with anticipation, and her pussy tingled as the blood rushed to her vulva, stimulating it hungrily. Her mouth went dry as all her energy was directed towards observing the erotic, tantalising tableau before her.

On the makeshift bed, Ling trailed kisses over Shazza's breasts all the way down her stomach to the soft, pink folds of her sex lips, parting them with her fingertips and drinking in the released perfume. There was a pause, and then Ling pierced the pouting pudenda with two of her fingers. Another pause followed, and then she replaced her fingers with her tongue, lapping up the nectar and teasing the engorged clitoris. Clearly, she was no novice to the pleasures of the female flesh.

Beneath Ling, Shazza stretched and moaned, but then commented in a deliberately nonchalant manner, 'I think I pulled a muscle on the pitch today.'

The indifferent comment made the circle of girls giggle, although not as freely as they had laughed previously. Now there was an almost tangible electric frisson in the air.

Shazza had admirable control, Tiffany had to grudgingly admit that to herself as she watched impotently, eddies of pleasure churning through her stomach with greater and greater intensity as she rubbed her thighs together, feeling them damp with perspiration. She could not control the unbridled sensuality that had been nurtured within her since she arrived at *Rache House*, and this was no exception, though she could not touch herself, not now. But she could imagine being touched as Shazza was being touched, and imagine receiving similar pleasure. If she concentrated hard enough, she could almost feel the touch of Ling's silky skin on her own, caressing and nurturing and demanding. It seemed so real that she wanted to close her eyes to picture it all the more vividly, but it was also extremely important to keep her wits about her.

Shazza continued to lie there, her folded hands propping up her head, while Ling worshipped her body. She could have been lying in bed daydreaming for all the reaction she exhibited to the other girl's passionate attentions, but then that was the point, and Tiffany was beginning to understand how, in an environment of sexual submission, the ability to conceal one's responses to someone's ministrations would be seen as a form of strength, and admired for that.

And as if to reinforce the illusion of strength, Shazza looked down at where Ling's pretty head worked between her generous thighs, sniffed indifferently, and asked, 'Are you done yet? We have to be up early in the morning.'

This time the giggles from the watching girls were even less evident, and even Tiffany surreptitiously let her hand drift down and squeeze between her tightly clenched legs. Ling looked up from between Shazza's thighs, her lips and chin glistening in the low, flickering light, and moved seductively up, her body caressing the king girl's as her hand reached down to take the place of her tongue. She fingered the king girl's pussy a moment, and then penetrated her with two fingers. When her right arm eventually tired, she seductively writhed into a different position and her left hand took over the duties, while Shazza hummed contentedly to herself, and occasionally studied her bitten nails.

At long last Ling gave up, slumping across Shazza as the circle of girls began chanting in a low whisper. 'King girl! King girl! King girl!' they chorused.

Shazza accepted their praise, and playfully slapped Ling's bottom to get her off her. 'Nice try, new girl,' she said disdainfully. 'I'll have a whole list of chores for you to do for me, starting first thing in the morning.' She sat up, reaching for what was left of her drink to quench her thirst. 'When will you pathetic bunch of girls learn?' she wondered aloud, indirectly challenging them to respond. 'I'm totally invisible.'

'That's *invincible*,' Tiffany promptly corrected her.

Shazza sneered. 'It was a joke, teacher's pet,' she said derisively. 'Irony, you know?'

All the girls looked at Tiffany, awaiting the next response in the tense exchange. There was always tension between the pair.

'Did you call Bonnie teacher's pet?' Tiffany demanded.

Shazza pretended to consider the question before answering. 'No, I didn't,' she declared, 'but then, I respect Bonnie. We all respect Bonnie. Don't we girls?' There was a general nodding of heads and murmurings of affirmation.

This was the moment, Tiffany knew. She took a deep breath and steeled herself. 'And what would it take for me to earn your respect?' she asked. 'What if

I took up your challenge?'

Shazza laughed, and the other girls took this as permission to do likewise. Then she parted her thighs lewdly to expose her pussy. 'Well then,' she leered, 'I'd say give it your best shot, princess.'

Realising this was all developing in her favour, Tiffany fought to stifle the smile threatening to creep to her lips. 'And I can do whatever I want to you?' she asked.

'Yeah, so long as you don't stop,' Shazza confirmed.

'Good,' Tiffany said, rising to her feet. 'Then I'll be right back.'

'Hey, where are you going, teacher's pet?' Shazza called after her, clearly amused both by Tiffany's effrontery at challenging her and by her sudden departure. 'My pussy's over here!' she added crudely, pointing down at it.

Tiffany did not reply. She went to her bed, stripped off her panties, and from beneath the mattress she retrieved the objects she had borrowed - smuggled - from Colbert's quarters. It was a little awkward strapping on the dildo, but she was gratified by the whispers of awe she heard from the uninvited girls who still lay awake in the dorm. Initially she was surprised that she had to suppress an acute sense of foolishness as the stout contraption sprouted and bobbed from between her thighs, but she grasped it by the base, assuring herself that it was securely attached to the harness, and how hard and real it felt instantly replaced her feeling of foolishness with a sense of strength and power. She quickly returned to the washroom, barely noticing the girls who slipped from their beds to follow cautiously but curiously behind her.

The confident smirk on Shazza's face disappeared when she saw Tiffany, and she got up from her position of exaggerated repose. 'What the fuck—?'

'You should see the look on your face now, king girl,' Tiffany goaded, and strode towards her, wanting to appear as resolute as possible, needing every ounce of determination to steel herself for the next few moments. The pink dildo bobbed before her with every step, and one cuff of the self-locking manacles hung from her hand.

Shazza pointed accusingly at the harness. 'Where'd you get that?' she demanded aggressively.

'Does it matter?' Tiffany taunted. 'Just lie back and think of England, or Cascara, or wherever.'

The king girl's face darkened with uncertainty. 'That's cheating,' she accused. 'You're not supposed to use anything but your own body.'

'You never said that before,' Tiffany countered. 'You said I could do whatever I wanted to you.' Tiffany's demeanour took on a confidence she began to enjoy, and in front of which Shazza visibly shrank. 'Ah, don't tell me king girl is afraid of anything the teacher's pet can do to her, is she?'

The words had the desired effect. Some of the girls in the circle, and others who had joined them from the dorm, also grew in confidence and began heckling their leader, ignoring her glare.

Realising no one was on her side, Shazza turned that glare towards Tiffany again. 'Okay,' she said, 'do your worst, bitch.'

Tiffany smiled and approached her. 'My worst?' she mimicked. 'I always try to do my best.' She held out the manacles and cuffed Shazza's wrists. The king girl stared at her bound arms, her breathing quickening. Then Tiffany reached out and gripped her shoulders, exerting a firm pressure. 'On your knees, bitch.'

Shazza stiffened, but then descended, as ordered, bound as much by her own rules as by the manacles. She sank down until her face was level with the pink shaft. The girls moved in closer, some silently they were so enthralled by the erotic scene playing out before them, others eagerly whispering to each other about who would win, or making vague noises of approval.

Tiffany looked down at Shazza. 'Well?' she said. 'You know what to do.'

Shazza parted her lips around the head of the dildo and licked, taking the large tip and then most of the shaft slowly into her mouth. Tiffany had to admire her courage as she let her fingers trail through the kneeling woman's short hair. Shazza looked up with her mouth stretched around the dildo, speaking eloquently with her eyes.

Tiffany smiled down at her devilishly.

'Yes, you love it don't you, you little whore?' she provoked. 'You love taking my friend into your mouth.' And she loved watching the king girl worship the dildo as if it were a real cock. What's more, there was a slight but noticeable rhythmic pressure exerted onto the base of the shaft as it was sucked, which pressed it deliciously against her clitoris, stimulating her even further. In fact, if the subtle pressure continued she might even come, which was not exactly what she had in mind, so she pulled Shazza away and ordered her onto all fours.

The other girls were urging her on even as they ridiculed her, so Shazza complied, trying to keep her balance with her wrists still bound. She braced herself as Tiffany sank to her knees behind her, and positioned the head of the dildo at the entrance to her sex. She paused for a moment, building the tension and savouring her victory, then eased her hips forward and slid in with little resistance. Either Shazza was extremely turned on by this surprising turn of events, or Ling's attempts to make her come had been a suitable warm up. Perhaps it was a little of both, but the fact was she could not help but groan loudly and lewdly beneath the sheer size of the shaft Tiffany drove into her.

'Yeah, that's it,' urged one of the watching girls. 'Fuck her. Fuck her good and proper.'

Tiffany complied with the request, moving her hips back and forth slowly, finding a suitable rhythm. Her nails dug into Shazza's hips, and even though she had never done anything like this before, within a few strokes she was pumping the large cock deep into the king girl's pussy as if it was something she did on a regular basis.

'You love this, don't you, you dirty bitch?' she taunted Shazza as she fucked her. 'You get so wet when you have a good solid length inside you, don't you?'

She paused long enough to deliver a few sharp slaps to the king girl's ample buttocks, until Shazza finally nodded and moaned in agreement. And onward Tiffany drove, realising she could carry on like this for much longer than any other girl could using just her fingers or her tongue, and best of all, unlike a man, she did not have to worry about ejaculating too soon.

Around them the girls had started a hushed but almost primeval chant in time with the dildo's thrusts, as if it all was part of some ancient tribal initiation. Then, unexpectedly, Shazza bucked and moaned, shuddered and stiffened, her body trembling as she fell forward so that the artificial erection plopped out of her.

She lay spread and exhausted across the mattress, unwilling or unable to look up at Tiffany as the girl rose to her feet and the others crowded around, their adoration shifted and solely focussed on the new king girl now; the dethroned forgotten; the dethroned finished.

It was a moment of supreme satisfaction for Tiffany, one she was glad to have experienced before she got away from the hellish place forever.

At last Shazza looked up, her expression one of anger and defiance, and when she spoke her quivering words quickly silenced the treacherous, fickle throng. 'You think you're hot shit now, Welborne?' she hissed. 'You think you've found the key to being popular? Well, you may be king girl until someone else takes the title, but that don't mean you're going to be any more popular in the morning.'

Some of the girls chided Shazza for her sour grapes attitude, but Tiffany knew the words carried an ominous truth, and suddenly her victory tasted less sweet.

CHAPTER THIRTEEN

Jude had everything worked out, which was just fine by Tiffany; it took a lot off her mind, and she could concentrate on whatever task was at hand, and on avoiding Colbert. The woman had been displeased at finding items removed from her quarters, and had privately punished her new assistant for it. The housekeeper's attitude had changed somewhat since their intimate encounter after the bizarre drama scene, and Tiffany wondered what had happened. Then she wondered why she even bothered wondering.

She was in the kitchens cleaning and scrubbing when she looked out onto the exercise field, and saw Quinn's crew practicing football with each other. It looked as hard, as rambunctious, as painful, and yes, as enjoyable, as she remembered from her experiences at the academy, and a sudden pang of longing made her pause as if in freeze frame. Her time helping out on the pitch had been more rewarding than she could have admitted to herself before now. Perhaps this was because, despite her pretensions to superiority, she recognised it as the one place where she could prove her worth without relying on her money and title and connections. There had been a sense of camaraderie amongst her academy teammates, and a genuine sense of earned achievement whenever they played a good game together.

If only she had joined Quinn's team from the beginning...

Tiffany opened the door to the sports bunker when no one answered her knock. 'Miss Quinn?' she called out tentatively.

The bunker seemed deserted, but the lights were on and Tiffany had not seen the woman emerge with her crew. Then she heard a noise, the slow, rhythmic clang of metal on metal like the pulse of a great mechanical heart that paused long enough for the familiar voice to call out, 'In here!'

Tiffany's nostrils inhaled the sweet scent of warm bodies and soap, her boots tapping against the stark concrete floor as she approached an open doorway that led her into what turned out to be a workout room. It was small but the walls were covered with mirrors that made it seem larger as they reflected countless weight benches and aerobic machines, along with a small army of Quinns lying on benches and raising and lowering heavy weights, using her legs with a precise and tireless motion. Her curves hugged her sweat-soaked T-shirt and skimpy shorts, and for the first time Tiffany was struck by the aura of power and grace surrounding the woman.

Quinn set the weights down and sat up, running a bare arm across her forehead as she smiled. 'What can I do for you, Tiff?' she asked breathlessly.

There was none of the animosity Tiffany had expected in her voice, and which she felt she deserved given her past behaviour towards the sports instructor, and it made her feel strangely humble. 'I just wanted to let you know that I think you've got a good team there,' she said.

Quinn looked surprised. 'Well, thank you.' She smiled.

'Tara's a good striker, but she overextends herself too much,' Tiffany went on quickly. 'A good defence could easily steal the ball from her.'

'So I've noticed, but thanks for the tip anyway.'

Tiffany paused, gathering the will to continue. 'Miss Quinn, I also wanted... I wanted to apologise to you.'

Quinn stared at her for a long moment. 'Apologise for what?' she asked eventually.

Tiffany suspected the woman already understood, but was feigning ignorance not to exacerbate her discomfort but out of courtesy. 'For acting the way I have. For thinking the way I have. I was wrong, and I'm sorry.'

Quinn seemed to consider her words. Then she nodded, and her smile was warm and affable. 'Let's put it behind us, okay?' she said fairly.

Tiffany could not help but smile back. It was amazing she could feel a lump in her throat about Nuala Quinn, whose imaginary sexual advances had so disgusted her at first. Still, she was glad she had managed to make some amends before she escaped.

She left, and jumped a little when she found Jude standing by the outer door, a finger to her lips in a gesture of silence before she signalled for Tiffany to follow her outside. Once in the open she whispered, 'Come on, it's time!'

'What, now?' Tiffany was stunned by the suddenness of this development. 'How did you get away from Kemp?'

'I told him I was sick, and I've bribed Dorothy to keep Colbert busy for the next twenty minutes.' Taking Tiffany by the arm, she led her quickly towards the garage. 'But security doesn't know about it. Colbert's still scheduled to leave in a few minutes.'

'Leave?' Tiffany was confused, her head spinning. 'I didn't know anything about Colbert leaving...'

'I heard Kemp talking about it this morning when he asked Colbert to pick up a few extra things from Cascara City. Security will see the van pull out at the expected time, and think nothing of it.'

Tiffany suddenly felt as if she was being swept along by an unstoppable tidal wave. 'But what about Wendy?' she asked.

'She's waiting for us in the garage,' Jude told her, apparently having every angle covered. 'Come on.'

There was an urgency to Jude's voice and manner that was one Tiffany should have shared, but she suddenly wished she'd had a chance to talk to Remy again before she left. Was it regret that kept her from feeling excited about her imminent freedom?

As expected, Wendy was alone in the garage. Less expected, however, was her state of undress.

'I found a copy of the prop room key,' Jude explained as she opened the van door and reached inside. 'And I found some suitable civilian clothes in yours and Wendy's sizes.' She grinned. 'It wouldn't do for three of us to be seen in prison grey. People would talk.' She patted Tiffany on the shoulder. 'Hurry up, lover.'

Tiffany began to comply, frowning. 'Can't we change on the way?' she reasoned.

'No, who knows when we might run into Cascaran security outside, and where?' Jude glanced at her watch. 'Now I have to get back to the house to take care of a last minute hitch. Wait here until I get back.'

Things were moving quickly, far too quickly for Tiffany's liking. The image of the tidal wave now had a waterfall added to it as she felt herself falling. 'What's the last minute hitch?' she asked anxiously.

'No time to explain,' Jude said mysteriously, then turned towards the door, and Tiffany suddenly remembered her last escape attempt, when she had deceived Jude.

'Where'd you get the watch?' she demanded abruptly.

'What?' Jude paused on her way out. 'I - I stole it off a guard,' she stammered unconvincingly.

'And the keys,' Tiffany pressed. 'How did you get them? In fact, how did you manage to do so much on your own?'

Jude was at the door. 'Don't worry, I'll explain later, I promise,' she said agitatedly.

'No, you'll explain now,' Tiffany insisted forcefully, then turned to Wendy, who was now dressed in civilian clothes and looking as nonplussed as Tiffany felt. 'I think she's set us up,' she told her, looking for support.

'What?' Wendy gasped. 'No, surely...'

Tiffany's accusing glare returned to Jude. 'The only subjects in *Rache House* who have watches are the security crew,' she stated with conviction. 'I should know, I was one of them for a while.'

Jude started to protest, but then seemed to change her mind and pulled her shoulders back boldly, her eyes steely and filled with disdain. 'Okay, yes you were, lover,' she acknowledged, 'and now I am.' She kicked the door open all the way.

Singh, Stuart and Keith entered the garage. The security chief surveyed the scene, and smiled. 'Well, well, well, isn't this a surprise?' he said.

Jude knelt in the conference room, her head bowed, silent and listening. Her no longer secret master, Armin Singh, was doing all the talking.

'Forrester had come to me a short time ago,' Singh was explaining, 'with the news that Welborne and Howard were planning an escape. I ordered her to continue with the charade of befriending them in order to keep me appraised of the details of the plan.'

'I don't suppose it occurred to you to catch her before today?' Kemp asked dryly, clearly annoyed at the amount of influence Singh had over one of Kemp's supposed mares.

The security chief remained confident. 'What for?' he asked with excessive politeness. 'She hadn't actually tried anything until today. Besides,' he nodded towards Rache, 'the director ordered me to review security measures following Welborne's last futile attempt. I had done so, and found Welborne could help me again with her next farcical plan. For instance...' He withdrew from his pocket a small brown leather wallet attached by a chain to a ring of keys, and dropped them onto the table before him as he fixed his gaze on Nuala Quinn. 'Recognise these?'

Quinn, still in her exercise gear from the bunker and looking distracted, sat up alertly and drew the items closer. 'They're mine!' she declared.

'Yes, they're perimeter gate keys,' Singh stated unnecessarily. 'And a wallet with cash in it, as well as credit cards. How did Welborne get her hands on these?'

Quinn was nonplussed. 'I - I don't know...' Then cold realisation set in. 'Wait a minute... she came to see me not long before you caught her... I was exercising and had left these in the office...'

'A serious lapse of security,' Singh declared, again unnecessarily. 'I'm surprised and disappointed in you, Nuala, as well as in you, Anne-Marie.'

Colbert steeled herself. 'It's hardly my fault,' she protested resentfully. 'I didn't make the same mistakes as the men with Welborne.'

'No, you made a whole batch of new ones,' Singh argued. 'Perhaps you're more like the men than you'd care to admit.'

Quinn spoke up again. 'Cyrus, what's going to happen to them?' she asked.

'Anne-Marie, assemble the staff and subjects on the pitch,' he instructed. 'Armin, can you ready the pillories?'

'Cyrus?' Quinn gasped, but Rache ignored her.

'If Welborne wishes to leave so badly, she just may get her wish,' he said, his expression allowing for no further discussion, and not even Chairman's attention-seeking exploits could distract him.

In a dark solitary cell with Wendy, their hands bound behind their backs, Tiffany fought the urge to gag on the rubber ball strapped in her mouth. It was difficult for her senses not to focus on it, difficult to ignore the urge to be free of the foul-tasting intruder. And from the muffled sounds coming from Wendy kneeling beside her, the other girl felt much the same way. Tiffany shifted to face her, though the darkness of the cell made the action seem pointless. Then, somewhat awkwardly, she leaned forward. Wendy tensed, but Tiffany was actually trying to brush cheek to cheek, the best physical gesture of affection and comfort she could muster under the circumstances.

Wendy's cheek felt wet, tearstained. Tiffany understood, and wished she could shed tears of her own. But all she could feel was disbelief - disbelief and rage against her situation in general, and Jude in particular.

How could that traitorous, two-faced bitch deceive and betray them like that? No, it was more than deception and betrayal, it was a conspiracy, and it was all so obvious now. How could she have done that? Had it been because of what happened, the closeness, between her and Wendy? When did Jude stop being her friend? Had she ever been her friend, really? And who had helped her, Singh or Rache? Wendy was all she had left, and she desperately wished she could hold and kiss her.

They both squinted at the sudden flood of light as the door unlocked and opened, and a tall, familiar figure was silhouetted there.

'Sorry to keep you waiting, girls.' Jude roughly helped them both to their feet, contempt marring her handsome features. 'I can see a thousand questions on your face, Tiffany. You're wondering when I turned against you. Remember our first escape attempt? Oh, sorry, I mean your first escape attempt, and how you clumsily drew me into your plans, not out of friendship but for your own ends? Remember when I was later brought into the kennels? I told you I'd had a good long talk with Master Singh, and I had.'

She paused to smirk at the memory.

'He offered me a place on his crew if I spied on you and grew closer to you and helped him catch you trying to escape again. He always knew you would try again.'

Tiffany mouthed furious obscenities, impotently muffled by the gag, but Jude understood them anyway. 'I know, I know,' she scoffed, 'the master and I should take the credit for planning this latest attempt, but we couldn't wait forever for an empty-headed bitch like you to work another one out for yourself, now could we? Oh, and don't bother trying to protest your innocence when you get to speak again. With your record and reputation, who'd believe you?'

She made a show of tapping her chin in mock contemplation. 'Now, have I forgotten anything...? Oh yes, the why. Or have you finally wised up as to how much everyone here loathes you? Have you finally realised that your selfishness and haughtiness make you completely unlikeable? I almost gagged when I made love with you in the kennels and held you in the showers. You know, I tried to be your friend in the beginning despite your insulting attitude, unless you think being called a "cow" is a compliment.' There was an undeniable undercurrent of pain in her voice. 'Now I see you for what you are, Tiffany Welborne, as everyone here always has. Even Remy's abandoned you.' She nodded towards Wendy. 'And this one's going to quickly follow after today.'

Hurt, anger and confusion welled up inside Tiffany and fought for release as if physically stoppered by the ball gag. An impulse made her kick out at Jude, but it was a foolish impulse as the other girl wore boots, and she was barefoot.

Jude laughed scathingly at the futile tantrum before reaching out and spitefully gripping Tiffany by the hair. Then she held her steady as she said coldly, a deadly look in her eyes, 'I'm on Singh's patrol crew now, just like you were. And as for your status as king girl, I'm taking it over. I trust you don't mind that. I trust you'll not complain.' She smiled at Tiffany's impotence. 'No, I didn't think you would.'

She drew closer as Tiffany tried in vain to back away, wincing as the fingers tightened in her hair. 'And in the short time you have left here, it won't be your little friend sharing your bed at night, it'll be me.' She kissed Tiffany on the cheek with an air of affection that would have been touching under any other circumstances - but in these circumstances was simply sinister.

Behind the gag Tiffany was desperate to ask the myriad questions buzzing around her head, and the one in particular that kept barging its way to the front in order of priority: what had Jude meant by, 'in the short time you have left here'?

The sky was only just beginning to turn red as the sun began to set, but the recent rains had left the air as fresh as morning all day long. The grass was still damp and birds sang happily, oblivious to the sinister proceedings below the relative safety of their branches.

Everyone appeared to have been assembled behind the main house; subjects, staff and guards. There were also, facing each other, two large, chest-high, T-shaped frames with holes in their horizontal beam. Tiffany knew their function as soon as she saw them. Although she had never seen them used, she had learned about them whilst working on Singh's crew.

She and Wendy were led before Rache, who was standing beside the stocks, and their cuffs were removed. Neither girl made an effort to remove her gag as the director scrutinised them both with obvious disdain, and then noted aloud for the benefit of the assembly, 'Tiffany Welborne, Wendy Howard, for attempted escape I give you both a choice of punishment. Howard, you may accept either lashes from the birch plus forfeiture of all accumulated work credits, or an extra month added to your sentence.'

Wendy looked to Tiffany for support, her eyes pleading.

'Well?' Rache demanded. 'Would you prefer the former?'

Wendy looked back at him, and nodded miserably.

Rache nodded in return, and then looked at Tiffany. 'As for you, Welborne, for your recidivism, you have a choice of birching and credit forfeiture, or a six month addition to your sentence.'

Tiffany's stomach lurched sickeningly. Six months? Between the two fruitless escape attempts she had added nearly a year to her original sentence. She had to appeal, she had to tell him the truth, and yet she knew he would not be interested.

'Well?' he pressed. 'Would you prefer the former?'

She nodded too, and again Rache echoed the gesture.

'Let the records note that both subjects freely accepted birching and credit forfeiture,' he announced pompously. 'They will receive one strike of the birch from each member of this establishment. All staff and subjects will participate.' Then he added, to seemingly no one in particular, 'These are not the uniforms I generously provided for them on their arrival.'

Jude, Hannah, Stuart and Remy moved in and began forcibly undressing the two captives. Wendy struggled instinctively, but Tiffany forced herself to relax. To be allowed to strip herself before the group would not have been as great an indignity for her crimes, she now realised. Her blouse was torn to shreds before being pulled away, and the bra followed with some passive assistance from her. The jeans were tougher, but her assailants managed to get them off, and her panties were no trouble at all.

Forty-three pairs of eyes feasted on their nakedness, but Tiffany could not tear her eyes away from Rache. His gaze was not on her body but burning into her very mind. It enervated her, and she could not find the strength of will to cover herself with her hands, as Wendy did. And his voice, a mixture of cultivated emotions, was equally inescapable. 'Prepare them!'

The two girls were dragged to the pillories as the assembly merged into a single queue behind Wendy. Tiffany watched the top half of her stock's horizontal beam being lifted, and then her hands were manoeuvred to rest in the appropriate hollows, as was her head, and the upper half of the beam was then returned and locked into place. She was now bent slightly from the waist, and if she strained her neck she could just see Wendy, who was in an identical position in her own pillory.

Someone was manhandling Tiffany's ankles, and she quickly realised they were attaching an iron spreader-bar, but longer than any she had worn before, so that her legs were parted obscenely, lowering the angle of her torso and adding to the strain on her neck and arms.

Rache observed the proceedings with an air of affected dispassion before nodding. Directly behind Tiffany someone stood, then made his or her presence felt by a single strike of a slim, pliable birch against her buttocks. The same fate was meted out to Wendy, but only Tiffany could see the birch being used on the other girl, and then passed to the person behind in the queue before they walked over to stand behind her. Everyone contributed to the punishment, as Rache had decreed.

It was very nearly unendurable, and it was not just the blows that hurt, but the looks on some of the faces delivering them that truly wounded Tiffany. It was not the sadistic glee of the opportunity to gain vengeance by someone who had been hurt by her, like Hannah, or the triumph she viewed in the gloating expressions of Jude, or Shazza, or Singh. It was the look of disappointment and betrayal on Nuala Quinn's face, and on Remy's. Tiffany saw herself in their eyes, and felt herself a worthless creature.

It came to Tiffany sometime during her punishment in a revelatory flash, that despite the innumerable indignities heaped upon her since her arrival she wanted to be worthy of these people. And this feeling was born not despite the regime that stripped her of her clothes, her dignity, her pride and her inhibitions, but precisely because of it. It had helped reveal what lay beneath her money and pretensions, and she did not like what she saw.

Rache was at the end of the queue. She tried to read his eyes, but could not. Above all others there, she wanted to be penitent before him, and not just because of his status. They shared an indefinable connection; she had felt it from the beginning. They were important to each other, somehow.

His parting words were more cutting than the birch. 'You and Howard will remain in the pillories until five minutes before lights out,' he stated. 'I suggest you say your goodbyes to her then. I'm arranging for your transfer to Cascara State Prison to serve out the rest of your sentence, which means serving your original six year term. I've given you more opportunities to reform than you deserve.'

The state prison? A month before she might have leapt at the chance, if only for the opportunity to tell the world about this place. But now... now she wanted to stay! She wanted to stay and serve them all. Above all, she wanted to stay and serve *him*. Helplessly gagged, she pleaded with him with her eyes, but to no avail; he simply turned his back on the crushed girl and walked away.

And Tiffany did not see the smile on his face as he departed.

The crowd broke up quickly afterwards, though Tiffany felt more than saw someone checking on them at regular intervals. Her back and neck ached, and the afternoon light felt warm on her naked bottom, a different, gentler heat than the one left behind from the birching. And though she did not want to be selfish now and titillate herself with the memory of the beating and humiliation, she could not help it. Her pussy was smouldering, a call no one would answer.

The sun had set and the sky was a burnt orange patched with dark clouds when Tiffany could no longer hold back, and released a stream of urine onto the grass between her feet. She tried to meet Wendy's gaze to see if her friend was watching. For some inexplicable reason she wanted to share this moment of intimacy with her, as she had shared other intimate moments. She saw that Wendy had indeed witnessed her release, and was copying her with a sigh of relief.

Not long after that, Nuala flitted through the dusk and released Tiffany. She removed the spreader bar from her ankles and then the ball gag from her mouth, and stepped back, unforgiving ire in her dark eyes. 'Why did you do it?' she asked Tiffany.

Tiffany straightened up gratefully, stretching and twisting, easing the stiffness in her back. Freedom was intensely welcome, but Tiffany was sufficiently distracted by the question not to be able to enjoy it properly.

'What have I done to you, Tiffany?' Nuala went on. 'I could have forced you onto my team if I wanted to, Cyrus said as much. But I knew how you felt and I didn't press the issue.' Her anger turned to hurt. 'And when I heard you apologising today, I really believed you.'

Tiffany was more disturbed by the woman's words than by her own aches and pains. 'What do you mean? I was telling the truth.'

'Yeah, right!' Nuala spat the words. 'And after you "told the truth" you went and took my wallet and keys from my office!'

'No,' Tiffany gasped in denial. 'I didn't do that.' And then her pulse quickened as she realised what had really happened. 'It was Jude,' she said slowly, the truth becoming clearer by the second. 'It was Jude, she did it! She'd planned it all at Singh's bidding! She pretended to be my friend, and... and...' Then the wellspring of emotion broke, the hurt and pain of the afternoon overcame her, and she fell into an astonished Quinn's arms, sobbing uncontrollably.

When Quinn spoke again her voice was softer, seemingly taken aback by the raw strength of the emotions at play inside the young woman in her arms. 'You're serious, aren't you?' she asked, and then sighed as she drew her closer, her anger washed away by Tiffany's genuine anguish.

Tiffany sat in Quinn's office, a large towel wrapped around her. She wished Nuala could have released Wendy as well, but she had refused point blank. It would be bad enough, she pointed out, if and when Rache discovered she had released Tiffany before her allotted time.

The fitness instructor sat opposite Tiffany, studying her face. 'Of course, you know there's no way we can prove any of this unless we can get Forrester to talk before you're transferred,' she said, and the frown punctuating her words told of her doubts concerning that possibility.

Tiffany looked around her. There was a pleasing, casual clutter to the office, where books of all sizes and subjects sat on shelves, and the desktop was strewn to capacity with papers and various knickknacks. Her attention was drawn to a number of framed photographs, and a closer examination revealed them to include a younger Nuala Quinn in public athletic settings with other female sportswomen. 'When were these taken?' she asked curiously, momentarily forgetting her predicament.

Nuala smiled wistfully. 'More years ago than I care to count up.' Then her smile evaporated. 'It seems like another person in those pictures, and I suppose it was.'

'You were a professional?'

'I almost made it to the Olympic team,' she said proudly.

Tiffany could not fail to detect the sadness in her voice. 'Did you miss it by much?'

The smile returned, but it was mirthless and did not quite reach her eyes. 'Only by a heartbeat, you might say. I had an affair with a fellow athlete, a really beautiful girl named Sinead. It was... very intense. She... well, let's just say our dirty laundry was aired in public, and somehow one of my drugs tests came out positive shortly afterwards.'

Tiffany was appalled to hear of such injustice. 'But, didn't you appeal?'

Nuala nodded. 'I did, until I realised it was all fabricated and only being used as an excuse to have me removed from the scene. There was too much and too many powerful people against me. So, I drifted for a while, and then eventually took coaching jobs like this one. Well, maybe not exactly like this one,' she amended with a wry smile. 'And then I met Cyrus through mutual... mutual contacts.'

'You didn't deserve what happened to you,' Tiffany said fervently.

'No, I didn't, but your point being?'

'Well, I deserved what I got,' Tiffany explained her thoughts. 'I can't really blame Jude for what she did.'

'Don't hog all the sackcloth and ashes,' Quinn said ruefully. 'It wasn't entirely your fault. Kemp, Singh and Colbert have been fighting to become Cyrus's replacement here.'

Tiffany sat up, her interest roused by this revelation. 'He's leaving?'

'So he says. And when you arrived, because of your reputation as a bit of a petulant young snob, he decreed that whomever was able to exert the most control over you would get the post.'

Tiffany felt as if she'd been struck again. Rache had been using her as a bargaining chip all this time? Was that the reason for the attention she had received from the other three supervisors? 'But why me?' she asked, dumbfounded by the news.

'Don't ask. I've already tried, to no avail, and I've known him for years. It just seems like one of his customary whims, at the time.' Quinn shook her head. 'It's a pity he can't be as straightforward as his photographs.'

'Photographs?'

'He was a photographer in Europe, very provocative, very controversial, under an assumed name, of course, to protect his medical qualifications,' Nuala explained. 'And he still takes pictures as a hobby.' She rose and reached for the shelf above her desk. 'Here's some of his early works.'

Tiffany accepted the book, curious about this aspect of the enigmatic man's life. It was a large volume fronted by a black-and-white photograph of a naked woman wrapped from the neck down in cellophane, and wearing a beatific smile on her face. The title above it read, *Bound Over: Images of Freedom in Submission*, by Cyrus Javert. The subsequent pages fulfilled the prurient subjects the cover promised - photos of men and women, alone and in couples or groups, displayed in rich monochrome tapestries of domination and submission. Tiffany's education enabled her to appreciate the artistic aspects of the photos, and her recent experiences enabled her to appreciate the erotic aspects.

'He was notorious in his day,' Nuala remarked. 'A celebrity in his own right. But back then the sadomasochistic scene was relegated to the domain of the pervert. The Left condemned his work for alleged sexism and the Right condemned it for alleged indecency. But the truth was he was simply ahead of his time.'

Tiffany was not listening now. She was engrossed in the volume. She had stopped on one page and was studying it with a fierce intensity. The photo was of a woman hooded in black leather, her arms extended, her body covered from the chest down with scores of wooden clothes pegs. Clothes pegs pinched her arms, her breasts and shoulders, her belly, hips, thighs, and pubes. The picture was cropped at the knees, but she suspected the clothes pegs extended to the woman's shins and feet. It was an image that, like the others, was both bizarre and highly erotic.

But it wasn't the image itself that captured her attention - it was the model.

And suddenly, everything made sense.

She looked up, her face earnest. 'If you help me, Miss Quinn, I swear to you I'll work my ass off to be the best team player you've ever seen!'

Nuala chuckled, more from surprise at the girl's sudden change of mood than from disbelief. Then she shrugged. 'Why not? In for a penny... but what do you need help with?'

'I need...' She exhaled tentatively, considering the task ahead of her. 'I need to make myself presentable.'

Cyrus Rache, a.k.a. Cyrus Javert, moved with the brisk energy of a man half his age, and with good reason. Once again his machinations had borne fruit and he had enjoyed another opportunity to punish that young temptress, the living embodiment of a long-ago betrayal, a wound that had festered over the years and refused to heal even half a lifetime later. That he had punished her in the open was less an attempt to involve the whole establishment and more an attempt to keep himself from losing control, which might have happened had he punished her privately. No, he preferred to savour the experience as much as possible, and there would be many more opportunities to do so over the coming years, no matter what he may have said to the contrary. He was not about to give her up now, oh no...

Nuala Quinn intercepted him in the corridor. 'Cyrus, I have to—'

'Doctor!' Singh quickly advanced from another direction, shooting a quick glare at Quinn before continuing. 'Doctor, I must protest. This woman freed Welborne early!'

'Oh?' Rache pursed his lips and furrowed his brow, but his eyes gave away the shallowness of his concern. 'Is this true, Nuala?'

'Yes, it is.' She turned around and presented him with her bottom. 'Will you spank me now, or later, sir?'

Rache released his mock anger with a chuckle. 'It would take years to make a dent in your muscular posterior, my dear,' he mused. 'I expect you have a reason for doing what you did.'

'Yes, I do,' Nuala said, 'and there's a package waiting for you in your studio.'

'Oh? Thank you. I do love packages. They can be so full of surprises.' He glanced at his watch. 'It's near lights out. Better go and release Wendy Howard, Armin.'

'But Cyrus,' Singh called after the back of his director as he continued on his way, 'what about Quinn and Welborne? What are you going to do about them?'

Rache paused, and seemed to consider the question before replying. 'If my decision requires your participation, Armin, I'll be sure to let you know,' he called back over his shoulder, and then continued around the corner, where he paused and listened.

'What are you up to?' Singh asked Quinn vehemently.

'I could ask you the same,' she retorted. 'But then I already know about how you and Jude set up Tiffany and Wendy.'

Singh hesitated, flushed in consternation, but his reply was laced with weak bravado. 'What are you talking about, Quinn? I don't know what you're talking about.'

In the shadow, around the corner, Rache allowed himself a fleeting, secretive smile.

None of her past ordeals had quite prepared Tiffany for what she underwent now. It was in fact far easier to be confined, bound or manacled. In those instances the body and the mind, once having tested their limitations, learned to adjust, but nothing kept her immobile now except her own stubborn will.

And then there were the clothes pegs... Nuala had placed them more or less evenly across Tiffany's naked body. The first dozen hurt terribly, yet as more and more were added the areas around the first began to numb, and she found herself in a delicious stew of mingled pain and pleasure.

Through the zippered open eye slits of the leather hood, she watched the studio door open, and only then wondered what she would do if it was not the director who entered.

But it was him. He stared at her intently as he closed and locked the door behind him. Then he approached her slowly, and a growing smile replaced the look of appreciative awe on his face. '*Cherie*,' he croaked emotionally, 'you look utterly beautiful.'

She turned, shivers of delight running through her as the clothes pegs shimmied and awakened her numbed flesh, to show off the birthmark on her breast. 'As beautiful as my mother was in this pose?' she asked.

His eyes narrowed, though the glint in them remained as focused as a laser. 'And how long have you known?'

'Barely an hour,' she told him. 'I saw the photograph in one of your books.'

He nodded. 'Celeste insisted on being masked, but her birthmark would be unmistakable to someone who knew her well enough. So you are her daughter, after all.'

Tiffany stared through the hood's slits at him, fascinated, the ache in her arms forgotten. 'And what were you to her?'

He sighed and turned away as if to survey the framed photographs covering the studio walls. 'Once I was an employer looking for models willing to bare all, and she was just a hairdresser looking for additional income. Later, I became her lover - her first lover. I introduced her to the delights of the whip and the chain. My tawse, used more than once on your cheeks, by the way, tanned her own delectable bottom many times. She took to it like a duck to water.' He glanced back at her, smiling. 'Nice to see such traits are inheritable.'

Within her mask, Tiffany blushed despite herself, and lowered her arms. 'I didn't know she ever modelled,' she admitted.

'No doubt you know little of your mother's life before she met your father. Keep your arms raised.'

She obeyed, and he went on. 'What is ironic, is that I introduced Celeste to Zak Welborne while I was in negotiation to design his band's next album cover. And the rest, as they say, is history. All she left me were my photos, my memories, and Chairman.' He bent by an uneven pile of assorted props, and lifted from it two red bricks. 'I had been her master, but I had also loved her too, and that was my downfall.' He set a brick in each of her hands, increasing her struggle to keep her arms perpendicular to her body. 'Even after she married that drug-addled, brain-dead musician, even after your birth, I would have taken her back. With you in tow, of course.'

Tiffany's arms cried out even as she wondered what life would have been like as the stepdaughter of a man like Cyrus Rache. 'They're... they're divorced now,' she pointed out.

'I'm fully aware of that, my dear.' He sounded faintly offended. 'And we both know why I won't be contacting her now.'

Tiffany blanched, thankful for the concealment of the hood. Her breathing quickened, and her arms shook. She did not think she could manage to keep them up much longer...

Rache idly flicked various clothes pegs, and sometimes twisted one to painfully reawaken the flesh as he spoke. 'Such was my depression following Celeste's departure that my career faltered, which was not helped by the contemporary conservative *zeitgeist*. But I persevered and left Europe for Cascara, the ultimate haven for exiles of all persuasions, where I found a new calling, the private prison service.'

'A way...' Tiffany panted, the pain in her arms almost too much to bear. 'A way to punish wicked girls like—'

'Like your mother,' he prompted, seemingly oblivious to her discomfort but in fact observing it carefully, his attention lingering on her nipples. 'My love for her refused to die. But it could reform into something equally potent - contempt. Contempt for her selfish betrayal and contempt for Zak Welborne, an alleged friend, for his betrayal and usurpation of what was rightfully mine.' His hand drifted to her pussy, and the tip of his index finger delicately brushed the pursed lips of her sex, making her tremble. 'I had made powerful friends from ex-lovers over the years, and one of them left me this estate in her will. Another helped equip me and my staff with false identities and qualifications, providing the backing I needed to make my new dream come true. I thought I had found contentment here at last; fulfilment.

But then you began appearing in Cascara, building up a lengthy record of troublemaking, and suddenly all I had achieved wasn't enough for me any more. It was no longer sufficient to punish women who reminded me of your mother; I had to have her daughter prostrate before me. So I kept an eye on you and waited, biding my time until your eighteenth birthday, when I sent you an invitation to visit my exclusive coterie in Cascara City.'

'The catacombs?' Tiffany gasped. 'You own them, too?'

'Yes, they amuse me during my erstwhile forays into the big city. And I needed to see how you'd respond to our particular tastes.' He smiled knowingly. 'And from all accounts, you responded very well. I even arranged to have a corrupt police officer discover a quantity of drugs in the car you were driving, but your own possession made that unnecessary.'

'Does... does my father know what's going on here?' she asked. 'You said once—'

'Zak Welborne has no idea what's going on here,' he interrupted abruptly. 'He doesn't know about me. In fact, I doubt if he knows what day of the year it is.' His finger finally pierced her, encountering a token, moist resistance that yielded readily to the invasion. But the sudden penetration was enough to make Tiffany cry out and drop the bricks as she sank to her knees before him.

Clothespins scattered around her as she curled up at his feet, overwhelmed by sensations, dizzying waves of torment mingled with bliss threatening to turn her inside out and make her pass out. She gasped for breath and removed the hood.

Rache reached for his camera where it rested on an adjacent table, and expertly snapped away. 'Perfect... just what I wanted...'

His eye still behind the lens, he continued his story. 'I contrived a rivalry amongst my staff so they would concentrate their special attentions on you. Had I openly ordered your specific persecution questions would have been asked, questions I would have been loathe to answer. Of course, when I believed you'd settled in too easily under Singh's command, I prompted you to consider an escape.'

Tiffany found her voice again. 'And to be punished...'

'Then you were caught a second time,' he went on, his mention of this making her look up. He seemed so tall, so commanding and omnipotent.

'No,' she protested, 'Singh and Jude, they did it all... they tricked me.'

He nodded. 'I know all about that,' he revealed. 'Absolutely nothing goes on here without my knowledge, Tiffany. Singh thought to punish you and hurt the others' chances of becoming the new director, augmenting his own standing by appearing to have foiled another escape attempt. He has failed on all three accounts, I'm afraid.'

'And Nuala's - sorry, Miss Quinn's wallet and keys?'

He leaned closer to her conspiratorially. 'Even if Nuala was negligent on that count, it would hardly change my high opinion of her.'

'Then you're not sending me away?'

He laughed, a soft yet dangerous sound that crawled down her spine like a tarantula. 'After all the trouble I took to get you here? Not a chance. Not a chance in hell.'

Tiffany let her head fall to the floor again. 'Good,' she sighed.

'Does that thought please you, Miss Welborne?'

She looked up at him again, this time with a fire in her eyes which in many ways rivalled his own. 'Yes,' she admitted passionately. 'Please let me stay. Let me be on Nuala's team and let me be the vessel that receives your anger, master.' Encouraged by his intrigued expression, she went on ardently. 'You wanted vengeance on my parents. What would be better - persecuting me without my knowing why, or having me as a willing, eager accomplice to your persecution? No games, no deceptions, just simple, raw, unwavering dominance and submission. Please let me serve you!' The words flowed unrehearsed from her lips with all the desperate energy of someone bargaining for her life. Standing before her was the one she had always sought without knowing it, the one who could do what daddy and mummy and the academy and even the law could not, or would not do. This man could discipline her. This man could break the spoilt, selfish brat inside her and make her a beautiful, generous, passionate woman. This man could tame and strengthen her at the same time. He could put her through the fire and make her a better person for it.

'There would be conditions,' he said quietly.

'I expected as much.'

'One of them being that you will keep silent about Singh's and Forrester's conspiracy against you, at least for the time being.'

She had no intention of refusing, but still she asked why.

'I have my reasons,' was all he said by way of an answer. 'Well?'

'Nuala knows about it,' she pointed out.

'She'll keep silent if she wants you on her team.'

'Yes, sir. Anything else?'

'I started a portfolio nearly twenty years ago starring your mother, but she left me before I could complete my work.'

'Then I'll finish what she started,' Tiffany suggested.

Holding the camera up again, he smiled. 'Crawl over to me on your front and beg my indulgence. And make me believe it.'

She did as he said, and he did believe it.

CHAPTER FOURTEEN

Anyone who says that girls are not as rough and competitive as boys at sports has obviously never seen them playing football.

Under Nuala's authority now, Tiffany trained twice as hard as the other girls to make up for time lost, not that she complained about it. Additional practice matches were set up in the free hours following dinner and before lights out using volunteers from other crews. It had rained again and the pitch was like a skating rink of thick black mud, and it was not long before both sets of players were practically unrecognisable.

Some of the subjects, and a few of the staff, emerged from the house to watch the practice match. They stood around the pitch at various vantage points, and some heckled Tiffany each time she made contact with the ball. But as they observed the frequency with which she scored, their cries of derision died away.

Up and down the pitch the ball was punted, sometimes getting stuck fast in the muck and producing a heaving ruck of kicking, pushing and shoving, before Nuala, acting as referee, blew her whistle. Despite the state of the pitch and her growing fatigue, Tiffany found herself performing with an ease that unnerved her. She was against her own teammates and volunteers now, but she suspected the visiting team from *Farrell House*, whom they were playing the following evening, would be even more competitive. And yet she could not deny that the team - and not just her - moved well and played well. It was like being back at the academy... no, it was better. At the academy there had been pretentiousness and unspoken hierarchies. Playing here was like a drink of mountain spring water; it was pure and refreshing and invigorating.

Shazza pounded the pitch towards her again, and Tiffany could not help but blanch at the prospect of more bruises on her shins from the ex-king girl, still playing on the volunteer's side, as she tried to seize control of the ball from her. Since the incident in the dorm, Shazza had kept her distance from Tiffany, minimising their communication to the absolutely necessary, and Tiffany was too busy and too tired to do anything about it. She could understand the other's ire, and if she had not been so absorbed by her catch up training under Nuala, she might have done something to try and assuage it. And now, on the pitch, seemed to be the moment when the tension between them was coming to a head.

Shazza kicked out at the ball, desperately doing her best to steal it. That she ended up making contact with Tiffany's shins more than with the ball was, perhaps for her, a bonus as their teammates, and the spectators, cheered them on. Tiffany endured the aggressive assault while all the time relentlessly leading the ball towards the goal. The mud splattered around her and her limbs ached, but she persevered. Suddenly she was there, and Shazza made a last ditch attempt to steal the ball, but to no avail. She ended up in the mud, and the ball ended up past the disbelieving goalie.

The cheers crescendoed - or was it just the blood pounding in her head? - and Tiffany could not help but grin at her triumph. They were ready for the forthcoming match. Desiree, Jodie, Yvette, Kamesha, Zoe, all of them, were ready. *Bring on Farrell House!*

She slapped hand after hand as each player came up to congratulate her, and then a grunt drew her attention. Shazza lay on the pitch covered in a mud. She sat up, disgust and defeat, not anger, visible in her pained expression.

Tiffany bent down and held out a hand towards the fallen antagonist. 'You play a good game,' she said generously. 'You should join us full time.'

Shazza looked up at her rival in disbelief. Yet gradually her belligerence melted, and left behind a measure of grudging respect, which was discernible in her eyes if not in her muddied face. Then with a growing, genuine smile, she let herself be helped back up to her feet, and held onto Tiffany's hand longer than was necessary.

Tiffany smiled back at her, as proud of this goal as she was of her previous one.

Tiffany adjusted the setting on the showerhead above her, turning the fine hot mist into a powerful jet to massage her aches away. The last of her fellow players had left the sports bunker, and the so-called star player was enjoying the water in peaceful privacy. She reminded herself that though she had played an important part in the team's success, it was still just that, a *part*. She would not be the whole game. Such vain notions belonged to another Tiffany Welborne.

Nuala appeared in the open doorway still clad in her mud-caked grey T-shirt and shorts. Having watched and listened to the other females over the past week, Tiffany had grown to admire her drive and professionalism. She took the game seriously, but not obsessively. 'How are you feeling?' the coach asked.

Tiffany sighed with pleasure. 'Can I sleep here tonight?'

Nuala laughed lightly. 'I'll see what I can do.' She pulled off her T-shirt, revealing a muscular upper body, firm but still feminine, her pert breasts held tightly by a white sports bra. 'You don't mind if I join you?'

Tiffany had waited for this moment all week, but allowed herself only a casual nod of the head. She watched intently as Nuala peeled off the rest of her clothes. The coach's body was, as she had expected, as striking naked as it was clothed. Her breasts were firm and pale and budded with dark pink nipples that stood at attention. Her pubic hair was a deep mahogany and trimmed neatly, only just covering the lips of her sex. Tiffany felt her own nipples tighten and her vulva swell expectantly.

Nuala tied her hair back with a band, and then stepped into the showers, selecting one nearby and sighing as the hot water washed over her. 'Oh... I think I'll sleep here, too,' she sighed.

'You're more than welcome,' Tiffany replied, knowing how the answer could be interpreted, and hoping it would, in fact, be interpreted that way.

Nuala smiled. 'You've made real progress here,' she said.

'Thanks, but you've quite a few good players in the team.'

'I'm not talking about your athletic abilities.'

'I know.' Tiffany smiled teasingly.

Nuala smiled back, but maintained a measure of sobriety. 'Especially in keeping silent about Singh and Jude. I understand she's taken the crown of king girl from you.'

Tiffany nodded. 'I didn't put up much of a struggle, though.'

'Nevertheless, you've managed to win over many of the girls. They can see genuine changes in you.'

'Thank you. Maybe Rache has done me a favour by having me keep silent.'

'I'm sure he wouldn't admit to it.'

'No.' Tiffany breathed in deeply, and found that she simply had to confide in Nuala. 'You know, there's a reason I used to hate the idea of women... being with women,' she started tentatively. ,My mother...'

Nuala helped her along unexpectedly. 'Your mother divorced your father when you were twelve to go live with another woman in America.'

'Oh,' Tiffany squealed indignantly, 'I should have known you people would know that.'

'I had Cyrus show me your psych profile as part of the price for my continued silence,' the coach explained, moving closer. 'You couldn't blame either parent for the divorce, so you turned against the woman your mother left with, and that turned you against the idea of lesbians.'

'I thought they were all predators abducting so-called normal women and taking them from their families and their children,' Tiffany admitted quietly, catching a glimpse of the woman's breasts, firm and lovely, and then looked away. 'It sounds like pat psychology, doesn't it?'

'That doesn't mean it can't be true,' Nuala pointed out gently.

'It's no excuse for my completely intolerant attitude, though.'

'It's not meant to be an excuse, it's meant to be an explanation, and you've changed. I'm only sorry it couldn't have been sooner. Had Rache not been so personally involved in your case, you would have been assigned to me immediately.'

Tiffany was silent for a moment. 'You're not like the other staff members,' she observed. 'You haven't tried to...'

'I was under the impression Cyrus was taking care of that now.'

At least once a day for the past seven days, Tiffany had spent time in his studio posing for his portfolio, the project he insisted would bring him back into the world of professional erotic photography. And under his tutelage she was reaching new levels of desire and ecstasy that, however, were never completely fulfilled. She could not understand why, and her frustration grew daily, but he had not yet fucked her after disciplining her.

'But maybe it's not enough?' Nuala suggested softly.

Tiffany looked back at her with renewed longing. 'I want to make love to you,' she suddenly confessed. 'I want to serve you. I want to worship you.'

The coach did not reply, and for a terrible moment Tiffany thought she would be refused, rejected. Then Nuala drew closer. 'Come here,' she whispered.

Tiffany obeyed, her stomach somersaulting as Nuala reached for a bar of soap. 'My sisters and I used to do each other's backs,' she purred seductively. 'I miss that. Let me do yours.'

'Only if I can do yours, too.'

She lathered up her hands and returned the bar to Tiffany. 'Sounds like a winner.' She stepped even closer, her breasts sleek and sliding against Tiffany's in a deeply sensual experience. Reaching under Tiffany's arms, Nuala began lathering her back, and Tiffany took the cue and did the same for her. As their breasts pressed and moulded together, Tiffany was conscious of her nipples becoming harder and tingly.

Nuala noticed it, too. 'Push harder against me, all over,' she coaxed, and Tiffany had little control over her body as she obeyed. Nuala was slightly taller, so she bent her knees until the soft down of her pussy met Tiffany's. They kissed, Nuala sliding her tongue into Tiffany's mouth and exploring exquisitely.

When they surfaced to catch breath, Tiffany nuzzled her face into Nuala's neck. 'How do you dominate your girls, mistress?' she murmured provocatively.

Nuala softly kissed the outer rim of Tiffany's ear as she whispered her reply.

'Do you really want to find out?' she asked.

Tiffany moaned and pressed her sex mound harder against Nuala's. Then she let herself be drawn out of the showers and over to the nearest wooden bench. Somehow Nuala's hands had snaked down and gripped Tiffany's wrists, and she tied them together with a discarded towel she found there.

'You made a few mistakes on the pitch this week, Tiffany,' she said hypnotically. 'You didn't listen to me.'

Tiffany understood, and could not suppress a smile. 'And what do you intend to do about it, Miss Quinn?'

The woman's eyes narrowed. 'In matters of sport, you will address me as coach. Now straddle the bench.'

'Yes, coach.' Tiffany did as she was told, enjoying the hardness of the wood against the front of her body as she spread her legs and gripped the sides of it. She faced away from the fitness instructor, and closed her eyes as she felt cool, strong, female fingers kneading her buttocks.

'You missed three opportunities for clear shots this evening,' Nuala said sternly. 'Sheer sloppiness on your part.'

'Yes, coach... oooh!' The first smack made Tiffany lift her head and arch her back. She moaned and writhed as Nuala spanked her, the firm skin of her open palm connecting with her flesh again and again as Tiffany's clitoris connected with the bench again and again with devastating effect. It was a rhythm of pain and pleasure she wanted to go on forever.

Nuala turned out to be as expert at punishment as the other staff, timing her slaps perfectly, allowing Tiffany's flesh to cool slightly before striking it again. And though it may just have been Tiffany's imagination, she seemed to detect an almost tender quality to the woman's discipline; recognition that it was a shared experience and that Nuala understood exactly what she was feeling.

When the spanking ceased Tiffany lay limp across the bench, but Nuala immediately eased her up and onto an adjacent mat, giving her no time to recover.

She caught her breath as the woman's eyes and hands roamed over her, cupping her breasts and squeezing them appreciatively before she bent over to engulf one of her nipples and suck it gently. Tiffany moaned, biting her lip beneath the delicious attention. She was conscious of Nuala's other hand descending her belly, and she opened her legs in anticipation. Nuala paused to stroke her mound a moment before delving between her yearning sex lips as Tiffany cried out and pushed her pussy up to meet her.

The coach raised her face from Tiffany's breasts, and smiled. 'Are you going to be selfish?' she prompted.

Tiffany could not speak. With her excitement mounting, she shook her head weakly.

'Yes, you are.' Nuala knelt down, and with Tiffany's thighs on either side of her head, her tongue continued what her fingers had begun. Tiffany thought she had reached incredible heights of ecstasy before, but she discovered they had been nothing compared with what she felt now...

Afterwards they lay clasped in each other's arms. 'I hope that's taught you something about performing consistently,' Nuala sighed contentedly.

'Remy!'

That he stopped when Tiffany called his name was a blessing. Less a blessing than a curse was the presence of Jude by his side, however. He and Jude were spending a lot of time together. But the treacherous girl's presence was not about to put Tiffany off now. She sprinted towards them across the exercise field before they had a chance to enter the woods on final patrol before lights out. 'Remy, I need to talk to you!' she shouted.

Jude turned to face her as she drew close, showing off the black patrol armband on her uniform. 'Some of us have proper work ahead of us, Welborne,' she said aggressively.

Remy, wearing a pained expression, stepped forward as if to block any further acrimony between the two young women. 'What is it, Tiffany?' he asked.

For a moment she considered telling him the truth about the conspiracy instigated by Jude and Singh. A part of her still wanted him - the incident during the stupid little period drama had confirmed she still desired him - and she was tempted to break her promise of silence to Rache. But she did not. Promises meant something to her now, and she was not there to try and rekindle their former relationship. 'I - I just wanted to apologise, Remy, for hurting you,' she said sincerely. 'And I wanted to apologise to you too, Jude.'

The words hung in the air along with the chirping of cicada.

'Is that it?' Jude said shortly. 'Can we get on now? I'm sure you have another failed escape to plan.'

Tiffany flinched at the barbed jibe, but she persevered. Without taking her eyes off Remy, she replied, 'Yes, that is it. I've nothing more to say.'

'Then run along, little girl,' Jude snapped, 'and stay awake for me tonight.' Her radio chirped, and she answered it. 'Forrester here.'

Rache's voice was deep and powerful. 'Forrester,' it boomed, 'report to my office, at once!'

'Yes, sir.' Switching off her radio, Jude glared at Tiffany as if she was somehow responsible for the interruption. Then she turned and boldly drew Remy into a kiss, which was less a display of affection than one of possession; possession of what had once been Tiffany's, had she wanted it.

Remy had to prise himself loose. 'You'd better get going,' he said.

Reluctantly Jude released him and started back towards the house, casting a warning look at the pair of them.

A pregnant silence hung between Tiffany and Remy for a moment, then he said, 'You'd better get going as well, Tiff.'

She nodded, not knowing what she had expected from him. She turned away, holding back her tears, inner confusion reigning.

'Good luck with the game tomorrow,' he called after her, and the tears won. She did not dare stop or look back so intense were the emotions churning inside her.

Jude had not returned to the dorm by lights out. Tiffany suspected Rache had her performing somewhere after hours, a privilege reserved for veteran subjects. Tiffany did not mind. Nor did Wendy, who was finally sharing her bed again after a week without her, though in fact Tiffany would have preferred to sleep alone. Not that her feelings for her friend had diminished. Wendy had been the one person who had shown consistent loyalty to her, and who trusted her. Only Tiffany knew the girl's true identity as a reporter, and she had managed to keep it a secret. Her reluctance to share her bed with Wendy was borne of a desire not to return to the one topic of conversation she knew the girl would bring up.

'Tomorrow night's the time,' Wendy whispered, snuggling against her. 'It'll be perfect.'

Tiffany sighed. 'Haven't you had your fill of failed escape attempts, Wendy? Or have you developed a taste for the pillory?'

'No, not escape, *exposure*,' she corrected enthusiastically. 'There'll be outsiders here tomorrow night, officials not on Rache's payroll. We can go right up to them and hand them the notes I've collected over the past month before anyone can stop us.'

Tiffany caught her breath. This sounded a dangerous ploy. 'I don't know, Wendy...'

The lovely young reporter pulled back and shifted onto her side so she could stroke Tiffany's cheek. Her touch was warm and comforting. 'They've brainwashed you, Tiff,' she said sadly. 'You've forgotten who you are.'

'I know who I was, and I didn't much like her,' Tiffany replied. 'I'm different now, Wendy, stronger.'

'Stronger? By being submissive?'

'Yes. As strange as that may seem, I feel... honourable now.'

Suddenly her friend's concern turned to a stony determination as she spoke in hushed tones. 'Honourable? How do you think we look to Rache and the rest of them when we're naked and bound and behaving like submissive little pets responding to their slightest word and touch, dancing to their tune just like trained dogs?'

'It's not like that, Wendy,' Tiffany argued, noting her own lack of conviction, 'it's—'

'Yes, it is. They're laughing at us and using us, and when they're through they'll discard us like soiled tissues. Is that what you want for yourself?' She did not wait for an answer. 'You promised me, you swore to me, you'd help me escape, Tiffany. I stuck by you when everyone else abandoned you, and if you're as honourable as you think or say you are now, you'll keep your word to me.'

And there it was, the moral quandary Tiffany had tried her best to avoid, the dilemma that would not go away. Rache and his little world had done more than just expand her sensual appetites and her taste for sexual submission; they had helped instil a sense of true pride and honour in her. Even if it was the honour of a slave, it was still better than the stifling, hypocritical lie that had been her old life. But if she wanted to be true to this new persona, and to her friend, she would have to let Wendy destroy Rache's world.

And in the end, there was really only one possible answer. 'Okay, Wendy,' she said quietly, 'we'll confront the visitors tomorrow night during the post-game party.'

Wendy's joy was almost palpable. 'Oh, I didn't think you'd let me down, Tiff!' she gushed. 'And don't worry; your name will be kept out of it, just like I promised.' She relaxed again, and her hand reached under the cover for Tiffany's pussy. 'I love you, Tiff...'

Her fingers followed a familiar path, and Tiffany parted her legs to accept the gentle approach. She was exhausted, both in body and spirit. Suddenly she prayed it would all be over by the following night. One way or another, it would all be over by the following night.

CHAPTER FIFTEEN

Jude was exhausted - exhausted beyond what she had once considered her limits. She'd lost track of how many hours Rache had kept her in the room, tormenting her. She had not received his personal attention before. Shazza, Kemp, Singh, they were mere shadows of the director, she realised that now. He was not as blunt or impatient as they were. He was more of a scalpel than a hammer, taking his time to maximise her pain and discomfort - and her pleasure, too. He had repeatedly brought her to the brink of ecstatic release, before pulling her back again cruelly.

At first he gave no reason for summoning her, simply ordered her to follow him into his studio, where he had her strip naked and kneel on all fours. Then he began his work on her, stopping only to secure her to a floor plate with manacles that immobilised her wrists and ankles and kept her thighs parted. An additional collar and lead were attached to her throat, serving no purpose other than as a vivid reminder of her status. Twin weights were clamped to her nipples by crocodile clips, and condemned her to a constant, excruciating torment. And, finally, wedged into her back passage was a large dildo held in place by a studded harness bisecting her sex.

And she loved it all.

Then he began asking her questions and she confessed all - her complicity with Singh in setting up Tiffany and Wendy in the escape attempt, and the fact that it was she who had stolen Quinn's wallet and keys. She confessed it all readily and repeatedly, because despite Singh's assurances of 'protection' she knew she was now under the thumb of the man who had probably taught Singh everything he knew about the art of erotic torture.

The following day was torturous for Tiffany. She could not think straight and it showed in her practice sessions, prompting awkward questions from Nuala and her teammates. She put it down to pre-match jitters, and this seemed to mollify everyone.

Rache held a special assembly following dinner. 'Our guests,' he began, 'including the inspector for prison services who will be acting as referee for the match, will be arriving shortly. Lights out has been extended an hour, and there will be wine and beer served on a limited basis tonight at the celebration party following the match. Unless the opposition wins, of course, in which case we'll serve them whatever we find at the bottom of the deep fat fryer.'

Laughter turned to cheers.

'It'll be a celebration, doctor,' Nuala assured him. 'We guarantee it.'

He smiled. 'But I expect everyone to be on their best behaviour, and to be discreet. Subjects at *Rache House* share unique privileges.' He paused, allowing the girls to absorb the meaning of his words. 'Privileges other houses such as *Farrell House* do not have. We would not want them to get jealous of us. I believe you all understand me.

'That's all for now... ah yes, Howard, report to security at once. Your behaviour this week has not earned you a place at either the match or the party tonight.'

Wendy, standing beside Tiffany, glanced at her ally in silent alarm. It was clear she could not think of anything she might have done, or not have done, to earn the director's displeasure, but Tiffany reached out and squeezed her hand in empathy as Remy appeared beside Wendy.

'We'll bring you a little food and beer later,' he said kindly.

Unspoken words were exchanged between Wendy and Tiffany through their eyes, reminders of promises made and obligations to be kept. Tiffany needed no reminding, however.

Amongst the staff, Singh had finally worked up the courage to approach Rache about an obligation of his own. 'Doctor, I've been meaning to ask about Jude Forrester,' he said.

Rache seemed distracted. 'What about her?'

'You've... you've kept her busy since last night in your studio.'

'And?'

Singh's mouth opened, and then closed, and then opened again. 'Is there any particular reason why?'

'I like her,' Rache said simply, then faced his security chief squarely. 'There's so much of her to chastise.'

'Is she okay?'

'Of course she is, but I don't think she'll be fit to attend the match and the party tonight. Is that loyalty I see and hear in your enquiries, Armin?'

'Of course, doctor.'

'Good, because I prize loyalty very highly, as you know.'

The locker room was a flurry of activity. The opposition girls had been allowed to change first, and they were now warming up on the floodlit pitch, which had thankfully dried out.

Butterflies churned in Tiffany's stomach. She had to somehow free Wendy, or at least get her notebook to the visiting inspector. Rache and the others did not have to know she was involved in the collapse of his regime. He was abusing his authority, she reminded herself, though she knew none of the girls were ever truly forced into anything against their will.

Kamesha approached Tiffany, followed by several other girls. She tried to look serious, but failed miserably. 'Tiff, I'm afraid you can't go out tonight.'

Tiffany frowned. 'Why not?'

'Well, I'm afraid you're not properly kitted out.'

Her frown deepened; they weren't even dressed yet. Then she understood, and looked around at all the shaven pussies before her. She smiled, momentarily forgetting her worries. 'Do we have time to make me presentable?' she asked sportingly.

Moments later she was lying naked on one of the exercise mats on the floor with a group of girls surrounding her. She parted her knees until she felt a tug in her groin, and Kamesha and Ling performed the actual procedure, Kamesha using a pair of scissors expertly on Tiffany's pale blonde curls, drawing them out with her fingertips before clipping them near the root and dropping them on an adjacent towel for disposal.

Then Ling applied shaving foam and used a safety razor. Tiffany let out an unwanted gasp as Ling's fingers brushed lightly against her parted sex lips, drawing forth the hardened nub of her clitoris from its fleshy hood. She heard the girl's fingers as they touched the slick moisture of her juices, and smelled her own arousal. Her body was completely open to their attentions, melting in submission.

When it was over she sat up and accepted pats of congratulation on her back as she stared at her naked pussy. It looked bizarre, but also undeniably erotic, and she wondered what it would feel like to have fingers, or a penis, slide in and out of it now.

Nuala strode in carrying a large canvas drawstring bag over one shoulder, and paused to stare at Tiffany, smiling. 'Nice look, Tiff.' Her accent was sharp, an indication of the level of her excitement. 'Listen up, ladies, you're not going out in those shorts and shirts.' She set the bag down and opened it. 'I have something special for you to wear tonight.' She withdrew a T-shirt and loose-fitting shorts, not the usual prison-issue grey but a more colourful navy-blue with gold and red striped trim, and they were even emblazoned with numbers and names. 'Just a little gesture of thanks for the hard work all of you have put in recently.'

To the cheers of the girls, the coach began distributing the kit while Tiffany felt herself cringing with guilt.

'Any last minute strategies you want to give us, coach?' Shazza asked. She was the team's newest member, albeit just a substitute for now.

'Yes, kick their arses!' Nuala beamed.

The girls cheered again, Tiffany included, though her heart was not fully in it. Then she chided herself. No matter what happened later, the next hour deserved her full attention and commitment, otherwise the past week's work would have been for nothing, and Nuala and her teammates deserved better than that.

It was sombrely quiet in the living room, its centre now cleared of furniture. Rache and Nuala stood before the girls, the football team in the front lines showered and dressed and once more in their house uniforms. Rache looked to the coach, but it was he who spoke. 'The one thing every athlete must remember is that it's not whether you win or lose, but how you play the game. However, winning is important, isn't it?'

Nuala held the trophy aloft again, and the room erupted with cheers as Rache raised a champagne glass to toast the *Farrell House* girls for their worthy performance.

Close to Rache and Nuala, Tiffany gratefully accepted the hugs and slaps of congratulation from her fellow teammates and subjects for her performance. She thanked them all, her exhaustion forgotten. It had been a terrific game, and though she did not see herself as a star player, she could acknowledge her own efforts. But she did not crave the limelight right now, not tonight...

The wine and beer flowed as Rache had promised, and the *Rache* and *Farrell House* girls mingled, as did the home and visiting staff accompanying the inspector - a tall, balding, nondescript man in his early fifties who returned to the main house after the match to change out of his referee uniform and back into his suit. He seemed decent and attentive, but Tiffany wondered if he would heed Wendy's accusations, or if he would not consider her written accounts worthy of his consideration since she was not present to submit them in person.

There was only one way to find out, so Tiffany, summoning all her courage, finished her drink and worked her way out of the room. With a sigh of resignation, feeling as though she was walking to the gallows, she ascended the deserted staircase to the classroom where Wendy had hidden her notebook.

Thankfully it was still there, so Tiffany breathed a huge sigh of relief, retrieved it, and was about to leave the room again when curiosity overwhelmed her and she flicked through the written pages. After all, she was sticking her neck out on the strength of whatever lay inside the thin book.

The notes were hastily scribbled, in various shades of ink and also in pencil, and they were in chronological order. They vividly described Wendy's processing and welcoming, and the numerous indignities she had suffered under Colbert, Shazza and others. Also included were the indignities she had witnessed other girls suffering. There was mention of Jude's double-cross and their last escape attempt, but no mention of Tiffany, as promised.

Until, that is, the very end of the damaging exposé.

And when she read it, Tiffany's stomach turned with shock and disappointment. There were numerous salacious descriptions of her body and her sexual responses, as well as accounts of her intimate sessions with Colbert and others, spiced up by other girls' comments. Beneath these was a list labelled *Prospective Headlines*, which included such subtle gems as, *Rich Bitch Turned Sex Slave*, and, *Wrightwood Welborne Woman Whipped Weekly*.

Disappointment quickly turned to anger, and that anger boiled inside Tiffany, galvanising her and giving her hands the strength they needed to tear the notebook to shreds, then with a shriek of frustration she slammed the remains into the waste bin. And how she would love to do the same to the author.

She returned to the party looking for Rache. 'Where's the director?' she asked Stuart urgently.

'I think he's in his office,' he told her. 'Why?'

'Oh, nothing,' she said noncommittally.

Wendy was crouched on the floor of her solitary cell when the door opened. 'Tiff!' she cried.

Tiffany forced her expression to one of neutrality. 'Are you ready to talk?' she asked.

Wendy's face broke into a smile of relief. 'Oh, Tiff, I do love you, you know,' she said with admirable sincerity. 'Let's get my notebook and—'

'We can't,' Tiffany snapped. 'The classroom's locked up.' She slipped an arm around the girl's shoulder and led her out of the dingy cell and down the corridor a short way, before she suddenly twisted Wendy's arm up behind her back, making her squeal in surprise and pain.

'Tiffany,' the girl shrieked anxiously, 'what—?'

'Be quiet, Wendy,' Tiffany said patiently, although her tone carried enough of a threat to silence the girl instantly, and then she marched her to Rache's office, only to knock and burst in without awaiting permission to discover the director was not alone. The inspector, the last person she wanted Wendy to come into contact with, was with him. They were sitting before Rache's desk, drinking wine. Chairman was on Rache's lap, enjoying the hand that stroked and pampered him, but jumped down and settled under the desk when the two girls burst in.

The director's eyes narrowed angrily at the intrusion. 'Would you care to explain this, Welborne?' he snapped.

Tiffany quickly recovered from the shock of seeing the inspector, and gave Wendy a shake. 'Sir, I've just caught Howard trying to escape,' she babbled unconvincingly.

Wendy looked at her in total shock. 'You've what?' she gasped.

Rache set his glass down. 'Indeed?' He reached across to his desk, and pressed the intercom. 'Mr Singh, Mr Baptiste, would you and the rest of the senior staff please report to my office at once?' Then he released the button and glared at Wendy. 'Such a disappointment, Miss Howard, and to think I was going to take pity and release you for the remainder of the party.'

Wendy looked at the other man in the room. 'Are you the inspector?' she blurted desperately.

He set his own glass down. 'Yes, young lady,' he confirmed. 'Why do you ask?'

Tiffany panicked; she had inadvertently given Wendy the opportunity she sought. 'Don't listen to her, sir, she's a pathological liar!'

Rache looked at her, bemused, and the inspector waved away her interruption as the summoned staff arrived in the office.

'Remy, be a good boy and bring Jude from my studio,' Rache ordered, and as Remy disappeared to expedite it, the inspector leaned forward in his chair towards Wendy.

'Did you wish to tell me something, young lady?' he asked.

Opportunity strengthened Wendy and she pulled her shoulders back determinedly, her eyes fixed on the inspector's face as if she was afraid he would vanish if she blinked. 'My name is Wendy Howard,' she began. 'I'm a British reporter working here undercover to investigate wrongdoing in the Cascaran private prison industry.' She stabbed an accusing finger in Rache's direction. 'This man and his staff are running an organised ring of sexual domination here. We've all been repeatedly beaten, abused, degraded—'

'That's a lie!' Tiffany cried.

'Quiet,' the inspector said firmly, his eyes never leaving Wendy's face. 'And do you have proof of this, young lady? Will any others corroborate your story?'

'I have notes on my experiences here, and I'm sure the newer subjects will back me up. The rest have been here too long and have been brainwashed.' She shot a withering glance at Tiffany.

'Indeed?' The inspector looked stunned as he turned to Rache, who appeared totally unaffected by developments. 'Cyrus, is any of this true?' he asked, and to the utter shock of both Tiffany and Wendy, Rache smiled casually and nodded.

'Oh yes, of course it is,' he said amiably. 'For the past six years all the young women I've had here have been taught the joys of submission. And I've yet to take one on I haven't been able to tame and condition.'

The room held its collective breath, awaiting the inspector's response.

'Well, my friend,' he said, nodding towards Wendy, 'you certainly have your work cut out with this petulant little madam.'

'Hardly, Jean-Claude.' Rache retrieved his wineglass, and settled back in his chair. 'I simply let the little bitch keep her secret for as long as it amused me.'

Tiffany's head reeled and she felt incredibly stupid that the obvious had not occurred to her before then. 'The inspector's in on all this?' she asked in disbelief.

Rache looked at her, but treated her question as a statement and did not answer her.

Just then, Remy returned with a naked Jude, who looked as if she had been dragged through a mile of hedges.

'Jean-Claude, would you give all of us some time alone?' the director requested.

'Of course, Cyrus.' He rose, casting a look of disdain at the stunned figure of Wendy as he left the room. Rache rose as well, but moved to sit behind his desk and give the others some breathing space. 'Yes, Miss Howard,' he said, 'I knew about you from the start.'

Wendy bristled. 'You found my notebook, or Tiffany told you.'

He shook his head. 'Even simpler, I talked with your employer, Victor Castlewell. He and I are old friends. He told me about your pitiful blackmail attempts, but he also told me about how well you responded to his tender mercies.'

Wendy seemed to shrink into herself, but the director was only too pleased to continue.

'So, when he seemingly relented and gave you the big break you'd always wanted, he arranged with me to have you sent here to get the full story on my corrupt regime.'

Wendy's lower lip quivered, but to her credit she still tried to salvage something from the situation. 'Then you can contact Mr Castlewell and tell him that I've learned my lesson and I won't be going to the media with this story,' she said, but Rache laughed softly.

'Oh, we both know you won't, at least not until your release. You did, after all, plead guilty to drug possession, did you not?'

'But - but I did that on purpose to get in here!' she shrieked, suddenly realising what he was implying.

'And you've succeeded. And when you eventually leave, you can return to Victor a docile, obedient, willing slave. You won't want to do anything but serve him. Remy, place her back in the cell until I have time to consider her punishment.'

Wendy bristled again, and Tiffany had to admire her strength of character. In her place she might have been blubbering by now. Wendy, however, stuck her chin out defiantly as she was led away. 'You won't break me, Rache!' she vowed.

But already the director's mind had moved elsewhere, and focused on Tiffany. 'I let her keep her secret with you in order to test your loyalty.'

'And - and did I pass?' Tiffany asked cautiously, not totally sure she wanted to hear the verdict.

He smiled enigmatically, and looked at Singh. 'Armin, I have some good news and I have some bad news. The good news is that you're receiving an immediate promotion.' The Indian beamed, his eyes widening in surprise and curiosity. 'The bad news,' Rache continued, after a short pause to allow his words to sink in more fully, 'is that it won't be here.'

The smile vanished. 'What?'

'I've made arrangements with *Farrell House*,' Rache explained. 'Their assistant director is leaving. Of course, theirs is a more conventional penal facility, so you'll actually have to work for your money.'

Singh looked as dismayed and disoriented as Wendy had. 'But, Cyrus, what have I done—'

'Don't, Armin,' the director stopped him, one hand raised. 'I knew about your conspiracy with Forrester from the beginning. Not that I blame you, any more than I'd blame a mosquito for trying to tap my blood, but your pitiful efforts indicate either sloppiness or an underestimation of my strength. Both annoy me.'

'But *Farrell House* is even more isolated than we are!' Singh protested. 'If they run things like an ordinary prison, what am I to do with myself?'

'You could try meditation,' Nuala suggested, with little or no sympathy.

'Cold showers help, too,' Tiffany added, suddenly feeling mischievous.

Singh shot her a glare before returning his attention to Rache, and mustering his bravado. 'And what would you say if I threatened to go public about this little operation of yours?' he threatened, unwisely.

Rache remained unperturbed. 'I'd ask you the names of the two daughters of that formidable gangster who once employed you in Cascara City. Weren't they Almira and Jarita? And how much of a reward is out for your head?'

Singh straightened up again, but his face was ashen.

'Oh, cheer up, Armin,' Rache continued, clearly knowing his veiled counter threat had quickly and effectively quashed any rebellion. 'If life has taught me anything it's that you can't expect to get everything you want out of it. So make do. Now go and pack up, you're leaving tonight.'

Tiffany felt more than saw the final glare Singh shot in her direction as he departed. The atmosphere in the room felt considerably lighter after that.

Then Colbert spoke up. 'You made a wise choice, Cyrus,' she said. 'I always knew he was a threat to you.'

'Did you?' Rache asked warmly. 'You're very sensible.'

She slinked closer to his desk. 'Why, thank you, Cyrus.'

'That's why I'm certain you'll agree that the perfect choice for my replacement is Nuala.'

'What?' Colbert and Quinn gasped in unison.

'But, Cyrus...' Colbert began.

'I don't want it,' Nuala insisted.

'And that makes you perfect,' the director said. 'You're honourable, not ambitious.'

'Well, if she doesn't want it, I'll give it a shot,' Tiffany offered, amused by the banter.

'No, you're too eager,' Rache countered, smiling. 'Well, Nuala?'

'Cyrus,' Colbert repeated, more forcefully this time and winning his attention. 'Cyrus, I deserve the post. All the effort I've put into my job—'

'Is thoroughly appreciated, Anne-Marie,' he said dismissively. 'Now please, don't interrupt me again. Nuala, at least act as assistant director for a while so I may prepare a new security chief—'

With a manic snarl Colbert kicked the front of Rache's desk with her boot. Her hands balled into fists, she practically screamed, 'Damn you, Cyrus Rache! I deserve better than this! I'd sooner quit than work under this conniving bitch!'

'As you wish,' the director said politely. 'It was a pleasure having you here, Anne-Marie. Don't let the door hit you on the ass on your way out.'

She froze, sheer disbelief petrifying her. 'And that's it? All the years of intimacy we've shared and that's all I get from you?'

'Oh, please, I've had deeper moments with my cat,' he said scornfully, and unable to take any more, Colbert stormed out of the room.

The tension lightened even more with just the four of them left; Rache, Nuala and Tiffany, and of course, Chairman.

Rache smiled. 'Nuala, you haven't accepted the position yet.'

'That's because I'm a heartbeat away from joining Armin and Anne-Marie and leaving here.' She drew closer to him, her words earnest. 'Your vendetta against this girl was an abuse of the trust that we - that I - put in you, Cyrus.'

'I know, and I apologise for that.'

'I've forgiven him, Nuala,' Tiffany said. 'So can't you?'

Nuala heard what Tiffany said, and considered her words for a while. 'Okay...' she eventually said slowly, 'okay, I accept the position.'

'I'm pleased,' Rache said. 'But now I still have two posts to fill. Or is it three, with you no longer the fitness instructor?'

'It's two posts,' Nuala said. 'Or rather, one; I accept mine on three conditions, the first that I still remain the fitness instructor.'

Rache nodded his agreement.

'The second, that you let me reassign Welborne.' Tiffany glanced at her, surprised.

'I believe I understand,' Rache said cryptically. 'And the last condition?'

Now the woman's eyes narrowed, and she pointed at the white old cat, now back on his master's lap and purring contentedly. 'Is that you finally tell me, after all these years, why the hell you named him Chairman.'

'Yes,' Tiffany chirped in. 'Why did you and my mother name him that?'

The director's face blanched and he grew visibly uncomfortable, a reaction Tiffany had not witnessed before, and he stroked the cat even more vigorously. 'It was nothing important, really...'

'Then you won't mind telling us now.'

He sighed. 'It was short for Chairman Meow, that's all.'

CHAPTER SIXTEEN

Tiffany Welborne was distracted, and did not like the feeling; she had too much to do to be sidetracked. She left her office, formerly the housekeeper's office but now hers as part of Nuala's staff restructuring. Tiffany worked as a trustee, supervising the other subjects in Colbert's old job even while remaining a prisoner, and she was answerable only to Rache and Nuala. She paused to glance at Shazza, bent over and scrubbing the floor diligently, her bottom gyrating invitingly with her efforts.

'I expect to be able to eat off that floor when I get back, Dewitt,' Tiffany said.

Shazza looked up at her, smiling. 'Yes, madam.'

Tiffany listened to her heels clicking against the polished floor. It was always quiet in the house at this time of day. The sound of Nuala Quinn putting the new girls on the team through their paces could be heard coming from outside as she descended to the first floor, and took the opportunity to open the front door and peer outside. Some of Kemp's crew were remodelling the front gardens. Jude was in harness in the cart transporting shrubs and paving stones around the estate. Stripped to her bra, panties and boots, her expression was as dark as her skin. Remy, standing nearby, saw Tiffany and smiled at her.

Once the truth about Jude's conspiracy with Singh had been revealed, she had been returned to Kemp's tender mercies. And when Tiffany was made trustee, the rest of the dorm anxiously waited for her to take revenge on Jude.

A revenge that might never come, as Tiffany took her new responsibilities seriously, and treated Jude no better and no worse than the other girls. Rache's situation had taught her much about obsession. Besides, it was fun watching Jude squirm as she waited for the hammer to fall.

As for Remy, he had approached Tiffany, and apologised himself. Theirs had been a sporadic relationship ever since, a pleasant diversion for them both, but neither had any illusions about some great romance blossoming from it.

Tiffany checked her watch again. She had an urgent matter to settle.

She found Rache in the studio with Chairman and Wendy. The young woman was naked except for a studded collar, and crouching on all fours over a yellow plastic animal food dish filled with dry, multicoloured chunks of feed while Rache zoomed in on the image with his camera. Of them all, Wendy had perhaps come the farthest in the shortest time. Once she gave up any hope of her publisher coming to her rescue, and gave in to her own secret inner desires, the last of her defiance crumbled and she soon fell wholeheartedly into the sublime delights of submission. Victor Castlewell would get himself a fine slave upon her release.

Rache himself was more animated these days. With Tiffany's encouragement he had remained in his post, released some of his more recent photographs under his old name, and now had a new book on the market.

'Doctor,' Tiffany said respectfully, 'I need to speak with you privately on an urgent matter.'

Rache sighed, but set aside his camera. 'Wait outside, Howard,' he ordered.

'Yes, master.' Wendy rose, grabbed her uniform from an adjacent rack, and padded away, avoiding Tiffany's eyes.

Tiffany waited until the girl had just passed her before rudely snatching the uniform out of her hands. 'Your master didn't say you could get dressed again, did he?'

Wendy's face flushed with anxious fervour, and she kept her eyes lowered. 'No, madam.'

'Wait ten paces down the corridor, on your knees, thighs spread.'

Wendy shuddered, her enjoyment as naked as her body. 'Yes, madam.'

Rache chuckled as the door closed behind the girl. 'You're quite a talent,' he complimented. 'Few people can truly enjoy being both dominant and submissive.'

'I'm my parents' child.'

'How true.'

She stepped forward. 'May I ask you some questions, Cyrus?'

Her use of his first name, a rare occurrence, emphasised the seriousness of her request. 'Have you been a good little trustee, Tiffany?'

'It's about the notebook Wendy kept. She'd promised to keep my name out of her exposé, but I saw written in it details about me - hurtful things.'

'Indeed?'

'Yes. I thought she would betray me, and that's why I turned against her.'

'A sensible decision.'

'But if she was going to betray me, why let me know the location of her notebook beforehand? Suppose I'd been curious before that night, and had a look at it?'

'Good point,' he agreed. 'How do you explain it?'

'I don't think she wrote anything about me at all. I think she meant to keep her word about protecting my identity. I think you knew about the book and had those things written in it, the same way you faked personal letters, to spur me into choosing you over her.'

'Indeed.'

'Yes. Otherwise, why were all the details about me at the end of her notes when I'd been involved with her from the very beginning of her stay here?' She paused. 'Well?'

'Wouldn't someone have put two-and-two together about you anyway in the ensuing scandal?' he pointed out.

'Maybe, but there's something else that's been bothering me.'

'Yes?'

'I've been helping you re-catalogue your old negatives. Some of them include my mother.'

'Do you intend to belabour the obvious, my dear?'

'You said mother left you two years before I was born, but the dates on the negatives of her extend past my birth date. And how old would that make Chairman? If that was true he'd be the granddaddy of all cats!'

'Miss Welborne, as much as I enjoy reddening your firm young backside, as I will be forced to do if you keep pestering me with questions, I have much serious work ahead of me—'

'Are you my father, Cyrus?'

He chuckled, either congratulating her powers of deduction or deriding her for such foolishness, and his subsequent words were just as ambiguous. 'Wicked, wicked girl, Tiffany Welborne.'